THE STATIONMASTER'S COTTAGE

PHILLIPA NEFRI CLARK

The Stationmaster's Cottage

Cover design by Steam Power Studios
Editing by NasDean.com

Written in Australian English for an authentic experience.

For my sister, Roshan.
You are always with me, not matter how many miles are between us.

A PROMISE MADE. A LIFETIME LOST

*O*ne final time, Dorothy Ryan prepared to play the game. The game from her teenage years when she'd squeeze her eyes shut and hope with all her might that when they opened, she would be on a stage on Broadway.

Solo in a dazzling spotlight, she'd sing her heart out to an enraptured audience. Music would fill the theatre as her voice soared to one high note and then, another. Thunderous applause followed, and her eyes flew open as she bowed with a flourish.

The disappointment was always the same. The stage was her bedroom. No audience, only dolls in a row on her bed. The music was her little sister singing to herself in the next room.

Her dreams vanished under the practical guidance of a mother who wanted her children properly educated. Dorothy left the game behind when she departed Rivers End at the age of twenty.

Now seventy-nine, Dorothy was back in her hometown after five decades, clinging to a final hope. She closed her eyes and wished— wished she was in her old bedroom in Palmerston House.

If only she was a daydreaming teenager again before this lifetime passed like the blink of an eye. Before she lost what mattered. Before her own choices shattered the life of the person she cared most for in the world, choices that destroyed true love.

Dorothy opened her eyes. She was still here, seated at a small table in a dingy motel room with a lumpy bed and peeling wallpaper. Her wrinkled hands were spotted from age, and her failing heart still pounded uncomfortably in her chest. So much for games.

She smoothed out an ivory page of delicate writing paper. Few people mattered to Dorothy. Her only grandchild, Christie, was one of them and this letter would say goodbye.

Her hand hovered over the paper, the expensive pen not making contact. There'd been another letter, one written and sent more than a month ago. Had Martha even read it and understood the urgency of her older sister's request? Dorothy sighed and put down the pen.

So little time left and so much to say. To explain herself and be forgiven. Surely Martha would accept Dorothy's actions all those years ago came from a place of love and concern?

I need you to understand.

None of this would have happened, none of it, had Martha ever cared about anything their mother, Lilian said, instead of following the rather bad example of their carefree father, Patrick. Martha was somehow the perfect combination of both parents, wild and stubborn, generous and passionate like Patrick, as well as proud and selfish, sensitive and protective like Lilian.

Ah, the beautiful one, the smart and funny child everybody loved. Especially me.

Her tea was cold in the thick white mug. It would have tasted better in her bone china and properly made by Angus, the only man she had not scared away over the years, no doubt due to the generous salary she paid him to run her house. She'd rather be there, or even at Palmerston House, than in this horrid room.

Dorothy shook her head with a frown. She needed to write her farewells to Christie. As she picked up the pen, a memory intruded, and her hand trembled. It was 1967. The year that changed everything.

Patrick Ryan stood by Dorothy's lounge room window, contemplating the hustle and bustle of Melbourne city several floors below. The outlook was straight down the main street filled with mid-afternoon shoppers, cars and workers. Patrick helped himself to a glass of whiskey from the small bar Dorothy kept, mostly for his visits.

"Father, you've got a long drive ahead!" Dorothy scolded.

Patrick tapped the window. "Do ye see the Clydies now?"

"The streets are getting too busy for the horses, Father, and besides, we don't have milk delivered to the apartment."

Patrick turned around. "All this progress—does it not make ye want to come home?" A third generation Australian, Patrick nevertheless spoke with the soft Irish accent of his father and grandfather. It was somehow out of place in Dorothy's modern apartment.

Her life had been in Melbourne since boarding school days, punctuated by long summer school holidays in Rivers End she tolerated for her mother's sake. The reality was she loved the progress, loved her job as a trainee manager at a department store, and rather loved the young man she was seeing. Going "home" would stifle her.

"Before I know it, Martha will be all married and gone as well. Both my girls disappearing in the blink of an eye." Patrick sighed.

"What do you mean, married? Martha won't marry Thomas Blake!"

"Have ye not spoken to yer sister in so long? She might not always like it, but Thomas has our girl all worked out. Them being wed will change her ways." Patrick chuckled and drained his glass. "Ye be coming to the engagement party when they have it?"

"Engagement? I think I must."

"I shall tell yer sister to hurry up and arrange the party so both my girls will be together again."

If Martha was engaged to this boy, Dorothy needed to speak with her. It may not be too late to change her mind, and if anyone could talk sense into Martha, it was her big sister.

In the dull motel room, Dorothy's heart overflowed with anguish.

Please, please let my letter have found you.

With both hands on the table to support her weight, Dorothy stood. Every bone hurt and her heart thumped oddly. She shuffled to an armchair in the corner of the room. The memories of that night in 1967 were crystal clear and she leaned back, closing her eyes.

Limestone cliffs towered above the perfectly curved, white sands of Rivers End beach. Midway along its one kilometre shore, a shallow river cut through the sand, forming a lagoon near the tideline. Close by, an old jetty resisted years of exposure to the open ocean to stand firm against the assault of the high tide.

Although after midnight, the air was hot and sultry with a bare whisper of a breeze to offer relief. Out over the Great Southern Ocean, a storm brewed.

Cut into the face of one cliff was a steep staircase of narrow limestone steps. Dorothy ran down them as fast as she dared. The beach was the last place she'd expected to be.

Where are you?

She reached the sand, almost tripping over shoes at the bottom of the steps. Martha's. She jumped as lightning flashed. But now she knew where Martha was.

Almost at the lagoon, long emerald-green dress hitched up to let her run, Martha disappeared into the dark. Not far behind, and closing fast, Thomas still wore his shoes. He must be desperate to reach her if he hadn't taken a few seconds to remove them. Dorothy pulled her sensible lace up leather shoes off, but kept hold of them as she took off after Martha.

Dorothy veered higher to the soft, dry sand. Surely Martha would run inland in a moment to follow the river back through the cliff to town. She aimed for the highest part of the lagoon, expecting to intercept her sister. Not finding her there, she ploughed through the sand toward the sea.

The sky lit up. Martha stood midway along the jetty as huge waves thrashed against its end. Dorothy opened her mouth to call out. But Thomas was there. On the sand, taking off one shoe, then the other, as though he had all the time in the world. What was he waiting for? He crossed his arms.

"Go away!" Martha's voice carried to Dorothy, and she came to a halt, unsure if she should show herself. "Don't follow me. You have no right!"

"Either you come off the jetty right now, or I'll come and get you. Martha, I mean it, I'll carry you back to the cottage if I must and I'll—" Thunder, directly overhead, cut off his words.

Horror paralysed Dorothy as a wave crashed over the boards where Martha stood. With a scream, she slipped into the swirling water and disappeared.

Even as Dorothy managed a few shaky steps, Thomas was on the jetty, tearing off his shirt. Then he dived.

Dorothy's eyes flew open. She sat upright on the armchair, disoriented. It was November 2016. Not 1967. The memories of that night almost fifty years ago were raw.

Martha had to learn the truth before it went to Dorothy's grave with her. As she stood, a wave of dizziness darkened the room for a moment. Somehow, she reached the table and dropped onto the chair. She scrawled a few words on the blank paper, pursing her lips as pain caught at her chest. The pen slipped from her hand.

Angus will know what to do.

Dorothy straightened her back as she shuffled to the bed, removed her shoes and placed them neatly on the floor. From an open cardboard box on the bedside table, she extracted a small photo album. Her breath ragged, she lay on her back, closed her eyes and willed her heart to steady. If only she'd done things differently that night so long ago.

Dorothy ran toward the jetty. Thomas surfaced amongst the angry waves for a second, only to dive under again. With a deafening crash, lightning struck the top of the cliff on the far end of the beach, and Dorothy screamed.

The seconds dragged like minutes, and still, there was no sign of them.

I cannot bear this!

As she tentatively stepped onto the jetty, there was a disturbance in the water, and Thomas burst up, Martha in his arms.

She was breathing. Martha was alive. Yet, Dorothy retreated. Back to the darkness near the lagoon as Thomas dragged himself from the shallows, Martha held against his chest. He staggered away from the water's edge, closer to Dorothy, who ducked down.

How he had found Martha was a miracle. He must love her so much to put his own life at risk. Perhaps she'd been wrong about him.

Thomas knelt, his arms tight around Martha. "Damn it, woman. You could have died, throwing yourself in the ocean!"

Martha pushed herself out of his arms, falling unceremoniously onto the sand. She glared at Thomas as she got to her feet, ignoring his outstretched hand. Her dress was torn. Sea water dripped from her long dark brown hair.

Why was she still angry when he'd save her life? Dorothy pushed herself a bit further away, still watching them.

"It's not what you think," Thomas said. "You don't understand."

"Understand? Oh my God, Thomas. I saw you! It'll be all over town tomorrow. She'll tell everyone. How could she? How could you?"

"Let me explain." Thomas stood.

"I don't want an explanation, Thomas. I saw what happened and I cannot endure this!"

The sky opened and hard rain pelted down. Dorothy was soaked in seconds, but couldn't take her eyes off the couple who were so close, yet unaware of her presence.

Martha twisted her solitaire engagement ring, then took it off.

"Put it back on before you drop it and stop being so damned melodramatic," Thomas said.

"Oh, how can you say that?" Martha cried. "Don't you get it? I'm leaving! It's over!" She threw the ring onto the sand, turned and stalked off.

Thomas scooped up the ring and pocketed it, before striding after Martha. "Where are you going?"

Dorothy followed, heart racing. Was this it? Was Martha about to end the engagement?

"Just wait for one god-damned minute!" Thomas bellowed.

Martha spun around, her eyes flashing with a fury Dorothy recognised. Martha always wanted her way. But when she grabbed at the pendant around her neck as if to tear it away, Thomas covered the ground between them and captured her hands in his. He leaned down and whispered to Martha.

Martha's expression had completely changed. Whatever he'd said, mattered. Now, she looked sad.

Thomas pulled Martha closer and traced the contours of her face with his fingertips.

The rain stopped.

The waves were the only sound.

The tenderness in Thomas' face as he wrapped his arms around Martha and held her against his bare chest tore a hole in Dorothy's heart.

For a long moment, it was as though even the elements held their breath.

"It's over between us." Martha stepped back.

Thomas held her wrist in his hand. "It will never be over with us."

"You see, I can't stay now. Not to face all those people and their laughter behind my back. After our engagement party of all times. And—"

Thomas cut her off. "That's what you care about? Your pride? Always your pride and your temper that gets between us! Well, go! Run away and think about what your pride is doing to us. No doubt your sister and your mother will be thrilled but know this, Martha Ryan, I will wait for you!"

"Well, you'll be waiting forever, because I'm not coming back!"

"I'll wait for you. There," Thomas pointed to the sea, "at the end of the jetty, I will wait. Every day I will be there to meet the dawn, as we have done so many times. Promise you'll come back."

Dorothy covered her mouth with both of her hands.

"Promise me!" Thomas insisted.

"Alright!" Martha cried out.

"No, Martha. A proper promise or it's not real. Say it."

"I promise! I promise I'll return, Tom! Now let me go!"

Thomas released Martha, and she sprinted back along the beach. Thunder boomed, and a flood of rain began.

"I love you, Martha Ryan!"

His voice must have reached Martha through the rain, for she glanced back. Then, she was gone.

Dorothy turned her eyes back to Thomas. He'd dropped to his hands and knees on the sand. As lightning hit the waves near the jetty, Thomas raised his face to the skies and cried out. "I will wait, Martha."

Now, on the lumpy bed in the dingy old motel room, Dorothy's eyes fluttered open. Against her chest, she clasped the photo album with both hands open on a photograph of Martha and Thomas, taken on the beach at Rivers End, holding hands and laughing.

A single tear escaped. "I'm sorry." Dorothy's final breath was like a whisper.

A CHANCE TO RECONNECT

*C*hristie Ryan gazed out of the window of the Qantas A380, recognising the landscape below with a sigh of relief. Only minutes now and she would be home in Melbourne. She had not slept during the fourteen-hour flight from Los Angeles, worrying, instead, about the last conversation with Derek Hobbs, her fiancé.

He had been abundantly clear about his expectations in a short, tense phone call two days ago. "You need to think about your priorities, Chris. Use your time on the flight home wisely, because we'll be talking once you're back. I'm over the separations." He hung up before she could respond.

The veiled threat still made her stomach churn. Derek knew from the beginning that her career as a specialist make-up artist took her away for weeks on end to film sets around the world. Their first glimpse of each other was during one of her shoots in London, where he had been doing business as a property developer. Since then, he had always been so proud of how sought after she was and often bragged to his friends about what he jokingly called her "brush with the stars".

She'd sensed a change in him over the past few contracts. He wasn't available as much to talk on Skype, and when they did, he'd dominate the conversation with his latest acquisition or recent success at the casino. The next few weeks were at home and Christie had every intention of spending some real time with Derek.

The plane banked over Brimbank Park, interrupting Christie's thoughts. She wanted to kick her shoes off, have a shower, and enjoy a cup of coffee from her own machine. She tightened her seat belt for landing.

Home was a tenth floor apartment close to Melbourne CBD. Christie dropped her bags inside the front door and went straight to the window of the living room to drink in the colour and movement that was Docklands. She never tired of the waterfront with its bright cafes, yacht-filled marina, and the myriad of visitors and residents who made it such a unique part of Melbourne. Across the narrow strip of water stood Etihad Stadium, the massive all weather sports and concert arena.

Christie draped her jacket across the back of a chair. She tossed her handbag onto the sofa, half of its contents spilling out. Only the view mattered. Taking her shoes off, she curled her toes into the carpet.

The soft tones of an acoustic guitar drifted in from next door and Christie grinned. She'd missed Ray and Ashley, her long time neighbours.

The front door clicked and she swung around. Derek was putting his briefcase onto the side table. She saw him glance at her jacket—which had slipped off the chair—and shoes on the floor, frowning at the spilled handbag on the sofa.

Christie smoothed her hair. "Hey there."

Derek half-smiled in return. "When did you get in?" His eyes darted back to the mess. Christie picked up her jacket and put it back on the chair before hurrying to him and sliding her arms around his neck. He wrapped his arms around her waist and brushed her lips.

"You look tired. Rundown." Derek said.

She regarded him with a smile. His face was developing lines that matched his greying red hair, but it suited him. He always dressed well and carried himself with the air of someone who knew he was not only handsome but successful.

"I need a shower." She slipped out of his embrace. "I'll only be a few minutes." After collecting her jacket and shoes, she sighed with happiness at the sight of their king size bed.

Soon. Sleep soon.

As she towelled her hair a few moments later, she saw Derek's reflection in the mirror. He'd carried her bags in. Suitcases on the bed, and professional make-up case at the end. He was still frowning.

"I'll unpack soon." Christie wished he would stop fussing. She had rented this apartment for three years before Derek moved in, not knowing until months later he purchased it soon after they met. He had been her landlord while they dated. He laughed it off when she questioned the secrecy. Business, he said. No big secret. Since moving in, he insisted the place be immaculate as if it was a show-home, rather than a real home. Christie tried, but her level of tidiness was not the same as his.

"Any chance of a coffee, honey? It was all I could think about on the flight."

He came to the doorway. "I hope you thought about more than coffee?"

"I did."

"And?"

"And I would love a cup of your coffee...and a talk." Christie peeked out from the towel.

Derek sat on the sofa, turning his phone around and around in his fingers, eyes drawn to the Melbourne skyline. Steam rose from two cups on a glass coffee table.

"Sorry I took so long." Christie joined him on the sofa. "Oh, yum, thank you." She picked up her coffee and savoured the first sip. "I've missed your blend."

"And I've missed you."

Christie dropped a hand onto his leg. "I didn't expect it to drag out for so long. Lots of reshoots."

Derek put his hand over hers. "But it's always that way, baby." It was a statement, delivered sadly. "Six weeks becomes ten. I might see you once in that time."

Christie dropped her head. "I know, and I'm—"

Derek cut her off. "No. Let me talk."

Christie put her coffee cup on the table and gave Derek her full attention. He was going to break off their engagement. Or tell her to change jobs. Her stomach tensed.

"I need to apologise," he started. "I've expected too much and not given enough."

Christie opened her mouth to reply, but Derek shook his head. "Still my turn to talk. Listen, when I told you to think about your priorities the other day, I was selfish. You work every bit as hard as I do, so here's the plan. When you have time off, I'll try to have time off. Like now." Derek jumped to his feet. "I've got a surprise."

He hurried to his briefcase and rummaged around, then returned with an envelope. He sat again and held it out. "Now, before you open it, I do know you've only just got home, but I really need this. I mean, we need this."

Curious, Christie drew out two airline tickets. Business class to Cairns, with connecting flights to Lizard Island.

"Six days there, baby. Just you and me at one of the world's most luxurious resorts. Okay?" His phone rang. He rejected the call. "So, we leave in the morning and get up there late afternoon. Just in time for cocktails. Yes?" His expression was like a little boy waiting to open a birthday present.

Another plane. Another hotel.

Christie took his hand. "This is wonderful, honey, thank you."

He lifted her hand to his lips and kissed it. "We can talk about a wedding date up there. It's time, don't you agree?" He did not wait around for an answer, getting to his feet and checking his phone as he walked into the kitchen.

Christie wandered back to the bedroom, where she stood for a while, contemplating the value of unpacking.

Derek had already packed a bag for Christie by the time she woke up the next morning. He brought her coffee and half-jokingly told her she only had an hour until they left. Jet-lagged, Christie longed to go back to sleep, but instead, she dragged herself into the shower.

She took extra care with her make-up, masking the lines of tiredness. Christie deliberately chose clothing for the flight she knew Derek liked. A light apricot silk blouse and darker designer pants showed off her figure, finished with flat suede shoes to keep her that fraction smaller in height than him, and the ruby pendant he had given her last Christmas.

The doorbell rang, and Derek called out from the living room, "That's our driver. Need to go."

It only took a moment for Christie to throw a small cosmetics bag into her handbag before she hurried along the hallway.

Derek was at the open front door with a tweed-coated man in his sixties. "Well, if you're not our driver, how can I help you?"

Christie squealed in delight and rushed to throw her arms around the visitor. "How wonderful to see you…oh, sorry." Christie said. "You haven't met. Derek, this is Angus McGregor, and Angus, this is my fiancé, Derek Hobbs."

She closed the door as Angus reached a hand out to Derek.

"Fiancé? Well, congratulations, Miss Christie." Angus nodded.

"Thank you. Derek, Angus works for Gran. He cares for the house and grounds, and drives her and…" Christie tapered off. Angus' face was drawn. Sad. "Gran?" Christie whispered. "Oh, Angus?"

"I'm so sorry, Miss Christie. It was a peaceful passing if that helps."

Christie covered her mouth with her hand. Derek put an arm around her shoulder. "Sorry, baby."

"Miss Dorothy left instructions. Her funeral is tomorrow, and she specifically wanted you to attend."

Derek released Christie. "Not possible, I'm afraid. We're about to get on a plane. But we'll send some beautiful flowers and make a donation to her favourite charity—"

"Where is the funeral being held?"

"Chris, no! It's not like you were close to her, I mean you hadn't spoken for years!" Derek stalked away to pick up his house keys and phone. "We have to go, or we'll miss the plane."

Angus was paler and thinner than she remembered. His thirty loyal years of service to Dorothy Ryan outlasted two husbands, and now, his world must have turned on its head with her death.

"Do you want to sit down?"

Angus shook his head. "The funeral is at 10 am tomorrow in Rivers End."

The name meant nothing to Christie.

"A town along the coast. Just off the Great Ocean Road. The original home of your family."

The doorbell rang, and Derek flung it open, startling the uniformed driver on the other side. Derek pointed to two suitcases inside the door, and the driver almost tripped over himself in his rush to pick them up and leave.

"Chris, I'm sorry about your grandmother, but we must go now." Derek collected Christie's phone from the coffee table and held it out.

"I have to go. It is the right thing to do. Come with me, Derek. Please?"

Angus shuffled away to stand near the window, his back turned to offer some privacy.

"Come with you where? To the funeral of a woman who didn't even care for you? I'm sorry to sound harsh but you know that's the truth. We have a chance to get away and reconnect. Don't you want that?" He took Christie's hands in his.

"Of course I do. I'm only asking for a day...to say goodbye. We can fly out tomorrow afternoon instead. Can't we?"

Why can't you see I need your support? Oh, Gran.

Christie pulled her hands away.

Derek scowled and turned to leave. One hand on the door handle, he paused. "I'm going. I'll change your flight to a later one tomorrow. Be on that flight." He closed the door behind himself.

"I'm sorry to have disturbed your plans, Miss Christie."

Christie hurried over to give him a hug. "Derek's disappointed. I'm sorry for the way he spoke."

Angus squeezed Christie's arm. "I'm quite immune. We both know your grandmother had her moments." He smiled at the understatement.

Gran had given Christie everything she needed. Everything, except her love and acceptance, the lack of which had driven her granddaughter away. Along with everyone else. Except for Angus.

Sorrow burrowed into Christie. For all her flaws, Gran had provided a home and a safe place to grow up. She certainly deserved to have two mourners at her funeral who cared about her. For now, Christie pushed aside the hurt Derek's departure caused.

"Tell me about Rivers End, and please, tell me why Gran is being buried there."

A LONELY COTTAGE

The white Lotus Elite S hugged the narrow, winding road as Christie, deep in thought, drove it a little too fast. The top was down, the speed whipping her hair back as the spring sun made occasional appearances through incoming rain clouds across the ocean to her left. The road was high above the water, with a flat expanse of saltbush-covered land to the right and not another car or sign of civilisation in sight.

After Angus had left, Christie packed an overnight bag and a black dress. Then, standing at the living room window, thoughts rushed through her head and emotions spun in turmoil. Derek...she needed him right now. Needed him to hold her hand and come to this unknown little town. She longed for his reassurance they would stand together. Instead, he had gone in the other direction, without her. Once again, she was facing a funeral alone. But this one was Gran's.

"Her heart had been playing up for a while. Not that she would admit it. I knew though because the doctor gave her pills and I made sure she took them." Angus had explained. "In the evenings, she'd sit for a while and talk of her childhood. Of growing up in Rivers End and of her family. Her sister."

Wide-eyed, Christie turned to Angus. "A sister?"

He nodded. "Martha is a few years younger."

"Does Martha live in Rivers End?"

Angus shrugged. "I don't know where she lives. Or if she is even still alive, although your grandmother believed her to be. Many years ago, your family owned much of this town. That is where Miss Dorothy and her sister grew up, and the family home was quite grand for the region. Now, one property remains in the family, and Miss Dorothy was determined to see it again."

The road had been climbing steadily, and now, as Christie rounded a curve a town came into view, at the bottom of the hill on the far side of a river.

Christie slowed as a road sign approached. *Rivers End. Pop 900.*

After pulling the car onto the shoulder to check Angus' instructions, Christie filled her lungs with sea air. From up here, the township was small, two shopping streets and houses scattered around. The lazy river made its way to the sea, pooling into a lagoon near a jetty on a kilometre-long beach. She nosed the Lotus back onto the road.

Fifty metres away was the turn-off. The road headed inland for a hundred metres or so before coming across an abandoned railway station. A single track ran beside it, overgrown with weeds and grass. The road on the other side was dirt, filled with potholes, and Christie grimaced as she navigated her low-bodied car around them.

Angus' sedan was parked in front of an old, neglected cottage that stood out from a mass of unkempt trees and bushes. Pickets hung onto the front fence under the weight of long-neglected rose bushes. The front gate lay rusting in the water-filled, shallow grass ditch.

Christie eased into the narrow driveway and turned the motor off. Behind the cottage, the driveway ended with a single garage, in no better repair than the rest of the property.

A drop of rain touched Christie's face, so she put the roof up. She stretched and glanced around, seeing only years of abandonment.

Angus appeared from the back of the cottage, raising a hand in welcome. Christie crunched her way along the rutted driveway as a shower began in earnest, joining him on a small porch. Rain tapped on the metal roof, and the temperature dropped. Christie shivered.

"Welcome, Miss Christie, to the Stationmaster's Cottage."

Inside, the neglect continued in the old-fashioned kitchen. A large window over the sink did little to reduce the dullness of the room. Against one wall, a heavy timber table might have not moved in a century. On the table was a cardboard box, sealed with packing tape. Christie peered down a long, dark hallway.

"Here are the keys." Angus dropped a key ring with three keys beside the box. "I've requested the power be reconnected."

"Probably not much point though. I'll be leaving straight after the funeral. I imagine Gran's estate will want to sell this?"

"I thought you understood. The cottage belongs to you now. Well, it will once the legalities are finalised. So, whether you sell it or keep it, no doubt some refurbishment is in order and that will take electricity."

"Mine? Oh, but no. Why would she leave it to me?"

"Why not leave it to you? Your Gran never did anything without reason."

That was true. Gran made decisions only after considering all the pros and cons. It might not always be clear why a decision went one way or the other to Christie, but Gran knew. So, why leave a rundown cottage to her jet-setting, estranged grandchild?

Angus checked his watch. "I have to meet with the funeral home in a few moments. There's a motel in town on the second street. I've arranged rooms there for us tonight, so unless you wish to accompany me now, I'll head off."

"Do you need me to?"

Angus shook his head. "Stay here for a while, wander through. We'll meet there for dinner?"

Christie hugged Angus, hoping he understood how much his presence meant. He patted her back before leaving with a small wave. In his wake, the fresh and vibrant smell of the wet garden wafted in.

Alone again, the tapping of rain on the roof interrupted Christie's thoughts, and she stood still to listen. She closed her eyes to concentrate on the soothing sound and the garden scent; transported for a moment to a rainy day in her grandmother's conservatory where the heady smells of roses, gardenia and jasmine filled the air. The memory faded as the old-house mustiness overwhelmed the kitchen again. Christie opened her eyes and wrinkled her nose.

She wandered along the hallway. On the left was a lounge room with an ornate ceiling rose. Old, heavy curtains sagged miserably, and a worn sofa slumped opposite the fireplace.

Across the hallway was a dining room, empty except for a couple of straight-backed dining chairs against a wall.

Next to the dining room was a small bathroom with grimy old fittings. In the bath was a torn shower curtain and large flakes of paint from the ceiling.

Does Gran want me to become an interior decorator or renovator?

Across from the bathroom was a tiny laundry with no washing machine, some cupboards and a sink. A small window beside an external door revealed a narrow concrete path winding to a broken clothesline.

At the end of the hallway, two bedrooms faced each other. In between was a built in cupboard. Inside it, Christie found several blankets, a broom, dustpan and brush, and a long-handled tool with a hook. Above her head was a trapdoor with a loop on it. Curious, she nudged it with the tool, bringing down a cloud of dust and debris. She tossed the tool back into the cupboard, closed the door and stood back, coughing.

After a quick check of each bedroom, which were both small but functional with double beds and wardrobes, she went back to the hallway to stare at the trapdoor.

What was up there?

More dust and debris, or hidden treasures? Shaking her head, Christie returned to the relative brightness of the kitchen.

The cardboard box had her name handwritten on it, so Christie used a key to slice through the packing tape. Inside were two items: a photo album and a cardboard cylinder about sixty centimetres in length. Christie opened the photo album to an old image of Dorothy. Aged around twenty, Dorothy stared gravely at the camera. The backdrop was a lush garden around an impressive limestone house.

Christie whispered. "So stern!" The grief that nagged all day started to rise, and she closed the album.

The cylinder was open-ended, and after a bit of fiddling, Christie eased out a canvas. Stiff with age and being confined, the canvas resisted Christie's first attempt to open it. She tried again, and with a bit of pressure, the canvas unrolled. Christie placed it on the table, a hand on either side to keep it flat.

It was a nocturnal seascape in oils. Angry waves pounded a timber jetty under the onslaught of a violent storm. Vibrant dark colours perfectly captured the fantastic terror of the moment. A savage streak of lightning hit the sea close to the jetty, illuminating the water around it. So incredible was the detail and clarity, even the droplets of sea spray reflected the lightning. Christie could almost smell the saltiness in the air.

Her phone beeped, and Christie reluctantly released the canvas, which rolled back up on its own. A text flashed on her phone.

Have emailed you a new ticket. Departs Tullamarine 3pm tomorrow. Don't miss the flight. D.

Christie frowned as she tapped a response. *Thanks. Love you.*

The rain stopped. Christie opened the back door and let the wet garden smell into the kitchen. She stared outside at the overgrown greenery, wondering how long it was since somebody loved it. Who had lived here? Not Gran, who Angus said grew up in a grand house. Where was Martha and why had Gran never mentioned her? Her sister should be the one to inherit the cottage. One question led to another and Christie told herself to stop. It was time to find the motel.

The box with its painting and photo album under her arm, Christie locked the door and made her way back to the car. The long grass was soaking wet of course, saturating her shoes in seconds. She hated wet feet with a vengeance, and her only other shoes were the black heels for the funeral. She put the box on the passenger seat, loathing the squishy sensation as her feet touched the pedals.

Christie backed out of the driveway and turned onto the road, the potholes now water filled. The late afternoon was misty from the rain and the deciduous trees, their leaves emerging, were like shadows lining the street. Behind them were paddocks dotted with cows. At the end of the road, Christie turned right and drove down the hill.

Not far along was a small graveyard, perched on the edge of a cliff and bordered by a gravel carpark. A digging machine piled soil to one side of a rectangular hole. A new grave.

Oh...it's for Gran.

Christie bit her bottom lip as her vision blurred. The car shuddered to a stop on the side of the road and she dropped her head into her hands with a soft moan.

Don't cry, Christie. Not here.

This wasn't the time or the place. She raised her head. Tasting salt on her lips, she swallowed to force the pain down.

Just before the township, a bridge crossed the broad, slow river which flowed through a gap in the cliffs.

Christie turned into the second street. The motel was old and rundown and proclaimed itself as "Rivers End Motel" with a vacant sign flashing. Angus' sedan was in front of one of six rooms in a row, so Christie parked beside it.

Angus was at the doorway before Christie turned the motor off. The deep lines on his face were more pronounced than usual, but he smiled as he came to greet her.

"I've checked you in, so all you need to do is go inside and relax for a bit." He took her overnight bag from the car and followed Christie inside.

"I'm sorry for the surroundings," he began, "not a lot of choice in such a small place."

"It'll be fine, Angus. Just for tonight, it's fine." Even to Christie, her voice sounded strained. "My feet are wet," she said and burst into tears.

Angus insisted Christie have a long, hot shower to warm up again. She emerged to find he'd laid out a pair of his own socks on the bed.

When she padded into the kitchen, she saw her wet shoes on top of the oil-filled heater, and mouthed "thank you" at Angus, who was flicking through menus.

"Ah, now how about a cup of tea?" Angus said.

"Stay there, I'll make us one." She switched the kettle on, put tea bags and sugar into two heavy white mugs, and found a small carton of milk in the bar fridge. "Oh, it's still two sugars?"

Angus nodded. "Not much about me has changed, Miss Christie. Just older."

Christie finished making the tea and brought the mugs to the table. She nodded at her shoes. "Thanks for that. And the socks. And putting up with my silliness."

"Unless you were in a swimming pool, you never liked having wet feet, even as a young child." Angus chuckled.

"The grass needs cutting. And the garden is overgrown. The bathroom is falling apart, and the windows don't open." Christie sipped her tea.

"So, you like it?"

"It's rundown and neglected and old. Why did Gran own it? Who lived there and where are they now? And what should I do with it?"

Angus shook his head. "So many questions I can't answer. What I do know is your great-grandparents owned it, back when they provided timber to many regional towns. The railway was extended here because of the timber trade. They built the cottage more than one hundred years ago for the stationmaster to live in."

"So the cottage is all that remains?"

Angus nodded and passed the menus to Christie. "There's not a lot to select from, unfortunately."

"You choose." Christie finished her tea and stood up. "If it's okay with you, I'd rather order takeaway."

After an early, small dinner of pizza, Angus said goodnight and went to his room.

Longing to hear Derek's voice, Christie dialled his number and sat, cross-legged on the bed, fiddling with her hair.

After a few rings, Derek answered with his customary "Derek here."

"Hi, honey. How was the trip?"

There was a pause before Derek answered "Lonely."

I'm lonely too.

"What's our room like?" Christie kept her voice light. "I'm in a dingy old motel room, so would rather hear about ours."

Derek audibly sighed on the other end. "It's a villa, and it's stunning. It overlooks the sea, which is like liquid gold. The bed is huge. But empty."

"I'll be there tomorrow night."

After another long silence, Christie began to rush her words. "There's a cottage here, near an old railway station. Gran left it to me for some reason, so I'll sell it of course. It's rundown and—"

Derek cut her off. "So your wealthy grandmother left you some crappy dump in the middle of nowhere. Sorry baby, but that sucks. That's why you should have come with me. I'm the one who loves you."

"I love you too. But, Gran did care about me."

There were voices in the background at Derek's end, laughter. "I have to go, baby. There's a couple here I've met before, and they want to do cocktails. I'll see you tomorrow, okay?" His voice was calm again.

"I can't wait. Sleep well." Christie said.

Derek cut the connection, and Christie was unsure if he even heard her. She had been reluctant to go to Lizard Island and now, because of Gran, they were apart. Christie curled into a ball and stared into the darkness.

A SAD GOODBYE

*C*hristie woke before sunrise after a restless night. Overnight, the rain had returned, leaving the bitumen outside glistening below the streetlights.

Over coffee, she downloaded the e-ticket to her phone and set a reminder for leaving Rivers End. When the soft light of dawn peeked through the clearing sky, Christie had enough of being in the gloomy room. She tossed her handbag into the car and got behind the wheel, glancing at the box on the front seat. When she got back from Queensland, she was going to get the painting framed and work out the significance of it. Of all of this.

The drive back to the cottage took little time, and Christie parked, thankful the drizzle had stopped. Instead of going up the driveway, she wandered along the road. From here, it was clear the garden continued well past the garage, extending alongside the railway for a couple of hundred metres. The fencing turned into old barbed wire and posts at odd angles but was part of the property.

She took a few photos with her phone. Perhaps when Derek saw them, he would soften his stance and be as intrigued as Christie was. Tonight she would be back in his arms and this awful day just a memory.

Old boom gates stood guard on either side of the railway crossing. A narrow stone platform housed an even narrower building. Curious, she followed a pathway up a slope to the platform. At least, it once must have been a pathway but weeds and time had taken over. The platform was a bit crumbly on the edges but otherwise solid. A sign hung from one screw on the wall of the building. *Rivers End Station.*

The building itself was little more than a covered waiting area and a boarded up ticket office. How sad that what once would have been a bustling little station had only ghosts to keep it company.

Years ago the station was vibrant and busy with the comings and goings of freight trains carrying timber to the city. Now though, it was quiet and overgrown. Like the cottage. Christie headed back to her car, wondering what happened in this sleepy little place all those years ago.

At 10 am, Dorothy Ryan went to her final resting place in the small clifftop graveyard. Her casket was the most elaborate the local funeral home had been able to source on short notice, with highly polished timber and gold fittings. White tulips—brought in from a Melbourne grower—covered the casket. All the arrangements were in line with instructions left by Dorothy and carried out by Angus, who was graveside with Christie, holding an umbrella over them both.

The return of light drizzle and grey skies fitted the occasion. Dressed in a plain black Armani dress and heels, her hair wound into a bun, Christie stood rigidly.

Gran had no other family to bid her farewell. No loved ones or friends who would mourn her passing. Apart from Angus, Christie only knew Jacob Bright, Gran's attorney. In his fifties, Jacob was tall, bespectacled, and immaculately dressed. He listened impassively to the celebrant.

Her gaze stopped on a middle-aged couple standing opposite. A woman with curly brown hair, and a balding man, both in black suits too tight for their frames, arm in arm.

The celebrant was the wife of the undertaker, and her voice was so quiet Christie had to lean toward her to hear the words of the ceremony. The sound of waves below the cliff and the cawing of seagulls almost drowned her out at times. These moments were surreal. To be in this beautiful place and see Gran laid to rest was hard to comprehend and in her mind, she had her own tribute.

Dorothy Ryan, a woman of strong opinions and principles, wealthy and successful in business. Ostentatious, private, intelligent, and often intolerant of those around her.

Perhaps beneath the cold exterior was a warm heart and love for those who had been in her life, although Christie had never seen a glimmer of it herself. One could hope.

This was just like another funeral. As if yesterday, Christie remembered the worst day of her life.

The hot outback sun scorched the red dirt beneath Christie's feet, uncomfortable in too-small lace-up shoes to go with her black, cut down dress, both borrowed for the occasion. Trishi from next door had plaited her hair in tight braids and told her to be a good girl and listen to the priest.

She tried to, she did, but her feet and head hurt, and she wanted this stupid speech to be over so she could run home to Mum and Dad. Except, they were here in boxes being lowered into the ground, and her eyes kept crying. Her dress was saturated from the heat and flies buzzed around her face, but all seven-year-old Christie knew was she would never see her parents again. She was all alone.

Then, a tall man in a hat squatted beside her and smiled kindly. He took her hand and said he would look after her. His name was Angus.

"Be brave, little one," he whispered.

Christie reached a hand out to Angus, and he squeezed her hand and mouthed, "Be brave."

She tossed a handful of soil onto the casket with a whisper, "Goodbye, Gran. I love you."

As she straightened, her eyes locked with those of a man standing back from the mourners. A shiver ran up her spine.

In jeans and a damp T-shirt, feet bare and metal bucket in one hand, he wasn't there to pay his respects to Gran. Not if the hostility in his dark eyes was anything to go by.

Angus closed the umbrella as the drizzle stopped, and went to speak with the celebrant.

"Hello, lovey. I'm Daphne." The woman with the curly brown hair appeared at Christie's side and squeezed her arm as though they were old friends. She followed Christie's line of sight.

"Oh, Martin's back."

"Martin?" Christie said. "He looks...angry."

Daphne dabbed her eyes. "I imagine he is, dear. Today of all days. Anyway, we wished to pay our respects to your grandmother." Close up, there were red streaks through her hair, and behind thick glasses, her mascara had run. "You must be so sad!" Daphne continued as she beckoned to her husband. "As I said, I'm Daphne, and this is my husband, John Jones."

John reached his hand out to Christie to shake. "We're sorry for your loss."

"Thank you for coming. You knew Gran?"

Daphne beamed and took John's arm. "John's the local real estate agent. He knows everyone! Now, how long are you staying, lovely?"

"I need to leave within the hour. I've got a plane to catch this afternoon, so a short trip this time."

Daphne glanced at John. "Oh. So, you'll come back to settle the estate up? I'm sure we'd be most happy to handle the sale of the cottage if you intend to sell it?"

Angus smiled at Christie from the other side of the grave.

"Um, I have to go, I'm sorry. But thanks again for being here for Gran." Christie shook both John and Daphne's hands.

Daphne patted Christie's arm. "It's been so lovely to meet you, dear. Now, here's John's card, so don't be afraid to call or drop in anytime."

The drizzle returned as Christie joined Angus. "Jacob would like a few moments with us. When do you need to leave, Miss Christie?" He put the umbrella up.

Christie wound her arm through his. "I've got a little time."

"We'll go to the café on the corner near the motel? It shouldn't take long."

Christie nodded and dug her car keys out of her handbag as she walked beside Angus to the carpark. They passed Martin, on his knees at an unkempt grave. Beside him, gardening tools lay scattered. His hair and clothes were soaked through. Christie forced a small smile when he glanced up, but his expression was every bit as uninviting as before.

She glanced back from the carpark. He had collected the tools and strode away, disappearing down the steps to the beach.

The small café was quiet, colourful umbrellas folded and its outdoor seating dripping wet. Christie, Angus and Jacob sat inside, beside a condensation-streaked window.

Jacob extracted a large yellow envelope from an expensive leather briefcase. Christie nursed a coffee between cold hands, watching Angus stir sugar into his tea. Jacob had politely refused a drink and now removed a pile of papers from the envelope.

"Right, well Dorothy was quite explicit with her instructions." Jacob began. Christie hid a smile, of course, Gran would have been.

"There has to be a proper reading of the will etcetera," he continued, "but this is the overview. The vast majority of her estate is to be sold and the funds distributed to several charities she supported for many years."

Gran never once mentioned charities. Christie was pleasantly surprised.

"Angus will receive an income equivalent to his current pay for the rest of his life, plus the choice of either the Bentley or the Range Rover. Of course, you are entitled to contest this."

"I won't be contesting her will."

Jacob shuffled through the papers. "Now, Dorothy made it a

condition you attend her funeral, and you visit the old cottage. You have done both, so it will now become your property."

"Why? I mean, what about her sister, Martha?"

"She's not mentioned in the will. Dorothy left you the cottage."

"What will I do with it?"

Jacob shrugged. "Sell it. Live in it. Rent it out. Dorothy signed a change of ownership several weeks ago on the basis the conditions were met, so once I action it, the cottage and its land will be yours."

Angus leaned forward. "If I may say so, Miss Dorothy left it to you for a reason. There are secrets in that cottage. Questions needing answers."

Jacob closed his briefcase and stood. "I must go, so thank you both for your time. I'll be in touch." After shaking hands, he nodded and left.

Christie turned back to Angus. "What secrets, Angus? What's in the cottage?"

"All I know is they concern your Great-Aunt Martha."

Christie glanced at her watch.

"Before you go, Miss Dorothy left a note. For you." Angus reached into a pocket and withdrew a neatly folded page of ivory paper. He held it out to Christie, and after a moment, she took it.

"Read it when you are ready. It was…unfinished. Left at the motel."

"Gran died at the motel? Not…" Christie gulped.

"No, not in our rooms. I'm so sorry, I should have told you."

"But why? Why did this all happen, Angus?"

"She had her reasons for coming here, and once she made her mind up, there was no changing it. I do know she wanted to see her sister again."

So Martha was alive. What had Gran wanted to tell her? Why had Gran thought Christie could uncover some old family secret in a cottage? The reminder on the phone interrupted her musings.

"Please keep in touch?"

"Of course I shall. I'll be packing up Miss Dorothy's belongings to dispose of as she wished. Should I come across any information on your great-aunt, I will let you know." Angus stood and offered Christie his arm.

As they walked to Christie's car, she didn't want to let go of his arm. She took a deep, steadying breath. Angus was one of life's gentlemen, and she had forgotten how much she cared for him. She made a silent resolve to visit him more often.

"Well, here we are. Now, you have a safe drive back and enjoy your holiday." Angus hugged Christie so tightly she was breathless. If there were tears, she blinked them away before he could see them.

A few moments later, Christie slowed the car as she passed the graveyard on the cliff, glancing across to where she had farewelled Gran. It was deserted, except for a woman who leant on a walking stick at the grave where that man, Martin, had been.

The phone rang, and Christie touched the button on her steering wheel to answer as she increased her speed on the open road.

"On your way, baby?"

"I just left Rivers End, so will get to the airport with time to spare." Christie passed the turnoff to the cottage.

"Glad to hear it. I was beginning to think you might not have wanted to come with me."

"Oh, that's not true. I miss you so much."

"Well, it's been a bit rough without you, Chris. A bit embarrassing, arriving here without you. I mean, this is a couple's paradise, and there I was more like a single."

You're joking. Right?

"A few more hours and I'll be there, honey. What's the plan for tonight?" The road started to curve.

"I made an appointment at the spa for you. Facial and hair first. We'll get you into something sexy for dinner and take you to meet some people I've met. Well, I already knew Ingrid from a conference in London and her husband, um, oh yeah, Leon, he's with her. Don't know what he does but you'll get on alright with him."

The phone went silent, and Christie realised a response was expected. "But, we'll have dinner alone, won't we?"

"It's already arranged for us to have dinner on the terrace with them. Champagne, lobster, the works. We can go dancing afterwards if you want."

"I was hoping to spend some time alone with you. I'd like to tell you what's been going on." Nothing sounded worse than having to meet strangers tonight.

There was silence from Derek's end. Christie took advantage of a wide shoulder to pull over. "Derek?"

"I think you're being a bit selfish, Chris. You know, I've been tolerant about you taking off for a road trip rather than come with me. The least you can do to make it up is meeting my friends when I ask."

"Road trip? It was my grandmother's funeral, Derek! How can you begrudge me one day to pay my respects to her? I've apologised for my change of plans more than once, but how is it selfish to want to spend tonight with my own fiancé?"

Christie turned the motor off, and the sounds of the nearby ocean filled the air. Her heart thumped uncomfortably, and her shoulders tightened.

"Don't get snappy with me." Derek's voice was hard. "It was your choice to go, and it's my choice who we'll socialise with and when on the holiday I paid for."

I can't lose you, too.

"Please don't be angry." She kept her tone even. "I feel bad about the poor timing, but I'm on my way now. Honey?"

"If a person you barely knew, and a pile of junk in a backwater town mean more than I do, well, of course, I'm angry. And hurt."

Christie started shaking as bewilderment swept through her, hands gripping the steering wheel until her knuckles turned white.

"Are you there, Chris?"

"Christie. You know I prefer to be called Christie." The shaking stopped as a heavy stone dropped into her stomach. "I'm going to have to call you later."

"And I expect you to be in a better frame of mind once you arrive. Understand?"

He hung up.

No, she did not understand. Not one bit. A weak sun forced its way through the clouds as Christie started the motor. After a moment's hesitation, Christie did a U-turn and headed back to Rivers End.

COMING HOME TO NOTHING

The woman in the graveyard glanced at the sports car as it drove past, distracted by the roar of its motor. Martha Ryan had quite a love of fast cars and seeing a Lotus here in this sleepy town was a bit surprising. Once out of sight, she lost interest and returned to contemplating the headstone in front of her.

Long grass and weeds masked the bottom half of a white headstone. There was a name etched into the stone. *Thomas Blake.* She silently mouthed the name.

Her fingers played with the pendant she wore, a simple chain with the letters M and T entwined.

"I came back, Tom. I did," she spoke to the headstone, "and look at you."

She turned her back on that grave and hobbled to Dorothy's. A white tulip lay forgotten on the ground. Martha leaned down to reach it, using her cane to keep balance.

"Until we meet again," she whispered, placing the tulip on the new earth.

Martha returned to Thomas' grave and with shaking hands, removed the pendant, holding it up to gaze at one last time before setting it upon the headstone. The sun broke through the clouds, and the pendant glinted.

Her injured ankle made walking a struggle and Martha took care on the uneven ground as she approached the edge of the cliff. She gazed at the white beach below, the jetty high above the tide. Then, Martha turned her eyes to the cliff all the way at the other end of the beach. How different things had been in 1966.

Near the jagged edge of a grass-covered clifftop, a blank canvas was on an easel. Thomas sat before it, deep in concentration as he mixed colours. Martha walked up the hill behind him wearing a simple white dress and hat. Her hair flowed over bare shoulders, and she was certain she had a hint of mischief in her eyes. Realising Thomas was unaware of her presence; she picked a daisy and tickled his neck. Absently, he brushed it away, so she did it again and this time, he reached up and captured her hand.

Martha laughed. She tossed her hat onto the grass and ran her hand through her hair, letting the strands fall. She loved the way the sunlight picked up the glints of gold in her otherwise dark brown hair.

"I just had to escape Palmerston. Mother is getting the house ready for Father's birthday party, and I simply couldn't bear listening to her going on and on about the guest list!" Martha walked to the edge of the cliff and glanced at the sea far below.

"Be careful," Thomas warned.

Martha stretched her arms out. She lifted herself onto her toes, her fingers wide as if to catch the breeze. Thomas was behind her, his arms whipping around her slim waist. Martha was startled but relaxed against his muscular body.

"I said to be careful. You could fall."

"You'd always catch me."

Thomas tightened his grip. "That's not all I'd do."

Martha laughed again, so Thomas spun her around to face him, taking a step back from the cliff edge at the same time. How she loved him! Martha gazed at Thomas. Ever so slowly, he lowered his mouth to within an inch of hers, and she closed her eyes in anticipation.

"You need someone to curb your wild nature. Someone with a firm hand," he whispered.

Martha opened her eyes. "You can't tame the wind. Or the ocean, except in your paintings."

He released her to return to the easel. Martha glared after him, hands on her hips as he picked up a brush. Had he just dismissed her?

Love him she might, but stay where she wasn't welcome, she wouldn't. She swept her hat off the grass and stalked down the hill.

"Bye, Martha."

"Goodbye, Thomas."

She sneaked a glance back and he was smiling at her, then blew a kiss. All the irritation drained away and she blew one back.

Clouds scuttled in front of the sun and Martha shivered, regretting her choice of a thin dress and no jacket. Her suitcase was back in the carpark, where the bus driver had kindly stopped to let her alight. There'd been no time to change since the airport. And still she'd not arrived in time.

Soaring on the updraft around the cliff, seagulls cawed and drifted. How lucky they were to fly where they chose. To care only where their next meal was. They lost interest in her and flew to the beach.

Martha followed them. The way to the stone steps was familiar but the descent was much harder than she remembered. One painful step at a time, leaning heavily on the cane, she drew closer to that beloved and hated place.

Her twentieth birthday was today and she ran down the steps without a care in the world. Thomas waited at the bottom, arms open and she threw herself into them.

The cane skidded and Martha grabbed the railing, barely keeping her balance on steps made slippery by the earlier drizzle.

Her arms wrapped around his neck and her body melted against him. She couldn't wait for the present he'd teased her about for days.

Martha rested at the bottom for a moment, her heart pounding from more than the effort of the descent.

With a laugh, Martha freed herself and sprinted away. Thomas's footsteps followed and she sped up, determined to get there first.

The sea reflected the overcast sky. Summer might be close but today the elements understood. There was no more sunshine for Martha. Dorothy was gone. Thomas was gone.

Impatient for Thomas to catch up, Martha danced along the jetty, dangling her sandals from her fingers. By the time he reached her, she'd settled on the end, feet dipping into warm water.

The old jetty creaked with every slow step Martha took. The tide was low, but wind whipped foam from the wave tops. Martha lowered herself onto the end of the jetty.

As she leaned against Thomas, Martha closed her eyes. What could be more perfect than the sun on her face, the sea lapping on her feet, and the man at her side? Her fingers played with the pendant, the one he'd had specially made for her birthday with their initials entwined. What more could a girl want?

She'd had it all. Martha glanced at the green-grey water. The last time she'd been here, the sea was black. And this jetty all but submerged. Tom had saved her life, and wanted her to listen to his explanation yet she'd run away.

"Promise me you'll return." And she had promised, before fleeing into the rain. His cry almost breaking her heart... "I love you, Martha Ryan."

She should have turned back, because she loved him with every ounce of her being.

A promise broken.

I am broken.

Even the seagulls were gone. Martha was alone. From some long, locked away corner of her heart, a sob escaped as raindrops fell, mingling with the tears she could no longer stop. She reached for the pendant. That was gone as well.

Trudging along the beach against sheets of rain, a fisherman pulled his hat further over his ears. Caught out on the rocks by the weather, he had given up the idea of fish for lunch and now wanted a steaming cup of coffee to nestle between his frozen hands. As he passed the jetty, a small movement caught his eye.

A hunched figure, an old woman on the end of the old structure. He dropped his tackle on the sand and stomped along the jetty. What was she doing out here, let alone in this rain? Drenched and with both arms wrapped around her body, she was deathly cold when he touched her arm. Her eyes stayed closed as he draped his oilskin around her shoulders. "Hold on, lady. Just hold on."

THE SECRETS WE KEEP

*C*hristie sat in her car, staring at the cottage. Parked halfway up the driveway, the dull scrape of her windscreen wipers periodically interrupted the pitter-patter of the rain on the roof. She had no idea what she was doing here. All she did know was that Lizard Island was off the cards. Unsure if she even wanted to be engaged to Derek anymore, she was numb.

Under heavy clouds and steady rain, the cottage melted into the foliage. Large trees overhung it, their branches brushing against the metal roof. Oversized bushes intruded on the windows and sprawled over garden beds. Across the front of the property, the rose bushes had grown into a hedge of sorts.

Christie knew a little about gardening, thanks to Gran's love of flowers, roses in particular. Tending to the beautiful array of plants in the conservatory and garden was the one thing they enjoyed doing together. Lilies, dahlias, roses and a multitude of others Gran taught her how to properly prune and feed. Yet, not one tulip Christie could recall, thinking back to the casket this morning.

She needed a bathroom stop and water. Christie dug around in her bag for the keys to the cottage. Her hand touched the letter from Gran.

Not yet.

Clutching her keys, she climbed out into the rain, stepping straight into a puddle, soaking her other shoes. This time though, all she could do was laugh. She laughed all the way to the porch where she tossed her heels off and shook the rain from her hair.

If Derek saw her now, he would be horrified. Shoeless feet, wet hair and damp clothes. Standing on the tiny porch of—what had he called it? Oh yes, a pile of junk in a backwater town. Christie played with the keys in her hand. Well, it was her pile of junk so he might have to get used to it. Before she could change her mind, Christie unlocked the door and went inside.

She turned the kitchen tap. The pipes groaned and rattled before delivering a trickle of brown water. She left it on while she checked the cupboards, finding some old glassware at the back of the one next to the even older oven. The water came out in a clear gush, and after washing a glass, Christie cautiously sipped the contents. It tasted fresh and pure. Through the grimy window, she spotted the source. A large metal tank was almost invisible within the grip of a blackberry bush.

She visited the bathroom. She ran the tap for a while there as well to wash her hands, before drying them on tissues from her bag. If she was going to stay here, she would need to shop soon.

Who said anything about staying?

No power, no food, no anything that made a house a home. But it is yours, a little voice insisted.

Worn old carpet in the hallway warmed her cold feet a little. She revisited the bedrooms, deciding the one on the left was in the best shape. Although missing curtains, its finely striped blue wallpaper was intact and the mattress on the post and rail bed was firm.

Remembering the blankets in the hallway closet, Christie went to check their condition. On closer inspection, only two of the blankets were usable, the others so worn and holey they would offer little warmth. Christie dropped the better blankets on the bed and returned to the hallway.

She glanced up at the trapdoor and hesitantly took the long tool out again. This time, when she hooked the loop and pulled, she stepped back to avoid the debris and dust. The trapdoor swung downwards. A pull-down ladder clunked its way to half a metre or so above the ground.

"Well, well." The attic in Gran's house always fascinated her with its treasure trove of unwanted furniture and old keepsakes. Not that you would want to be caught there, as it was deemed off limits.

Christie put one foot on the ladder. Probably should have worn shoes, but she wanted to see what was up there. The ladder swayed alarmingly as she climbed. It was awkward climbing in a narrow skirted dress, but she got to the top and took her phone out. Finding its flashlight, she cast the light around. It was a surprisingly large space with the roof high in the middle. Christie pulled herself onto the floor of the attic and stood.

The rain thundered like a relentless waterfall on the metal roof. There was one cobweb-covered window. Beside it was a small armchair with a throw rug tossed over its back. An empty workbench ran along one end of the attic, covered with layers of paint splashes.

There was little else to investigate. No hidden rooms or secret passages. Disappointed, Christie hesitated at the edge of the open trapdoor, flashing the phone torch around one last time. In the furthest corner, where the roof was low, a dark shape was just visible. It was a small wooden trunk, pushed so far back that Christie had to get onto her knees to reach it.

Crafted from timber, it was about the size of a small suitcase with a curved top. It was locked. Christie sat back on her heels. Was this where Gran kept her secrets? If the cottage had been the home of the stationmaster until the trains stopped, who had lived here since? Not Gran. Would Martha have lived here? Maybe this trunk was empty, and there were no secrets.

Only one way to find out. Christie pulled the keys from her pocket. There was the key to the front door, a small key that might be for a padlock, and a long skeleton key.

"Private Investigator Ryan!" Christie giggled as she inserted the long key and turned it. It went around, and around again, and with a small "click", the lock opened.

Almost holding her breath, Christie opened the trunk and flicked the light inside. Adorned with a red velvet ribbon was a shoebox. Nothing else. Christie picked it up with a frown and carried it to the armchair where there was a little bit of natural if dull light.

The box on her lap, Christie tugged the ribbon, and it slipped off. The shoebox must have been decades old, as the brand was indiscernible and the cardboard was spongy. Inside, a black ring box perched on top of a bundle of letters tied up with more red velvet ribbon. Christie removed the lid of the ring box.

On a bed of black silk lay two rings. A simple gold wedding band and a solitaire ring.

"Oh, my." Christie held the box up to the window to see them better, but it was too dark, so she replaced the lid and put it back in the shoebox. Now, this might qualify as a secret. Or, it might be someone's rings accidentally left behind. Whichever, Christie knew she needed more light and something on her cold feet.

Half an hour later and Christie was more puzzled than ever. Taking advantage of a break in the rain, she made a dash for the car to retrieve her overnight bag and the box from Gran. Dry socks warmed her feet, and her shoes were now perched on the windowsill facing where the sun would be, should it decide to make an appearance.

She picked up the wedding ring and squinted at the engraving on the inside.

Forever Taming the Wind

The ring was exquisitely made, as if by a master jeweller. The solitaire was every bit as beautiful in matching yellow gold, with a stunning brilliant cut diamond in a six claw setting. Christie removed her own ring and tried this one on. It fitted as if made for her finger.

Christie compared her ring with the solitaire. Her three stone, halo diamond ring was set in platinum, and while it was sparkly and expensive, lacked the simple perfection of the other ring. She pulled it off, filled with guilt for thinking that way.

She needed to let Derek know her change of plans. Before she put it off any longer, she dialled his number. It went to voicemail.

"Hi honey," she began, "please call me when you get this. I'm sorry, but I won't be there today. Um, I...I need a few days to myself. The funeral and everything was hard, and I need a little time to work through it all. Sorry. Please don't worry about me. Just enjoy your time up there. I'll talk to you soon. Love you."

No doubt he would be upset and probably had every right to be. Instead of enjoying a long-awaited break together, he was alone and disappointed by the turn of events that were outside his control. Christie pushed aside the thought she would be on her way to him now if he had been more understanding.

Instead of dwelling on it, she took the bundle of letters out of the shoebox and slipped the ribbon off. There were a handful of letters, each addressed to Miss M Ryan, care of Miss D Ryan at a Melbourne address. The handwriting was bold and masculine with the return address of T. Blake, 37 Station Street, Rivers End. This cottage. All the letters had stamps, and postage marks and all of them remained unopened. How strange. There was no return to sender message on them, so presumably, they had found their way to Martha and been ignored.

Christie flicked through them. The timespan ranged across three months in 1967 and 1968. Who was T. Blake? For that matter, how had they come back to the cottage where they originated, and who kept them in this shoebox for all of these years? Angus had been right about secrets!

The sun came out, bringing instant warmth. Christie peered out of the window. Outside, the wet trees glistened under a clearing sky. There was peace here.

The sound of heavy footsteps on the porch, followed by a creak and a bang, interrupted this new found peace. Christie waited for the knock that did not come, so after a moment she looked outside. Nobody there. She went to the driveway, watching her step. A van was pulling away, with Municipal Power across its side.

Back inside, Christie tried the light switch, and was rewarded with a brightly lit kitchen. Well, that made the decision easier. At least for tonight, she would stay here, and tomorrow she would work out what she wanted to do with the cottage.

STRANGERS AMONGST US

*W*ith the sun out, it was as though all the people living in town emerged. Christie circled the block for a parking spot, aware her car was drawing the interest of almost everyone she passed.

The town was old, with late nineteenth-century architecture modified to accommodate modern trends. Shops had housing behind or above them. Along one side of the main street were cafés and take-aways, a jeweller, a couple of clothing shops, a bakery, and a pharmacy next to a house converted into a medical surgery. On the other side was a small supermarket, two real estate agents, a newsagent, a bank, also a post office and a butcher. Public hotels were at either end of the main street, one with a bottle shop attached. Further along was a police station converted from a house.

The small supermarket was bursting with products on high shelves. Christie could not believe her luck finding a sheet set, pillow, and a towel. To those she added toilet paper, paper towels, garbage bags, cleaning products, and a kettle hiding behind some vases, some long life milk, and instant coffee, plus a mug, and plastic cutlery set.

At the checkout, two middle-aged women—one on either side of the counter—were deep in conversation, but as Christie approached, they stopped and stared at her. She smiled and loaded her purchases. In silence, the woman behind the checkout scanned Christie's items and packed them into a box. The other woman stood back to watch.

"How are you?" Christie asked them, getting only a grunt in return. Unfazed, Christie took her purse out and found some cash. "Nice to see the sun."

Finished, the shopkeeper merely held her hand out for the money. After thoroughly checking each note, the woman handed change and a receipt back without a word.

Next, she went to the bakery, which boasted a tempting array of pastries, cakes and all manner of baked delights. Doubting the quality of the oven in the cottage, she decided to buy lunch and tomorrow's breakfast now, and come back into town this evening for dinner.

The girl behind the checkout was about eighteen, excessively made up, with rings through her nose and eyebrow. Her name badge said Belinda. She openly admired Christie's clothes. "Is that your car outside? The white sports car?"

"Sure is."

"Wow, cool. You must be pretty rich."

Christie laughed. "Hardly. Just a bit lucky to get an amazing deal."

"Wish I was lucky! Don't think I'll ever own anything that fantastic. Now, what delicious offerings may I help with?"

Christie chose a couple of croissants for tomorrow and a freshly made salad roll for lunch. As Belinda got these, a younger girl dressed in school uniform and carrying a backpack hurried into the shop and straight around the counter.

"Hey Jess," Belinda glanced up, "there's lunch on the table."

Jess glanced around on her way to the backroom, giving Christie a glimpse of her face. About twelve, she was pretty but had a long, light coloured birthmark on her left cheek.

"Thanks," she mumbled as she rushed through the door.

Belinda put Christie's food into a carry bag. "There you go, the croissants are a local favourite. Next time, try the éclair. They're a bit spesh too."

Christie paid and thanked Belinda. What a different reception from the supermarket. Small towns!

MIXED MOMENTS

As she eased the car into the driveway, Christie unexpectedly smiled. The rainy skies were now blue, and the air was warmer. For some reason, the cottage was calling her. It might have caused a rift with Derek, but something was appealing about this funny little house.

Christie ate her roll perched on the corner of the kitchen table, her eyes drawn to the open shoebox. This whole mystery surrounding Gran and her sister was puzzling. Something had driven a wedge between them, and the answers might be in those letters. She intended to find an address for Martha and let her know, as gently as possible, that Gran had passed away.

Before doing anything though, she made the bed and cleaned the bathroom. The methodical job of cleaning was oddly relaxing, and the result of a serviceable bathroom and ready to sleep in bed left Christie satisfied.

She glanced at her watch. Almost three. Her flight would be leaving, and she should have been on it. How could her life have changed so fast? She should have been able to handle the whole thing better, and make Derek happy as well as fulfil Gran's final wishes.

Her relationship with Derek had always been tranquil. No arguments or hurtful words, until the last day or so, when Gran's funeral derailed his plans. He had to be hurt to have written off Christie's loss as less important than his own needs.

Christie got a glass of water and sat at the table, mentally shaking it all off. She unrolled the canvas.

So beautiful.

The top right corner had a small tear needing attention before any more damage occurred. There was no apparent signature on the painting.

She laid the letters to Martha out on the table by date, oldest to newest. Their postmarks stretched from 7 December 1967 to 19 March 1968. Some dates were within days of each other and others, more than a week apart. All in a bold, male hand and addressed to Martha. Each was unopened. How odd.

So, there is an old painting of the ocean and a handful of unopened letters. And the rings.

What was the connection, if there even was one? Christie knew now her predecessors owned this cottage. Built for the stationmasters. Had T. Blake been one of them? What did the painting have to do with the cottage?

There was a jetty on the beach she'd seen when she arrived. The painting featured a jetty, so had it been painted here? The paint splashes on the long bench in the attic could easily have been those left behind by an artist. For Gran to leave Christie the painting, it was either valuable or part of the so-called secrets of the cottage. She discarded the first idea, as Gran would never permit anything of value to be neglected. So, what was its secret?

Was T. Blake an artist who lived here? Had he—a man, going by the handwriting—painted the seascape, which for some reason had significance to either Gran or Martha? A gift or a commission, or maybe payment for something?

Christie's brain was going around in circles. She wanted a big piece of paper to write out what little information she had, to see if any of it matched up.

Her hand strayed to the ring box, and she found herself holding the solitaire. Who had worn this beautiful ring? She almost threw it back in its box and closed the lid to stop herself putting it back on. Instead, she sat playing with her own engagement ring, turning it around and around while she thought about Derek.

He had purchased this in London a month before he proposed. Then, at one of Melbourne's most exclusive restaurants and in typical Derek fashion, he proposed. On one knee in the middle of the place, much to the delight of other patrons and Christie's discomfort.

The ring had been on her finger for two years now. There had never been a proper conversation about wedding dates or plans until Derek's throwaway comment the day Christie came home. She would have happily set a date. If only he had shown a little compassion and concern, instead of tearing her down.

Dusk approached as Christie drove into the carpark beside the grave-yard. She stopped at Gran's grave and squatted to touch the tulip.

Who put you there?

Christie wandered to the edge of the cliff. The sky was clear and the air already cooling as the sun sank toward the horizon. Beautiful slivers of colour stretched across the mirror-like ocean. The stone steps tempted Christie, and before she could change her mind, she ran down to the beach.

She took off her shoes and meandered along the shoreline, drinking in the natural beauty, and marvelling in this place so unknown. She was glad it was almost untouched, as progress could easily spoil such a region. Derek would have loved it here, but for the wrong reasons, with ideas of housing estates, high-rise hotels, and shopping malls.

She kept half an eye on the incoming waves, adjusting her path each time one came too close to her feet.

The jetty reached about twenty metres into the water, high enough to keep above the level of an average high tide. The old timber boards creaked and groaned with the undertow and above, seagulls cawed to each other. Endless waves rushed in, ever higher, leaving a trail of sparkling foam on the sand as they slipped back again with a soft whoosh.

As daylight faded, she made her way back. At the bottom of the steps, she gazed longingly again at the beach. Turning to go, something on the cliff face caught her eye.

In the flat, limestone rock to one side of the steps, someone had carved a love heart. It was quite deep and on closer inspection, had a letter T above it and a letter M below.

"T loves M," Christie said, tracing the engraving with her finger. She stared at it for a moment and took her phone out of a pocket. Standing back a little, she took a few photographs of the love heart. She glanced back at the jetty, deep in thought. From here, under the imminent onset of night, the jetty most certainly was the same as in the seascape.

Finding the keyhole in pitch black was almost impossible, let alone while juggling bags of Chinese food and a bottle of wine. Christie's phone had a flat battery now, so she could not even use its torch. After a few failed attempts, the key found its home, and the door opened. Christie flicked on the light switch with a sigh of relief.

Christie plugged in the phone and opened the first container as her stomach rumbled. She scooped up the first mouthful of noodles dripping in satay sauce into her mouth, closing her eyes with pleasure. The peanutty, spicy mix was filled with crunchy fresh vegetables and was delicious.

The phone beeped, and Christie groaned when she saw it was a missed call from Derek. Of all times for him to ring when the phone was off. There was no voicemail and no follow up text message. She dialled his number and reluctantly pushed her meal away.

Derek answered with a terse "Give me a minute."

There was background noise of people talking, and soft music and Christie heard Derek speak to someone, followed by laughter. The sounds faded as if he was walking somewhere and then, "Why have you done this?"

"I'm sorry I couldn't get there." Christie's heart sank.

"Couldn't? You mean wouldn't. Tell me, do you even want to be my wife anymore?"

"Of course I do! Oh, Derek, please understand how much Gran dying has affected me. It's brought back a lot of memories and a lot of grief."

"Which is why you should have done as I said and not gone to the funeral. You should be here with me, not in that nowhere town. A couple of days up here, some friendly company and a few cocktails and you'd be yourself again. Not moping about someone who rejected you."

"Why don't you understand how I feel?"

"I do understand. That's the problem, Chris. From the day we first met, I knew you needed a man who would guide you through life. You're too trusting and generous. I mean, those are admirable qualities, but it doesn't get you anywhere, and you'll end up being badly hurt."

But you're hurting me now!

"You need to learn to stand up for yourself. To say no more often. No to jobs that take you to the other side of the world. No to those pro bono sessions at the hospitals. No to people who want you to drop everything to suit themselves." he laughed shortly. "Even no to me sometimes, instead of always saying sorry. Just tell me what you're thinking instead of going along with my ideas all the time. You should have said you didn't want to come with me."

There was a long silence, and the music and laughter got louder again.

"I did want to go with you, Derek. I did."

Why are you lying?

"Well, you're not here. Are you in the apartment?"

"No. I'm staying at the cottage tonight."

On the other end of the phone, a woman called out, "Derek, your entrée's getting cold!"

"Just think about what I've said. You need to change yourself if you want our relationship to go forward. It's over to you."

"What do you mean?"

"Just think about our conversation, Chris. I'm not happy at all, and that's your doing." Derek hung up.

Eyes wide, Christie stared at the phone. "Christie," she whispered. "Not Chris. Christie."

Her pro bono hospital work meant so much, helping people regain their confidence after an accident or burn with special make-up techniques. It was something she loved doing.

I thought you were proud of me.

Dinner was a write-off now, but the wine was delicious. It warmed her and took the edge off the anxiety and pain from the phone call. In the absence of a real wine glass, she half-filled a water glass.

She took the bundle of letters and her glass of wine to the bedroom. Sitting cross-legged on the bed, she sorted them again, from the first date to last.

It went against her nature to read someone else's mail, but who would this hurt? Fifty years old, never opened. Nobody but the author apparently ever read them, so who knows what they contained or why they were in Gran's cottage. Christie reached for the oldest letter from 1967.

AFTER SHE'S GONE

1 *967*

Rain thundered on the metal roof of the attic. Motionless, Thomas stared into the night, a towel tossed over bare shoulders and pants clinging to him, soaked through.

The storm was directly overhead and relentless lightning turned night into fractured day. In the centre of the attic were two easels, each with a canvas. One was blank; ready for the first strokes of a brush, but the other was a completed portrait of Martha sitting on the cliff top, surrounded by spring flowers, her eyes brimming with amusement.

The long bench held pots of paint, brushes and rags. The armchair beside the window was almost new, its fabric bright and a throw rug tossed over its back.

A shuddering rumble of thunder stirred Thomas and he moved away from the window to stand in front of the blank canvas. Contemplating it for a moment, he slipped his hand into a pocket and retrieved Martha's engagement ring. It was cold between his fingers as he placed it on the edge of the easel.

Taking the towel off his shoulders, he dried his hair, his expression as empty as the canvas.

After stripping to boxer shorts, Thomas made his way to his bedroom, the one on the right of the attic staircase. He dangled a whiskey-filled glass from one hand and carried an almost empty bottle in the other. The single bed was a mess with blankets and sheets thrown about and the pillows side by side. Two empty glasses perched on a bedside table.

Thomas pushed the other glasses aside to make room for his whiskey glass and the bottle. Straightening the blankets and sheets, he piled one pillow on top of the other, before dropping onto the side of the bed.

Lying back, Thomas stared at the ceiling as his mind replayed the events of the evening. Martha falling into the sea and his desperate swim to save her. Martha's anger. Her sorrow and stubborn pride. Martha running into the night.

He reached out to pick up his glass and his arm touched something on the bed...a pendant. Not Martha's, with their initials intertwined. This one was on a silver chain with the letter F as the pendant. Thomas picked it up, his knuckles turning white as he crushed the letter within his palm.

A week later Thomas had waited long enough for Martha to come to him. He'd gone to Palmerston House, prepared to accept the contempt of her mother, the anger of her sister, even the half drunken forgiveness of her father, if only to have one moment with Martha.

A moment would be enough. He would apologise for letting her believe for even a second there could ever be anyone other than her in his life. He would slip the ring back onto her finger and kiss her tears away. Stubborn or not, Thomas knew Martha loved him.

Nobody was at the sprawling, two level limestone and timber house. Deflated, he trudged back along the long driveway. As he reached the road, Patrick drove through the gate, winding down the window as he stopped the car.

"Give ye credit for trying, lad. Just too late."

"Too late for what? Where's Martha, sir?"

"Sworn to secrecy. Lilian made me promise I'd never tell ye."

Thomas felt his shoulders slump. Why had he expected Martha to be here? She had said she was leaving, so why had he waited?

"Thank you, sir. Goodbye." Thomas nodded to Patrick and turned to leave.

Patrick sighed. "Wait a bit. Here." Pulling a pen and notebook from his coat pocket, he scribbled an address, tore the page out and held it out.

"She's with her sister in the city. But ye need to know her mother's staying there for a while, so maybe write her a note, don't just show up. Ay?"

Thomas visibly brightened. "Yes, I mean, thank you. I'll never tell you gave me the address."

Patrick shrugged. "I'm always in trouble so it is of no matter. She does love ye, son." Winding the window back up, he continued to the homestead.

Thomas put the page in his pocket. "And I love your daughter, sir. Very much."

An hour later, Thomas posted his first letter to Martha.

THE TRAIL BEGINS

2 016

Christie unfolded the letter. The paper was thin and fragile and had a masculine scent. It was a few lines long.

Dear Martha,

I know you are hurt and must feel disappointed in me. For that I am deeply, truly sorry. But sweetheart, being away will not make things better. Being home again, here, in my arms, will help heal your hurt feelings. I promise to explain everything when I see you. No more running and no more secrets. Please come home soon.

Love, Thomas

A lover's quarrel, with Martha running away upset. What had Thomas Blake done to hurt her? No more secrets…what secrets?

Christie put the letter aside and opened the next.

Dear Martha,

I know only a few days have passed, but it feels like months to me. The other night—I was wrong to let you leave like that. I thought you would feel differently in a day or two. I will never go against my instincts again. Once we are married, you will not run away if we argue because I will deal with it differently. You will listen to me, talk with me, instead of using your pride as a barrier. I hurt you, yes, but what you are doing now is hurting us both, so time to end this ridiculous separation and come home. If your mother and sister refuse to bring you home, phone me and I will be there in a few hours. No matter how difficult it might be for you to return, it will lead to our life together.

Love,

Thomas

Christie read the letter twice, trying to understand what Thomas meant. The tone of his words was different from the first, being more resolute than apologetic.

After putting this letter into its envelope, Christie picked up her glass and sipped the wine. The way Derek sometimes spoke to her was similar to the last letter. Listen to me. Do as I tell you. Somehow, it was different though. Thomas wrote with love and equity of blame. Derek just blamed Christie.

The glass was empty. Well, she had no plans to drive anywhere tonight. Christie wandered barefoot to the kitchen, surprised at how warm the cottage had stayed after the sunny afternoon.

Back in the bedroom, she changed into soft pyjamas and slid into the sheets to continue reading. The next letter was postmarked four days later.

THEIR JETTY

1 *967*

Thomas stood at the end of the jetty as the first flicker of dawn lightened the starry sky, contemplating the calm water lapping against the pylons. All he could think about was the moment Martha slipped off the jetty and into the stormy sea. The hair on his skin rose as he recalled the heart stopping moment he thought he would never find her.

Either way, she was gone. Her absence left his heart empty and he longed to turn around and see her running down those stone steps, her face alight with happiness. How this happened was still something of a blur. He had been at fault, yet not at fault. Certainly, this had been none of Martha's doing but her leaving was making this worse.

What mystified him was the lack of communication from Martha. She never stayed angry for long and yet not one reply to his letters. Even if she wanted time away, he would have thought it a safe bet she would have written back. She must be hurt to stay silent for so long and that cut at Thomas. To know he had been instrumental in damaging their relationship was incomprehensible. Time to fix things.

The sea glistened in front of Thomas as the morning rays touched it and he sat on the edge of the jetty. Removing his shoes, he dropped his feet into the warm water, as he and Martha had done together so often.

This jetty meant so much to them both. It was here they had first spoken. Thomas often came to sit on the jetty early in the day, before anyone was about. It cleared his head and let him paint pictures in his head before committing them to canvas. One spring morning two years ago, he walked halfway along the timber boards before seeing someone sitting on the end.

Irritated at the intrusion, he stopped. Before he could leave, Martha turned around and flashed a stunning smile his way. "How gorgeous is this view?"

For a while, they sat in silence and then began talking as if they were old friends. A month later, they kissed at the same place and became inseparable.

This jetty was where he proposed. On one knee, trying not to let the ring fall into the sea and having to contend with Martha bursting into laughter until she realised he was serious. Her expression turned to pure love and she had thrown her arms around him, nearly over-balancing them both. His heart overflowed from so much love and the beauty Martha brought into his life.

He had to remind Martha of their past and let her see into his heart.

OUR LOVE IS NOT ORDINARY

2016.

As she blinked tears away, Christie reread the final few lines of the letter.

...so you see, sweetheart, we are meant to be together. Our love is not ordinary. It defies time and will live forever. Let me come and bring you home where you belong, in my arms, where I can protect and cherish you for a lifetime.

I love you,

Thomas

This was so real and poignant. What could have torn these two apart?

Had they reconciled? Surely, they must. Thomas sounded ready to go straight to Gran's home and whisk his beloved Martha away. No doubt, Gran and their mother put up a fight and perhaps that was the reason for the two sisters parting ways.

She reached for another letter.

Dear Martha,

I sold a painting! The one from our special place on the mountain, over-looking Rivers End and out across the sea. It was a lady from the city, an art collector. Perhaps she will come back and buy another? Once you are home, we will take a picnic up to the lookout there and celebrate the sale with champagne.

You always believed in my art, even when I did not believe in it myself. Remember the first time you saw my paintings? You told me I should move to France and become a famous artist. I laughed at the notion, but you were serious, my darling. You said my eye for detail would be appreciated by the art set in Paris and my charm would sell the paintings.

I do not feel much charm now. Just sadness and loneliness without you by my side. We belong together. It is time to come home, Martha. Please come home now.

Love,

Thomas.

An artist? Perhaps the seascape was his. This would explain the bench upstairs with its paint-splattered surface.

Christie yawned. One more.

Dear Martha,

Another week has passed and not one word from you.

Today, I waited in the rain. All day, from dawn to nightfall and I am frozen to the bone. Today of all days, I could not risk being absent from the jetty should you have returned. It is a full year since you accepted my marriage proposal and I had hoped, with every fibre, you would come home today. It seemed fitting, yet I am still alone.

Why, Martha, why not return and let us work this out? I know you love me with every ounce of my being. You are too strong to allow Dorothy and Lilian to stop you, so where are you?

My heart is breaking. There. I have said it. My heart is breaking for you.

Thomas.

The letter slipped from Christie's fingers. Asleep, her face was wet with tears.

LOST AND FOUND

*S*unlight streamed through the uncurtained window, stirring Christie from a deep sleep. She took her time opening her eyes and stretched, loving the warmth of the sun. Her night had been free of any dreams she could remember and she had to think for a moment of where she was. Her watch told her she had slept close on twelve hours. The remnants of jet lag had disappeared at last.

As she swung her feet over the side of the bed, Christie noticed the last letter was on the floor, so scooped it up and returned it to its envelope.

Poor Thomas. Whatever did you do?

The last thing she expected from these letters was the eloquent outpouring of love and loss an apparently young man in the sixties penned. How the pieces fitted together was beyond her.

The shower was refreshing but too short, as the hot water ran out after only a couple of moments. Towelling herself dry, Christie decided she needed more information about the cottage if she was to make an educated decision about its future. Starting with Daphne and John Jones.

~

Rivers End had two real estate agents, but only one with brightly flowering pot plants along its front. For some reason, Christie knew Daphne was responsible for this. Pushing the door open, she was right, with Daphne having a loud and happy conversation on the phone behind a dated laminate counter.

"Of course! Yes, Beth, I know exactly what you mean!" Daphne laughed then spotted Christie.

"Now, Beth…yes, yes, I agree, but Beth, I need to go now. Sorry darl, I've got an important client here so I'll phone you back. Okie dokie!"

Daphne replaced the receiver with a sigh. "Oh that one, she can talk! How lovely to see you! I thought you were leaving yesterday, lovely?"

"It seemed a pity not to stay for a little while." Christie leaned her arms on the counter. "It's a rather…enchanting little property under the dust and neglect."

"Indeed! And will be worth quite a bit if you were to sell. Would you like John to do an appraisal?"

"Oh, not at this point, but thanks. Could you refer me to someone who knows how to fix houses? I mean, it needs some electrical work and carpentry and painting. And gardening. Maybe a new fence?"

Daphne reached for a notepad and pen. "Well, let us know when you're ready and John will be most happy to give you some ideas. Rivers End is about to boom so it will certainly be a seller's market, mark my words."

"I promise I'll talk to John first, should I decide to sell." Christie hid a smile.

"Now, this is the number for Barry who is a local builder. Have a chat with him and see what he can do."

Daphne tore a page from the notepad and handed it to Christie. She stared at Christie's engagement ring. "What a beauty! So, is your young man going to join you here?"

Christie shrugged. "He's away, so we'll see once he's back. Daphne, at the funeral you mentioned you knew my Gran? Did you happen to know her sister?"

Daphne's eyes flew wide open. "Oh, no, I'm afraid Martha hasn't been seen in these parts for many a year. Of course, there's always been stories about her."

"You mean idle gossip." John walked out from an office behind the counter. "Hello again, Ms Ryan." he nodded.

"Please, call me Christie."

"But John," Daphne pouted, "even if it's gossip, there's always truth in talk."

"Not after all these years." John dropped some paperwork on the desk beside Daphne. She sighed audibly, but winked at Christie as John went back to his office. The whole town might be a haven of secrets still living in the last century.

"The other thing is I have a painting that needs some attention. It has a small tear and is old and I know it's a long shot, but is there a local gallery or the like?"

"Ah!" Daphne held her hand out for the piece of paper she gave Christie. When Christie handed it back, Daphne drew a map.

"That's easy, lovely. Amongst other things, young Martin is a framer. You take your painting to him to fix."

"Martin? The man at the graveyard?"

"Oh, you saw him at a bad time. He'll do the right thing for you."

I doubt that!

Something about that man had shaken her emotions and sent warning signals to her brain.

"Thanks, Daphne, you've been such a help." she said with a smile. "I'll let you get back to work."

"No, my pleasure, lovely. You drop in anytime and come and have a coffee one day."

She leaned forward and whispered. "There's always truth in talk!"

Christie nodded at Daphne, but had no idea what she meant. Daphne was a pleasant woman if something of a gossip and she hoped she might be able to talk to her away from John sometime. Even if it was gossip, anything at all about Martha was more than she had.

Driving back up the hill a few moments later, Christie glanced across at the graveyard. It was empty and Christie would have continued past, except a glint on top of a headstone caught her eye. Almost unconsciously, she found herself parking the car and wandering over to where the glint came from.

It was a pendant, its fine gold chain draped over the top of the rounded headstone. Christie picked it up, almost dropping it again when she saw the two letters entwined. *T and M.*

It must be pure coincidence the initials matched those of Thomas and Martha! Someone must have found it and left it on a random headstone for the owner to find. Almost holding her breath, Christie walked around the headstone to read the inscription.

Thomas Blake

Christie gasped and put her hand to her mouth. Thomas Blake, the man whose letters she had read, was dead. Buried here, overlooking the jetty where he had waited for his girl to come home.

A chill crept through Christie and she knew she had to stay until she found some answers. Somehow, in a day, the secrets of the cottage had captured her imagination and drawn her into its world.

A MAN AND A DOG

*C*hristie followed Daphne's map over the bridge to a narrow
road that by-passed the township, zigzagging close to the
beach. Soon, the road wound upwards around a cliff. It forked and
Christie took the left, noticing an elegant old guesthouse tucked
around the corner of the other road.

The road stopped at the top of the cliff. Christie pulled over and
checked the map. Yes, this matched the map, yet there was only one
house up here, right in the middle of a meadow behind a gate. There
was no driveway or path, nor any sign of life.

After leaving the graveyard, Christie had collected the painting.
Her resolution to find out about Martha and Thomas forced her to
ignore her instincts that this man, Martin, was trouble better avoided.
Daphne liked him. Not that she knew Daphne enough to trust her
judgement, but she had to start somewhere.

Christie checked herself in the rear vision mirror. She reapplied
lipstick and fiddled nervously with her hair. "Stop being silly," she
scolded her reflection, grabbed her handbag and the cylinder and
climbed out of the car.

The view from up here was incredible. At the distant reaches of
the ocean was an endless, hazy horizon. On the cliff to the left was the

graveyard and further on, the turn-off to the cottage. The beach was nestled between both cliffs, white and enticing. Inland, the town was like a toy village and beyond it, thick bush led to mountains. It was magical, like something from a storybook.

Looped around the heavy timber gate was a padlocked chain. Christie giggled as she climbed the gate. Ha! Would be hilarious if she was shot as a trespasser. Not. The grass was long and soft and would be lovely to walk through bare-footed, but Christie kept her shoes on and pushed herself forward.

The front door was as unwelcoming as the locked gate, cobwebs covering the handle and hinges. A dead pot plant reinforced the message that visitors were not welcome and Christie gulped and stepped back. There were no windows on this side of the house and Christie turned away before knocking.

This was a bad idea.

From around the corner, a golden retriever bounded toward her, tail wagging madly and soft, brown eyes warm and friendly. Christie's face lit up and she let the dog sniff her.

"Hello there. You're a beauty!" she scratched behind his ears.

Just as fast as he appeared, the dog ran off again, back in the same direction. After a moment's hesitation, Christie followed. If Martin owned this dog, he could not be all bad.

Dogs know.

This side of the house was different. Facing out to sea, a long timber deck ran along its length, its railings dripping with jasmine. Heavy wind chimes murmured from one end. There were a couple of deck chairs and a small table, along with a covered barbeque. Two railed steps led up to the deck, another to a sliding glass door, which was wide open.

The dog must have gone inside and Christie followed as far as the door. She knocked on the glass with no response. "Hello?"

No answer. Her senses were on high alert and it was time to go. She turned to leave and stopped dead.

Martin stood at the bottom of the steps with a hand on either handrail, forming a human barrier to her escape, which she wanted very, very much.

A white T-shirt hugged his chest and broad shoulders, whilst board shorts left his muscular legs and bare feet exposed. Strong, sun-bronzed arms and three-day growth gave Christie a vision of him on a surfboard, controlling the waves. An unwanted surge of attraction rushed through her. She forced it into the background. It occurred to her she was staring at him.

Christie swallowed. "Um, hi. Daphne—at the real estate agents—gave me your address."

Martin watched Christie without changing his expression, which was neither hostile nor welcoming. His eyes moved briefly to the cylinder, then straight back to her face.

"Daphne didn't give me a phone number, so I'm sorry I couldn't call ahead."

No response, just a silence that hung between them.

"Daphne said you might be able to help me, with my painting."

"Daphne talks too much." Martin took both steps in one movement and brushed past Christie to go into the house. "You have five minutes."

Christie glanced longingly at the stairs, but she followed him. She stopped a few steps inside the door. The room was a large, open plan living area, with floor to ceiling windows on two sides and furnished with natural timber and neutral fabrics. Behind a long, timber break-fast bar was a roomy kitchen.

Martin stood on the far side of the room, arms crossed, openly inspecting her. Heat rose to her face, colouring it. Flustered, she introduced herself.

"I'm Christie Ry—"

"I know who you are," Martin interrupted. "Do you always follow dogs to their home?"

"Only the ones that like me."

"He's a terrible judge of character."

"He must be!" As soon as the words left her lips, Christie's eyes widened. "I'm sorry. I didn't mean to imply..." Her voice trailed off.

"Sure you did." Martin uncrossed his arms, showing no sign of being offended. He stalked across the room, like a panther to its prey. Wide-eyed, Christie gazed at him as he approached. Her heart pounded, and when he stopped close enough for her to feel the heat from his body, she stopped breathing altogether.

Very deliberately, he brought his mouth close to her ear. "Never apologise," he slipped the cylinder from her hands, "it weakens your position."

With that, he took the cylinder to the kitchen counter. Martin eased the painting out and flattened it. He studied the canvas as if memorising every brush stroke. Christie joined him, curious at his concentration. His eyes turned to her.

"You got this from your grandmother?"

"Yes. But how did you know? Have you met her?"

"Where did she get it?"

"I'd never seen it until yesterday."

"You have no idea? None?" Martin allowed the canvas to roll back up.

Christie shook her head. "Just a theory."

"Which is?"

"I think maybe it was painted by...a local. Perhaps it was a gift to Gran."

"Have you ever been to Rivers End before, Miss Ryan?" Martin captured Christie's left hand, and held it up to inspect her engagement ring. "Expensive. Like your car. Not once have you visited your home-town, so why now? That cottage is worthless, unless you're a developer?"

Christie pulled her hand away. "Me? No, of course not. But the cottage does have value and secrets that need discovering."

"What secrets?"

"Let me ask a question," Christie began, "that grave you were tending?"

"What are the secrets of the cottage?" His face was hard.

Christie reached for the painting but Martin stepped between her and the counter. "The damage will worsen if it isn't framed. The tear needs repairing."

He picked up the canvas and the cylinder as if it was agreed upon. "Write your phone number down—there's pen and paper beside you. I'll phone when it's done."

Without another word, Martin stalked out of the house. Christie stared after him, unconsciously rubbing her left hand. Now he had her painting. Insufferable and not at all helpful, he nevertheless seemed to know a lot more about her and her family than she knew about him. Which was almost nothing.

SETTLING IN

*D*usk was closing in when the Lotus passed the *Welcome to Rivers End* sign. Instead of going to the cottage, Christie drove to the clifftop carpark and stepped out into the cooling air. She stretched to relieve the stiffness in her body and headed to the top of the stone steps.

After leaving Martin's house, she'd driven home to Melbourne. If she was going to stay in the cottage for a few days, she needed clothes and her laptop. Any doubts about her decision vanished as she breathed in the clear air.

The ocean resembled a postcard, deep blue with highlights of aqua and pink reflected from the horizon. High tide was a couple of hours away, so the waves near the beach were full and rolled in from a long way out. Long enough for a lone surfboarder to take advantage of.

Christie perched on the top step to watch the setting sun, but instead, her eyes focussed on the man riding the waves. Although a fair way out and in fading light, she was certain it was Martin. A moment later, she spotted the dog rolling in the soft sand.

Her earlier mental image of Martin surfing was a pale shadow of the reality. He radiated power and control as he effortlessly navigated the surfboard out to sea, then back in on a wave. There was an artistry in every move.

Christie's car keys slipped out of her fingers onto the step. She picked them up, but not before the dog heard the small sound. Bounding across the beach and up the steps, he planted a wet kiss on her nose.

"Shh, doggie, no!" she giggled. "Go back to your master!" Instead, he dropped himself at her feet, his tail madly wagging. Martin was paddling back out to sea but it would only be a moment or two before he caught a wave back in again.

"Seriously, you have to go. So do I!"

After giving the dog a quick hug, Christie got to her feet and hurried back to the car.

The small wardrobe in the bedroom had just enough room for the selection of dresses, pants and tops, plus a couple of jackets Christie had chosen rather randomly. She had been a bit more conscious about lingerie, socks and shoes, with the drawers filled to capacity and shoes ranging from high heels and boots to slippers and runners lining the bottom of the hanging space. Her stomach growled as she closed the empty suitcase and slid it under the bed.

Back in the kitchen, Christie plugged in her laptop and left it charging on the old table whilst she prepared dinner. On the way back, she had shopped at Green Bay, the previous, larger town. Now, she made a meal from sliced tomatoes, salad leaves, olives, feta, grapes and shallots. The sourdough bread from the bakery was crusty, freshly baked and a perfect accompaniment drizzled with a little olive oil.

Christie tethered her laptop to her phone to use its internet. She scrolled down the emails to the one Derek sent from the airport with her revised e-ticket. She read the brief message. "Don't miss this flight, Chris." It could read as a loving reminder he was wanting to see her soon, or as a warning of some sort. She sat back in her chair, sad again.

She could have told Angus her commitment was to Derek and although she loved Gran, she could not attend the funeral. Derek would have felt supported and Angus would have understood, even if he would've been disappointed. Without the cottage, instead of puzzling over secrets and difficult men, Christie would be sipping a cocktail on the beach with Derek.

Yes, that would have kept Derek happy and she would have done her best to enjoy the holiday. But her heart and mind would have been here in Rivers End, knowing she let Angus down and failed Gran.

It was a no-win situation. At least now, she had said a proper farewell to the woman who had taken her in all those years ago. She had also learnt more about Derek than in all of their previous time together.

Christie closed the laptop and left it to continue charging. Even though it was still early, Christie changed into pyjamas and dressing gown and put her slippers on. How indulgent was this? Derek would have thought her ill to be dressed for bed straight after an early dinner.

In her bedroom, Christie relaxed on the bed and reached for the box of letters, hesitating at the memory of Thomas' headstone. Before, she had imagined him still alive and with Martha. Now, she knew that not to be the case and their paths would never cross.

Why she even thought that possible or desirable was a mystery, as some fifty years had passed since these letters were penned, and Thomas could have been anywhere in the world. What a heartbreaking story this was turning out to be. Christie opened the next letter.

Dear Martha,

Today I found a photograph. I remember the day it was taken, how cold the wind was and how cross you were with me...at first...

IMAGES

1 *967.*
It was a windswept, wintry day on the beach. Thomas and Martha walked hand in hand toward the lagoon. Trailing behind with a camera in her hand was Frannie Williams, Martha's best friend.

"Um, aren't we meant to be taking photos?" Frannie called out. Martha stopped to let Frannie catch up, but Thomas kept walking.

"Tom? Frannie's taking our photo!"

He glanced over his shoulder, eyebrow raised. Martha struck a pose for Frannie.

"He's so rude!" Martha remarked. "Just take my photo, 'cos I'm better looking than him."

Dramatically, she gazed off into the distance while Frannie played with the focus on the camera.

Thomas sneaked up behind Martha and grabbed her. She squealed and tried to escape but he wrestled her onto the sand.

"Thomas Blake, let me go! Oh, there's sand in my hair now!" Martha pushed against his arms as he laughed and held her even tighter. "It's not funny!" she fumed.

Frannie took a few photos of them on the sand. Thomas captured Martha's lips with his and kissed her until she stopped struggling. As soon as she did, Thomas let her go, getting to his feet and extending his hand.

Martha pretended not to see it and stood up on her own, shaking the sand off her clothes and out of her hair.

"Stubborn girl." Thomas said.

He laughed as Martha stalked off, back toward the stone steps.

"You shouldn't do that!" Frannie scolded. "She's sensitive."

"Sorry." Thomas sprinted after Martha. By the time Frannie got to the steps, Martha was sitting on Thomas' lap, cuddled up in his arms.

AND RESEMBLENCE

2 016.

So Martha's friend, Frannie, was a budding photographer. And found Thomas annoying.

Looking at that photo, I remember the taste of salt on your lips and the way the wind made your hair into a silken ribbon. Those memories comfort me but they taunt me as well. I need you back. Please, Martha? Please come home.

Love,

Thomas

Christie opened the photo album that had been in the box with the painting. This time, she went past the photograph of Gran and found one of a striking young woman on a windswept beach, posing in a theatrical stance. Her eyes and cheekbones were much like Christie's and her long hair had the same wave in it. "Hello, Great Aunt Martha."

The next photo was again of Martha, but this time with Thomas, his arms around her and his eyes on her face. Christie drew her breath in sharply. Through his letters to Martha, she had visualized him as being a handsome man with strong features. What came as a shock was his resemblance to another man. Thomas Blake and Martin could almost have been brothers.

THE PIECES DON'T FIT

*C*hristie sipped on hot coffee whilst she stared out of the kitchen window into the night. Her mind overflowed with possibilities about this little town and the two families connected by more than a broken engagement.

Martin must be a descendant of Thomas Blake. Probably his grandson, which led to an interesting question. Who was Martin's grandmother? If Thomas and Martha had reconciled, Martin was Christie's second cousin. Family.

Yet, it did not fit. Martin knew she was Dorothy's grandchild, so why not introduce himself as her cousin? Why this hostility and why, for that matter, would Gran not tell Christie herself?

No, Thomas must have married someone else. Or, what if Thomas had been unfaithful to Martha during their engagement, which resulted in the broken relationship and a child?

The letters spoke of loyalty, love, and total commitment, so there must have been another reason for the split. She needed to know if they reunited before she spoke to Martin again. She had to keep reading.

Christie contemplated the bundle of letters. Why had Thomas not gone to where Martha was staying? Was Lilian—Christie's great grandmother—so intimidating a grown man feared to confront her? He seemed to get on well enough with Patrick, so why had he not gone to him for more information? For that matter, why not pick up a phone and call her? It was all a mystery. The next letter was a few lines long.

Dear Martha,

Today is one month since you left. Christmas has come and gone and my gift to you is at your house, left with the housekeeper. It is almost the New Year and this must be our turning point.

Meet me on the jetty on New Year's Day, Martha. If you do not, I shall accept you no longer wish us to be together.

It is entirely up to you now.

Love,

Thomas

An ultimatum? Such a risk when one party was clearly not interested in engaging. What would she have done, had Derek insisted she made a choice between Lizard Island and Gran's funeral? It hurt Christie's brain to think about that too closely, so she unfolded another letter instead, dated a day after the last.

Sweetheart, forgive me.

I put pressure on you to act when you may not be ready. The last letter means nothing.

That night, you nearly died when you fell into the sea and I could not find you. I was almost at my own final breath when, by the sheer fortune of a lightning flash, I saw you. Your dress had snagged on a pylon and your hair drifted around your face. You were like an angel, your hair floating like a halo. At that instant, I knew I could never let you go and yet, only moments later, you were gone.

Everything was my fault, my doing. Regret and sorrow overwhelms me at times. We were happy, so happy.

Is it possible, my darling we can be together again? Tell me there is a chance, that I have not ruined this. You are my one true love, the only love I will ever know.

I will meet you anytime, anywhere you want me to. We can move to Paris if you wish. Get far away from Rivers End and start a new life for ourselves. Just do not give up on us.

Love,

Thomas

Wow! Martha almost drowned. And, Thomas saved her life, apparently in the middle of a storm. Something happened between them that drove Martha to run away and so far, not return.

Christie had to know what happened next.

Dear Martha,

I no longer know where you are or if you are even getting my letters. Palmerston House is boarded up and people say your parents have left for an extended trip to Ireland. No staff are there; even the horses are off the property. Is it possible your father gave me the wrong address and not one of my letters reached you? My enquiries about your sister's address have not been successful. I am unfamiliar with the city and at a loss at how to find you.

The railway is closing the line next month so my father will retire. The last stationmaster. They have been offered the cottage to rent cheaply, so will stay for a while at least.

There is nothing here for me, yet how do I leave? Every morning I wait on the jetty for you and every morning I go home disappointed. I paint no more. I work enough hours a week to pay my way and that is all I do. Work and wait.

Martha, this cannot continue. I love you as much this moment as I ever have and I need to find you. I had to speak to one of your friends. Forgive me, but I had to...but it did not amount to much as you have not spoken to your friends in town either. Nobody is to blame except for me, so at least let your friends know you are okay.

I will come to Melbourne if I do not hear from you soon. If it is over between us, I need to hear you say it.

Love,

Thomas

Christie folded the letter. Which friend had he spoken to? He had apologised for doing so, but why? It was so hard trying to read between the lines—to fill in the gaps of information from so long ago.

He mentioned Palmerston House again, which must be the original family home. Gran had never spoken of it, not that she had ever spoken of Rivers End.

Who lives there now?

Christie turned the light off and slid under the covers. The moon shone brightly through the trees. It was so peaceful here. Far enough from the main road to keep almost all traffic sounds away and only the occasional mooing between the cows up the road. So simple a life, and somehow, already making inroads on Christie's heart.

THE JETTY AT DAWN

Christie ran toward the village, puffing misty breaths. Morning hadn't quite arrived but there was sufficient light to see ahead. Once on level ground near the river, muscle fatigue set in, reminding her how long it had been since her last run. She slowed to a jog, then a walk, panting heavily.

Below the bridge, the slow, shallow river meandered to the beach. On its far side, a narrow track was just discernible, so Christie crossed over and scrambled down the embankment.

The track followed the river through a gap in the cliffs, straight onto the beach. It brought Christie out not far from the jetty, so she took off her shoes and socks and jogged to the tideline.

The air was still and the water incredibly calm. Low tide fully exposed the jetty, even the pylons Thomas mentioned in his letter. Martha's dress had caught on one and held her below the surface until he found her. Christie shivered as she imagined Martha's terror and the power of the ocean in the midst of the storm.

Dawn broke as she stepped onto the jetty and walked to its end.

How happy Thomas and Martha had been at this place.

Their first meeting, the proposal. Many early mornings spent together enjoying the beauty of the ocean from this vantage point.

Christie gazed into water so clear she could see the sandy floor and fish swimming in small schools around the pylons. Thomas had come here in hope, and in growing despair, waiting for his girl to return. So sad.

"Miss? You okay?"

Christie jumped at the unexpected voice nearby, and turned to see a weathered older man, fishing pole and tackle box in hand.

Exhaling a startled breath, Christie said, "I'm fine thanks."

With a brief nod, the fisherman trudged off toward the end of the beach.

Christie ran after him, catching up as he headed toward the stone steps.

"Excuse me? Why did you ask if I was okay? Is there a problem with the jetty?"

He kept walking but muttered, "Just with tourists who should stay off the beach this time of year."

"I'm not a tourist."

The fisherman reached the steps and stopped to adjust his load. "Old lady was. Caught exposure, sitting out there in the rain."

"Who? Did you get her name? Is she okay?" Christie sprinted up the steps behind him.

"Full of questions," he said, going to an old truck and tossing his tackle in the back. "Ambulance came. End of story, miss." He opened the door and got in.

"Sorry, please wait. She went to hospital. Where?"

"Only one round here. You sound like a tourist." With that observation, the fisherman closed the door.

A dog barked in the distance. Christie returned to the steps and sat on the top one to put on her shoes and socks whilst she mused over the man's information. Some small memory was just out of reach. It nagged at her as soon as the fisherman mentioned the old lady.

The dog barked again, closer this time, drawing Christie's attention. It was the golden retriever, engaged in a game of Frisbee with Martin. Christie watched unnoticed, smiling at the sheer excitement of the dog every time the disc went up in the air. It headed toward the steps with the dog in hot pursuit, but instead of trying to catch it, he raced up the steps to Christie, his tail wagging furiously.

Christie scratched behind his ear as Martin approached. Stopping for a second to retrieve the toy, his eyes met Christie's, before he jogged off in the other direction.

"Randall? You coming?" he called over his shoulder.

"Ah, Randall is it? Go on." Christie nudged the dog and he tore back down the steps to race after Martin.

For a moment, Christie considered following Randall and trying to speak with Martin about Thomas Blake. First, she needed to get her painting back and gather more information. She might get one chance at asking questions and it would be prudent to have thought through what she wanted to ask.

Much of what she had already learned came from a few old letters and some throwaway comments. The fisherman's words added more speculation and Christie knew she had to get some facts.

Back at the cottage, Christie took a quick shower, wishing it were longer but not enthralled by a dramatic drop in water temperature after a few moments. The fact-finding would have to wait a bit whilst she found someone to help her get things right here.

After breakfast, Christie rang Barry, the builder Daphne recommended. Over a background of hammering, he agreed to call by. That done, Christie worked her way through the cottage to list the areas to address with Barry.

Every room had problems, from the ceiling in the bathroom to the flooring in the majority of the cottage. Light switches and power points were loose. Some were more cosmetic in nature, such as the drooping curtain rails in the lounge room that Christie thought she could fix herself. Others though would require professional attention.

For the first time, Christie had a proper walk through the gardens. The front fence was ready to collapse, so a new one was in order, along with a replacement gate. The clothesline was another casualty and a decent path to it would be safer than the crumbling, old bricks.

The outside of the cottage was difficult to evaluate behind the overgrown bushes and trees. The weatherboards might have rotted and the cottage subject to rising damp. Or, they may only need sanding back and repainting.

The back part of the garden was divided by a fence covered in a passionfruit vine on one side, a flowering wisteria on the other, and a wrought iron gate in the middle. With a bit of persuasion, the gate opened with a protesting squeak and Christie stepped through. Although the grass was long and the trees years overdue for proper feeding and pruning, Christie was delighted to find an orchard.

She wandered from tree to tree; identifying apples, apricots, plums, lemons, pears and what appeared to be a cumquat. She laughed in pleasure at the discovery of an old vegetable patch and compost heap. *What a wonderful find.*

Christie gazed around at her lush, if bushy surrounds, overcome with a sense of belonging. Without a doubt, she had fallen in love with this little place. It was a world away from her apartment, and even further from the glamorous hotels, movie sets, and lavish parties her career afforded. Filled with character and charm, it was hers.

SMILES AND SUSPICION

*T*he growl from the Lotus turned heads as Christie drove along the main street in town. She parked outside the bank, checked her makeup in the rear vision mirror, and stepped out into the early afternoon sunshine.

Over on the far corner at the café, patrons sat under open umbrellas enjoying a late lunch or coffee. Such a difference from the other day in the rain, when she met with Angus and Jacob to discuss Gran's estate.

Was it only two days ago?

The bank was a community brand with a generic ATM in the wall. Christie withdrew a few hundred dollars, in case the tradesmen wanted cash. Next door was a newsagency, perhaps a place to buy the tools to make a mind-map.

Mouth-watering smells of freshly baked pastries wafted out of the bakery and Christie peered at the enticing selection in the window. Belinda waved with a huge smile, sending an unexpected surge of happiness through Christie.

After passing a dress shop, hairdresser, and the Chinese take-away she'd used, Christie pushed open the door to the real estate agents.

John stood behind the counter, leaning down to write something. He glanced up with a welcoming nod. "Miss Ryan, how are you?"

"Christie, please. I'm well, thank you."

"Got in touch with Barry?"

"He dropped by this morning, and sent someone around to install a new hot water system, so I wanted to thank Daphne for the referral."

"Excellent. Daphne is off work today so I'll let her know. What did Barry suggest?"

"He is sending me a quote on repairs."

"A quote? Ah, so we'll be seeing more of you. Or..."

"Let's see what Barry recommends. I did want to ask something though. Is there a property around here called Palmerston House?"

"Well, yes. It's a bed and breakfast now, but is one of the original homes in the area."

"Oh! The one around the fork in the road near the cliff?"

"That's it. Owned by Elizabeth White for a number of years now."

The phone rang and John answered it with an apologetic nod. He put his hand over the mouthpiece. "Sorry, I might be a while. Is there anything else I can help with today?"

"You've been a big help, thanks John. Say hello to Daphne, please."

Christie wandered back out to the street. So, Palmerston House, the original Ryan family home, was now a B&B. Maybe the owner, this Elizabeth White, would have some history to share.

Christie crossed the road to the jewellers, admiring the beautiful brickwork and gleaming windows. It was an old building, almost lost in time. The windows displayed porcelain ornaments, brass figurines, crystal pieces and jewellery. Above the door was a simple sign. *Rivers End Jeweller. Est. 1902.*

Inside, the shop was dark and cool. Behind a long glass counter was a wall of clocks, tick-tocking in a staggered rhythm. In every cabinet, Christie saw quality, sparkling creations. A genuine, old-fashioned jewellery shop.

The door closed behind her with a jangle, and a woman emerged from a doorway in the wall of clocks. In her late forties, she had a stern face with greying hair piled up in a messy bun.

"Can I help?" she said. Then, she forced a smile. "I mean, what can I help you with? I have some lovely diamond earrings that would suit you so well."

Christie returned the smile. "Perhaps another time. I was wondering if you have someone here who could help me with a couple of rings. Just hoping for some information on them."

The woman stopped smiling. "What kind of rings? What kind of information?"

"A wedding ring and engagement ring. They're quite old and—"

"If you want them valued, you need to see George. He's not here."

"Okay. When should I come back?"

"Later. Or tomorrow." The woman stared at Christie.

"Okay. Well, thanks for that. I'll try again later. Or tomorrow." As Christie left, she wondered if this woman was related to the ones in the supermarket. Should she laugh or feel offended? The extremes in this little town were surprising, as though split between super friendly and super suspicious folk. Something bothered her though from the brief encounter.

She stared at her reflection in the window. Her hair was in a slick ponytail, fastened with a pretty butterfly jewelled clasp. Her makeup was perfect, her shirt and pants were casual but designer. She wore low-heeled leather sandals and carried a small Valentino shoulder handbag.

The woman had been quite curt at first, as though Christie had interrupted her. Then, she offered what was probably an expensive pair of earrings. Christie knew the Lotus gave an impression of wealth, but did the way she presented herself intimidate some of the locals?

Christie sighed and decided she had enough of window-shopping for today.

The supermarket yielded locally made cheese and a selection of fresh vegetables and fruit. As Christie approached the checkout, her heart sank a little to see the same woman serving as on her last visit. Nevertheless, she smiled and said hello and this time the woman nodded and grunted something that might have been a greeting.

86

On her way to the car, the lure of the bakery was too tempting for Christie and she found herself inside, almost drooling over the delicious array of baked goods.

"Here for eclairs this time?" Belinda beamed.

"Enticing, but that apple slice has my name on it!"

"Oh, well let's see!" Belinda opened the glass cabinet and peered in. "Now, what was your name and I'll find it."

Christie laughed. "I'm Christie."

Belinda slid an apple slice into a bag. "Yes, definitely has Christie written on it," she grinned as she closed the cabinet. "I'm Belinda."

"I know." Christie pointed to the name badge and Belinda rolled her eyes at herself.

"I might take a sourdough loaf as well, please."

"Awesome choice. Mum uses her own starter so each batch is quite unique."

"So this is a family business?"

Belinda finished wrapping the sourdough loaf in crisp paper and placed it next to the slice on the top of the counter. "Mum bakes and runs things. She's the real deal, a single super-mum. I help out. Jess, well Jess studies a lot. She's smart. Now anything else today? I have some cupcakes I iced myself!"

"If I took you up on all of your suggestions, I'd be waddling not running every morning!"

"You'll be back for more once you've had the apple slice." Belinda warned as she rang up the sale.

"I fear you may be right." Christie answered solemnly, before both of them burst into laughter. Christie was still smiling when she opened the door to leave.

The woman from the jewellery store was reaching for the handle on the other side and there was an awkward moment while they worked out who would use the door first. It was Christie, who thanked the woman and got "You're welcome" in response.

As she went back past the window, Christie glanced in and saw the woman behind the counter, putting on an apron. She was Belinda's mother.

EYES TO HER SOUL

On the other side of Martin's house, past a shed storing surfboards and an old motorbike, a long, low building faced the sea.

Inside, it was part workspace and part gallery. A solid timber workbench filled one wall. Wood turning tools were neatly stored underneath. Paints and brushes occupied an end.

The windows were floor to ceiling on two sides and the roof was dotted with skylights, flooding the room with light. Below the skylights were half a dozen easels, each with a finished painting. All were abstract, in bold and vibrant colours.

In front of the window facing the sea was a deep cushioned sofa. There was a small, beautifully crafted bar in the corner and a dog basket where the morning sun would shine.

Randall lay flat on his side in the middle of the studio, fast asleep. Martin glanced at him when he murmured in a dream, his feet twitching.

Martin swept cut offs and shavings from the workbench, tossing them into a bin. He wiped the area with a clean cloth before going to an easel in the middle of the room.

It was the seascape, repaired and framed in locally grown mountain ash. The subtle timber brought out the beauty of the painting even more and Martin struggled to take his eyes off it.

He could paint, but never a scene as complex and heart stopping and detailed. This painting captured a moment in time and held it still forever. It told a story of unleashed power that could crush...yet had a wondrous life about it.

The work of a Master.

This painting had been stored away for decades to the point of risking its viability. Somebody had deliberately hidden it from its artist and its intended recipient, making Martin angry and sad at the same time.

Randall woke and stretched, lifting his head. Martin glanced at his watch. Squatting beside the dog, he scratched his chest, smiling as glazed pleasure filled Randall's eyes.

"You like her."

Why are you still in Rivers End, Christie Ryan?

He glanced back at the seascape. Was she being honest about this? Did the granddaughter of Dorothy Ryan truly not know the family history?

The woman whose eyes revealed her soul. So expressive. So unattainable.

"Go back to sleep, doggo. I won't be long."

PUZZLES TO SOLVE

*C*hristie arrived home in time to pay the cheery young man who showed her how to work the new hot water system. It was just a second hand unit but would suffice until she decided what to do with the cottage.

On the kitchen table, Christie laid out several large pieces of white card, a ruler, coloured markers and a couple of pencils. The man at the newsagency had been most helpful with her request, proclaiming the sunny weather was here to stay and giving her a copy of the local paper as she left. Christie made a coffee, leaving the newspaper on the counter as she went over to the table.

With a black marker, Christie wrote *Cottage* in the centre of the card. Like the spokes of a wheel, she drew lines outward with the ruler and gave each one a name.

Gran, Martha, Thomas, Painting, Rings, Letters.

With a blue marker, she connected Thomas and Martha with a line and on it wrote—*engagement ended 1967.*

Under Martha's name—*Left Rivers End 1967,* and *Returned?*

In pencil, she added information to Gran's and Thomas' lines. *Deceased*

For a while, she sipped her coffee as she contemplated the circle of information. What else did she know? The painting? That came from Gran, so she put her name underneath it, as well as *artist unknown*.

Below *Rings*, Christie added *Found in shoebox in attic*, and *Forever Taming the Wind*. She turned her attention to *Letters*, writing—*Found in shoebox in attic*, and—*Sent but unopened and kept by persons unknown*.

Oh, it was so complicated! There was no obvious answer, no inspiration from mapping it out. At least, not yet, Christie thought. More information would help.

The remains of her coffee were cold, so Christie threw them out and rinsed the cup. She picked up the newspaper and flicked through it until a small article caught her attention.

Bad weather almost claims life. An elderly woman was rushed to hospital after collapsing on Rivers End Beach. A local fisherman sounded the alarm after finding the woman on the end of the jetty in pouring rain on an unseasonably cold day earlier this week. Unable to speak and with low body temperature, the woman—thought to be a tourist—was lucky to be found before her situation worsened.

This must be the tourist the fisherman mentioned. Christie went back to the table and stared at the card. *Martha Ryan. Left Rivers End 1967. Returned?*

It was too far-fetched to be true. The tourist could have been anyone. Wouldn't Martha have contacted Gran before coming here? Why not come to the cottage, or to her family home?

Christie picked up her phone and googled local hospitals. The fisherman had said there was only one, in the next town. Green Bay hospital. She had to find out.

The twenty-minute drive to Green Bay was a waste of time. As polite as the receptionist at the hospital was, she refused to provide any details about the woman in the paper. Christie pleaded this might be the great-aunt she had never met, the last family she knew of. Although sympathetic, the receptionist would only say the patient was no longer there.

Nosing the Lotus out of the carpark, Christie frowned. Gran was gone, leaving behind a mystery with few clues and turning Christie's life upside down. The problems—her damaged relationship with Derek, trying to find Martha, the meaning of the secrets—all gathered like one crushing rain cloud above her head.

Christie found a rock ballad on the radio and pumped the volume up as she accelerated on the open road toward Rivers End.

Back in town, Christie went straight to the jewellers. The shop was empty, so she browsed for a while, lingering over an emerald and diamond pendant. The emerald was the same colour as her eyes and beautifully simple.

Christie caught the reflection of someone watching her from the doorway behind the counter. Martin leaned against the doorframe.

"How many expensive toys does one woman need?"

Christie gathered herself and turned around.

"You assume a lot about me." she said.

He stared back and the silence drew out.

The jangling of the door interrupted them and Christie glanced away.

George Campbell, dapper in a crisp white shirt and dark navy pin striped suit, hobbled past Christie without noticing her. "Ah, Martin my boy, thank you. Such a long council meeting today. If it wasn't for you, and Sylvia, I'd have needed to close the shop."

"My pleasure, George." Martin patted George on the shoulder as they passed. "You have a visitor."

"Why, thank you." George went behind the counter and pulled a spectacles case from his top pocket.

"How are you going with my painting?" Christie asked Martin as he opened the door.

"I'll phone when it's ready."

"You said that the other day."

"Why must I repeat myself?" He let the door close on its own behind him.

Christie watched him jog across the road, aware her heart was racing and not at all happy with the unbidden reaction.

"Now, young lady," said George, "how may I assist?"

Christie smiled and approached the counter.

George's face paled. "You have to be a Ryan."

"I'm Christie. Dorothy Ryan was my grandmother."

"Dorothy. Of course. I thought for a moment…"

She took the ring box from her bag, opening it to reveal both rings. "The wedding ring is engraved and I know it's a long shot—"

"Forever taming the wind." George said.

A GIFT OF LOVE LOST

"*Y*ou know the rings?" The young woman asked. Christie. Dorothy's grandchild.

Who would have thought this possible?

He did know the rings. All too well. It might have been yesterday, not more than fifty years ago when he'd last seen them.

Twenty-four-year-old George hummed as he polished the glass counter. The door jangled and Thomas, aged twenty-three, rushed in with an expectant expression.

"Well, I'm here! So, what's the panic?" Thomas said, and George raised his eyebrows.

"Must you be so melodramatic?" George folded his polishing cloth.

"Frannie said I needed to get here right away. Is something wrong?"

"Frances is as bad as you are." George put the cloth away. "Nevertheless, I do have something to show you."

He reached below the counter and brought out a ring box. He opened it to display Martha's engagement ring and the wedding ring.

Thomas picked up the box. "Brilliant work, George! Perhaps the finest yet. Do I know the lucky couple?"

"Call it my wedding gift." George located a black velvet pouch. Taking the ring box back from Thomas, he slipped it into the pouch.

"What wedding?" It was clear from his expression that Thomas was confused, more so when George held out the pouch.

"Well, there never will be a wedding if you don't ask Martha to marry you."

Thomas stared solemnly at the pouch, then at George. His face lit up with a delighted grin. Taking the pouch, he tossed it into the air.

"Oh my, take care!" George was horrified.

Thomas deftly caught, and pocketed the pouch. He grabbed George's hand to pump it vigorously.

"You are right! Thank you! Thank you again."

Thomas waved and ran out of the door, leaving George smiling in his wake, but shaking his head at the same time.

Thomas flung the door open again with an evil expression.

"Just remember, my friend, it is you I shall blame when I am in misery in years to come!" With that, he closed the door, leaving it jangling.

"George? Do you know who made the rings?"

Christie's question brought George back to the present.

He sighed. "I made the rings."

"So, you knew them? You knew Martha?"

"Martha was the most beautiful girl in town. Rich, of course. Kind. And wild. That was the real attraction for Thomas."

How he adored her.

"But they never married?"

George handed the ring box to Christie. "No, they never did." He removed his glasses. "I thought I'd never see these again. I thought she'd sold them."

"Do you mean Martha?"

The door jangled behind Christie as a customer entered.

"No. Not Martha."

"Then, who?"

So many questions. None he wished to answer. The past belonged in the past. "I must attend to my customer, if you would excuse me."

WHAT IS LOVE

*C*hristie gazed at the paper on the table, remembering the words George said so sadly. They never married. The couple that loved each other so deeply and once held the world in their hands. Separated forever.

Taking a pencil, Christie wrote—*Never Married* below the line she had drawn between Thomas and Martha's names. Under *Rings*, she penned—*Made by George. Thought sold by unknown woman.*

Whom had George meant? Most likely Martha had given her ring back to Thomas so it must have been someone else in his life. His mother? Sister? Future wife? If George thought someone in Thomas' life sold the rings, how had they ended up in the cottage, with the unopened love letters?

Christie found a piece of paper and wrote a list.

- Visit Palmerston House and speak to Elizabeth White.
- Get painting back.
- Ask George about unknown woman.
- Read remaining letters.
- Find owner of pendant from graveyard.

That made Christie stop and think about where the pendant was.

She remembered holding it at the grave of Thomas Blake but what had she done with it next escaped her. What had she been wearing?

Christie went into the bedroom and opened the wardrobe. The pendant was nestled inside the pocket of a light blue jacket. She held it up, taken with its simple charm. This was also a quality piece of jewellery and lovingly maintained. Perhaps it was another of George's collection. Another thing to ask him about.

Christie's phone began to ring and she sprinted back to the kitchen to find it, pendant in hand. The ringtone was Derek's and the phone was buried somewhere in her handbag. She emptied it on the table with coins, lipstick and keys spilling onto the timber. The note from Gran fluttered down, catching Christie's eye as she grabbed the phone. On its last ring, she answered, breathless.

"Derek? Um, hi honey." She flopped onto a chair.

"Were you running?"

"The phone was down the other end."

"The other end? Are you still at that cottage? Thought you'd be at home."

"I'll head home in a couple of days."

There was a long silence and Christie could hear talk and laughter in the background. It was as though Derek always surrounded himself with people who had fun.

"That won't help me. I needed you to check my passport for the date I was in London in 2012. Can't if you're miles away."

"Why do you need to know?"

"Settle a friendly debate. Told you I knew Ingrid already and we were trying to work out the first time we met. That's all. Doesn't matter."

"I'm sorry." Christie wondered if this was just an excuse to call.

"Well, I'm sorry you're missing all of this, Chris. Serious fun and so much food. Must have gained kilos so I'll have to do one of those detox things next week. I bet you're sorry too."

"I can't wait to hear all about it." was the best Christie could manage. She was not sorry she had come to the cottage, only that Derek made things so much harder than they should have been.

"Ah, the crew are ready on the yacht for our sunset cruise. Gotta go, babe. Just be at the apartment because I'm over the absences. Bye."

"Derek, wait!"

She slumped back in her chair. Why could he not have a normal conversation or even ask how she was and tell her he missed her. That he loved her. They had some talking to do when they both got home and Christie's stomach tensed up.

After tossing everything back into her handbag, she unfolded Gran's note. The handwriting was a fragile version of Gran's and hard to read. This was probably the last thing Gran had done before she passed away.

The enormity of being in Dorothy's thoughts at the end was too much. Before the tears came, before her heart broke again, she folded the note and put it away.

~

It was dark by the time Christie had her promised long, hot shower, going over the phone call with Derek in her mind. He had mentioned Ingrid again. If he wanted some sort of response from Christie, he would be disappointed. Games like that were of no interest to her.

Christie reached for a glass of wine resting on the edge of the sink. She took a long sip, loving this Chardonnay. It was local, dry and pure gold in colour. Replacing the glass, she slipped back under the shower.

For a few moments, Christie stood directly under the stream of hot water, letting it surround her and wash away the negative emotions that bubbled up. She loved Derek and when she got home, would do her utmost to show him how much he meant to her. They'd make things right again.

Wrapped in her dressing gown, she made dinner from local cheese and olives, some of the beautiful sourdough bread from the bakery, and a fresh salad. These and the wine accompanied her to the bedroom where she laid the letters out on the bed; putting aside those she had already read, she opened the next one.

Darling girl,

These past few months have been the worst of my life. I miss you as much today as the moment you ran into the night. Our connection is so strong I believe—deep inside myself –you feel the same way. Whether it is pride, fear, or anger that keeps you silent, I do not know.

What I do know is I still see our future together as clearly as ever. Our plans remain in place. Our wedding—well that was postponed but when we do marry, it will be away from here. I have been working a lot and saving for us. We can go to Paris if you wish and be married at the foot of the Eiffel Tower.

We can live there or in England or Amsterdam…all places you long to visit. I will go because you inspire me to. You inspire me by being in my life. Our children will be raised in a home filled with laughter and love. With you as their mother, they will learn to enjoy life and be generous and kind. As their father, I shall teach them to draw on inner strength and to strive for the stars. Such lucky children we shall have!

One day, in the far future, our grandchildren shall sit on our laps as we gaze out over the ocean. We will share our stories and teach them to be strong, loving, and self-aware.

Imagine this. It will be ours, my love, starting the moment you come home.

With all of my heart, my soul and being, I love you Martha.

Thomas

Christie read the letter twice. Knowing now they never married, she could only assume Martha never read this letter. If she had, how could she have stayed away from Thomas Blake, whose love was true?

If only that kind of love was in her life. If only Derek loved her this way and knew exactly what to say to make her pain go away. Was anyone out there like Thomas?

Martin's studio was in darkness, save for a spotlight near the window, where Martin sat on the floor, sketching in an art book. Deep in concentration, he worked on a portrait like a labour of love.

After a while, he sat back and picked up a glass of whiskey. Sipping it, he stared at the portrait.

It was Christie on the steps at the beach. Leaning down to pat Randall, her eyes were alight with happiness. Around her neck was the diamond and emerald pendant from the jewellery shop.

Martin shook his head at himself.

"Fool."

He closed the art book and finished his drink.

FIRE IN HER EYES

*C*hristie woke to rolling thunder, followed by a downpour. Staring out of the window at the heavy, dark clouds, she was tempted to snuggle further under the covers and go back to sleep. She'd eventually read Gran's note, once she could so without the emotion. Not that she could decipher it all.

Dearest Christabel,

My last request is you find my sister and give her the diary. In the box. It is...

The words became too hard to read. Maybe Angus would know about a diary in a box. She would see him once she went home. With a reluctant yawn, she slipped out of bed and stretched.

On the way to the kitchen, the dark lounge room took her attention. She stared at the fireplace, admiring the marble mantelpiece. Above it was a hook in the centre of the wall, as if waiting for a painting to hang. The seascape would be perfect there.

The walls had brown striped wallpaper and the heavy curtains allowed no light in at all. So dark a blue, they were almost black, and as worn as the sofa. They also refused to slide along their rod.

It was time these curtains came down.

The rain stopped by the time Christie, dressed in jeans and a T-shirt, went hunting for tools in the garage. The double doors were hard to open but with enough pressure, one yielded with a groan. Inside, the floor was hard dirt and a single lightbulb hung from a beam. Along one side, narrow shelves held old pots, some gardening tools, and a collection of empty glass jars. At the end, a wooden ladder leaned at an angle.

There was nothing else of any substance, so Christie took her toolkit from the boot of the Lotus. It was basic, with a hammer, a screwdriver set and mixed screws, tape, some nails, a paint scraper and a wrench. She had bought this kit during her house-sharing days, finding it easier to fix most things herself than wait for a landlord. Derek thought it ridiculous she would take on the work of a tradesperson, so the kit ended up in the Lotus for emergencies.

After shooing a couple of spiders off the ladder, Christie part dragged, part carried it into the cottage and set it up in the lounge room. It was old and wobbly but seemed stable enough. It was oddly exciting to be doing something for the cottage and she could hardly wait to see the room in decent light.

In the cottage driveway, Martin stood holding the painting—wrapped in a sheet—in his arms.

I shouldn't be here.

As he turned to leave, a thud emanated from inside, and another. Instead of going, Martin hurried to the back door and knocked.

From somewhere deep inside came a muffled "It's unlocked. I'm in the lounge room!"

Martin shook his head as he opened the door. He glanced at the mind map on the table on his way to the lounge room, where he stopped.

Half of the curtain rod had been liberated, its end almost on the floor and the curtains in a pile around it. Christie was near the top of the old ladder, leaning at a precarious angle as she worked on a screw with both hands. The rungs creaked loudly with every move.

Martin placed the painting on the sofa before stalking to the window.

"Are you crazy?" he grabbed the supports.

Christie glanced at him. "Oh, I thought you were one of the tradies."

"Get down, now!"

"Oh, that's better. Stay there for a moment please. I'm almost done." Christie put all of her strength into turning the screwdriver.

"I'm not joking! This thing is about to collapse and you with it." Martin wanted to reach up and remove Christie from her perilous position, giving her no say in the matter. Instead, he gripped the timber until his knuckles turned white.

Christie seemed oblivious. "Can you spare a hand in case this falls...oh!"

The rod fell with a bang, narrowly missing Martin. Christie gaped down at him in horror.

"Climb down now or I'll lift you down." The frustration in his voice must have got through to Christie and she clambered off her perch.

At the bottom, she spun around, trapped between Martin's arms and the ladder. And he wasn't moving.

"Are you always so bossy?"

"Do you always put yourself at risk?"

"You mean the ladder? I don't just put makeup on human faces; I work on larger than life creatures and effects and know my way around scaffolding."

"This isn't scaffolding. Your door was unlocked. You don't know what sort of person might come into your house."

"I can see that."

And there's that fire again...

Martin managed to avoid grinning. He released the ladder and turned away to unwrap the painting and lean it against the back of the sofa.

"It's so beautiful!" Christie knelt down to see the painting better, her eyes bright. "You are amazing, Martin! Thank you so much."

She smiled up at him. "Thanks for bringing it to me, but I would have been happy to have picked it up."

A long, uncomfortable silence fell.

"What's wrong?" Christie ventured.

"I wish to buy it." Martin said.

"The painting?" Christie got back to her feet. "I couldn't. It was Gran's."

"No, it wasn't. Regardless, I'll pay whatever you ask. So?"

"If it wasn't Gran's, then whose? Martin, who owns it?"

Does she really not know?

"How much? That necklace you admired at George's is worth seven thousand—"

"You think I'm so shallow?" Christie stepped in front of the painting protectively. "It's not for sale."

"It is no more yours than it was Dorothy's. Think about selling."

"Who should own it? Please tell me!"

Martin spun around and stalked off. Another minute and he'd succumb to her confused plea.

"Martin! How much do I owe you?" Her words followed him as he left, slamming the door in his wake.

AND SO IT BEGINS

One by one, Christie threw the remains of the ladder in the garage. As soon as the door slammed, the ladder groaned and fell in a heap. Another thing to replace.

Martin was impossible. One moment bossing her around, then the cold mask came down. She had seen him smile at her implied insult, so he had human emotions. The secrecy about the painting's ownership was ridiculous. As if she would wilfully keep it from its true owner.

She pushed aside the way her body had responded to his closeness when she'd climbed down the ladder. His hand on either side of the rails, heat had radiated from his body. The scent of the sea still lingered on her skin. Then she'd insulted him. Again.

At least I didn't apologise.

This cottage and its secrets weighed heavily in her thoughts. Those who could help, would not. Either deliberately, like Martin, or unintentionally, like George and Daphne. Her instincts told her to go home and forget all of this. Stop worrying about a mystery from half a century ago.

Christie sighed heavily and wandered to the front gate. The sun was drying up the puddles from the earlier downpour. Over the road was a parked, black Maserati. Three men were huddled around a large map laid out on its bonnet. One of the men was John Jones.

Whatever where they up to?

Curious, Christie picked seaside daisies along the side of the driveway, making them into a small bouquet as she kept an eye on the men. They were deep in discussion, turning to point at the parcel of land next to the cottage.

John saw Christie and raised a hand in greeting. One of the other men walked over the road toward her, straight into the driveway and extended his hand to shake.

"Hi, I'm Bryce Montgomery. Lovely day."

Christie shook his hand. He was about her age and handsome in a well-dressed, slicked back hair kind of way. He wore a Rolex and a diamond stud through one ear.

"Yes, lovely morning now the rain has cleared."

"So, John mentioned you inherited this place?"

"Did he?"

Bryce checked Christie out. "You don't strike me as being a country girl."

"I don't?"

"A Lotus. You have excellent taste."

"Thank you." Christie glanced at John, who headed her way.

"Interested in selling? The cottage, I mean."

"You don't seem like a country boy."

He smiled, but his eyes were hard and cold. Like Derek's when something was out of his reach. Must be a property developer trait.

John joined them, red faced. "Morning, Miss Ryan."

"Christie, please. Nice day for a drive?"

"Oh, um, Bryce and Allan are interested in local real estate. Just showing them some of the areas that might be worth considering."

"Ah, property developers." Christie said.

"You make it sound like a dirty word." Bryce said.

"Not at all. My fiancé is one."

Bryce glanced sharply at John, who shrugged his shoulders and turned away. "We'll leave you in peace."

"Please say hello to Daphne."

Bryce held out a business card. "I like this area. A lot. I'm prepared to negotiate with your fiancé."

"He doesn't speak for me and the cottage isn't for sale. Enjoy your day." Christie ignored the outstretched card and went back along the driveway. She glanced at the Maserati as the three men got in. After a moment, it did a U-turn and drove toward the main road.

She stopped and stared up at the cottage. "You're not for sale, are you? Just like the painting, you're not for sale."

Christie perched on the arm of the sofa with a cup of coffee, happy with the results from a two-hour cleaning spree. The daisy bouquet adorned the mantelpiece in a glass from the kitchen. Above it, the seascape added warmth and vibrancy to the room.

She would renovate the cottage with the help of Barry Parks and decide whether to sell, or keep this as her hideaway. With images in her mind of how pretty she would make the cottage and its grounds, she knew Derek would love her plans. This could be their weekend retreat.

The painting caught her attention. What was its significance in all of this? Gran had custody of it, hidden away in an unsuitable cylinder as though it meant nothing.

Perhaps it meant too much.

Back in the kitchen, Christie sat before the mind map. What was the connection between the painting and the cottage? Was there one, or had Christie assumed so because Angus left it here for her? What did she know about it? Christie picked up a pencil and scribbled under the word *Painting*.

- Artist Thomas Blake lived here, at least as a young person
- Subject is the jetty Martha fell off in a storm
- Painting hidden for years in a cylinder by Gran
- Martin wants to buy painting for persons unknown

That last point bothered Christie the most. From the first moment, he recognised it, or its artist. If, as Christie suspected, he was related to Thomas, perhaps he had more of his paintings. It may be he collected them and wanted this one for himself.

If Martin was the last of the family, assuming this was the case, and wanted the painting as some sort of heirloom, he could have asked. All the theatrics mystified Christie. As did her response to him.

Over the past few years, Christie had been close to attractive men. Actors, including superstars who made hearts flutter across the world. Make-up meant being a hair's breadth away, touching skin, hair, lips. In spite of the physical closeness, she had never been tempted to be other than professional. Even before Derek, her relationship with her clients never went beyond the job. Since Derek, her sole focus changed to him. Her man, who made her feel safe.

Martin did not make her feel safe. Instead, he shook up her senses with his eyes and confused her with his words. She barely knew the man, but he intruded into her thoughts too much. His scent was like the ocean and if she touched him…

Stop it!

She pushed the mind map away and stood up. What she did need to do was pay him for the work on the painting. Maybe, if she kept her cool, he would answer her questions this time.

ANOTHER HOUSE OF SECRETS

*P*atrick Ryan's grandfather won Palmerston House in a game of poker. Built in the 1850s from local limestone and surrounded by timber verandas, it was an iconic homestead in the small community and home to generations of the Ryan family.

The driveway circled around an ornate, but unused fountain dating back one hundred years. Christie nosed the Lotus past it and pulled over to park. On her way to see Martin, she found herself taking the other fork in the road.

Out of the car, she gazed around in awe. The gardens were extensive and immaculate. Not only perfect, but clearly loved. The plants were heavily European rather than native, which given Gran's Irish heritage, was understandable. This was where Gran grew up.

Christie noticed a curtain on the upper floor open. It closed again and she lost interest. Going up several steps to the double front door, Christie wondered what life here would have been like in Gran's childhood. A plaque on the wall beside the door proclaimed this was Palmerston House. Below was a modern sign asking visitors to enter and wait in the lobby. Christie pushed open the door and stepped inside.

The lobby was a vast and open common space featuring a curved staircase with beautiful timber railings leading to the mezzanine level. Behind the staircase, a picture studded hallway led to the service areas of the house. Beside the staircase was a small desk with a phone, old-fashioned guest book and a selection of brochures on local attractions.

Behind the desk sat an elegant woman in her sixties, who acknowledged Christie with a faint smile. "How may I help you? I'm Elizabeth White."

"Hello, I'm Christie Ryan. I'm staying in the area and believe this beautiful home once belonged to my family."

"I see. That does seem unlikely though, as the original owners moved back to Ireland many, many years ago."

"Oh. I understood Dorothy Ryan's parents owned Palmerston House at one time?"

"You're related to this Dorothy Ryan?"

"Gran passed away a few days ago and I came to her funeral. You didn't know her?"

Elizabeth fussed around straightening the items on the desk before glancing up. "I wish I could be more help, dear. All before my time, I'm afraid."

"Oh. I was hoping…" Christie let her words trail off.

"What, dear?"

"It's just I'm searching for Dorothy's sister, who may still be alive. Her name is Martha. Martha Ryan."

Elizabeth took a moment to reply. "I'm sorry I can't help you. Now, if that is all, I do have to leave. To shop."

Christie opened her mouth to ask another question but Elizabeth's closed body language told her to tread lightly. She nodded. "If you should think of anything, I'm staying at the old Stationmaster's Cottage up the hill. I'll be there for a couple more days…if you remember anything?"

Elizabeth stood up. "You're leaving soon?"

"In a day or so, yes. Palmerston House looks lovely."

"It is. I'm sorry I can't give you a tour. Perhaps on your next visit?"

"I'd like that. Well, thanks for your time."

Elizabeth nodded and hurried up the staircase.

Christie let herself out. What a strange encounter. Maybe Elizabeth thought Christie would make some claim on the property. Or, was it possible she was hiding something?

"Along with everyone else in town!" Christie muttered to herself as she started the motor.

Elizabeth tapped on Martha's half open door.

Martha rested on the made bed, staring at the sky through the window.

"Would you like some tea, dear?" Elizabeth asked.

"Yes please." Martha sat up, glad for the company. "Who was that?"

"The young woman?" Elizabeth stood by the window, watching the Lotus drive out. "After directions, that's all."

"I've seen the car before. She must live around here."

"Visiting. I've pointed her in the right direction. I shall go and brew some tea and bring it up here."

Martha reached for her cane and stood up. "No, I shall come down. I'm spending too much time alone again and I would much rather hear about your last few years. We've not caught up at all."

"And there is plenty to catch up on! Alright, well, let's go together and I'll see if I can find a slice of cake, assuming you still like chocolate?"

Elizabeth put her arm through Martha's. She had just sent away Martha's great-niece and now she was lying to her old friend. All she wanted was to protect her from more hurt, so why did it seem like a terrible mistake?

Why is everything such a secret?

A CHANGE OF VIEW

*C*hristie also wondered if she was making a mistake by being back at Martin's property. She sat in the car staring at his house across the meadow, remembering the door slamming as he walked out of the cottage. She reapplied lipstick.

The gate was unlocked, the chain and padlock missing, so she slipped through and crossed the grassy land. Martin was working on the area around the front door. Randall sat on the top step of the small porch and barked a welcome before rushing to her, his tail wagging madly. Martin turned around, broom in hand, and watched Christie as she stopped to pat the dog.

The dead pot plant was in a wheelbarrow and the area around the door was free of cobwebs and debris. Martin leaned the broom against the wall and crossed his arms.

"Changed your mind?"

About what?

"About my offer?" he prompted.

"Oh, that was an offer? Well, no, I came to pay you for repairing and framing the painting."

A flicker of disappointment crossed Martin's face. "No payment required."

"You're sure I'll sell it to you?" Christie said.

"Yes. But beside that, it was a work of love."

"Tell me about the painting. You said it was never Gran's so who does it belong to? Who is the mystery owner?"

"Why do you care? This isn't your real life, is it? It's not as if you're staying here."

Christie saw the wall in his eyes and something snapped. She was at the end of her tether with the secrets and poorly formed opinions since arriving in Rivers End.

"It's not as if I've been made welcome, is it? Secrets everywhere, as if something from the past could matter so much now. I'd never even heard of Rivers End until a few days ago yet I'm still here. Martin, I'm still here, trying to honour my grandmother's final wishes."

She paused to glare at Martin, who remained impassive. "And I have you wanting the painting she left me and developers wanting to buy the cottage I just inherited!"

"Sell it to them."

"And let them bulldoze it into the ground?"

"Best thing for everyone." There was a bitter tone to his voice now.

The anger drained away. "Well, I disagree. It is not for sale. And nor is the painting."

Martin reached for the broom. "Anything else?"

Christie walked away but called over her shoulder. "Yes. How did you get such a nice dog to live with you?"

By the time she reached the gate, she thoroughly regretted those last words. How could she be so rude? Why the loss of control?

Get a grip, Christie.

A couple of minutes later she was regretting her temper even more. The car refused to start and the petrol gauge defiantly stayed on empty. How she had overlooked the warning signal was beyond her, but here she was, stranded outside the only house in the area, which happened to belong to a man who made her lose the ability to behave normally.

Christie started searching Google on her phone for the closest petrol station, hoping there was one within walking distance who would sell or loan her a petrol can. The deep rumble of a motorbike drew closer. It was Martin, riding something out of a 50's movie toward her over the grass. There was a petrol can propped in front of him.

He eased the motorbike through the gate and pulled up beside Christie. "Put the roof up and lock it."

Christie did not move.

"Or you can walk," he continued. "It's only a couple of k's each way."

That galvanized Christie, who raised the roof and locked the car. She slipped the keys into her handbag and looped the strap over her head. Martin motioned for her to get on the motorbike behind him and she cautiously climbed on.

He powered the throttle and Christie grabbed around his waist as he steered off the grass and onto the road.

"What about a helmet?" Christie called over the motor, but the only response was a quick acceleration.

A few minutes later, Christie returned to the motorbike after paying for the fuel. Martin was on the bike, the can again tucked in front of him.

"Thanks. I mean it, thank you."

Martin contemplated her.

"What's wrong?" she said.

"There's something you should see."

"Okay. Where?"

Martin started the bike. "Coming?"

Christie clambered on and gripped Martin.

"I won't let you fall." he said and she loosened her hold as they left the petrol station.

~

Christie decided the sea air must have gone to her head and caused her to lose all caution and common sense. The motorbike was surprisingly powerful and careened too fast up a narrow track filled with twists and turns, fallen trees and potholes.

After a short ride inland, Martin made an abrupt turn into the forest. Was he so intent on getting the painting he was heading to a place to hide her body? She giggled. The track kept going up and up through increasingly dense bush before ending at a flat clearing, right on the side of a mountain.

Martin stopped the motorbike and turned off the engine. Relieved, Christie hopped off and stretched, checking she was all in one piece.

The clearing was a natural lookout, with mountains going off one way and the ocean in the other. Christie wandered to the edge. Far below, Rivers End was a miniature village. The river wound its way from the mountains right to the lagoon near the jetty. At high tide, the sea and river would meet.

Martin joined Christie. "Be careful. The rocks can give way."

"But you said you wouldn't let me fall." Christie flashed a smile at Martin. She turned her attention to the township.

"Oh look! I can see your house."

"Forget my house. See that area?" he pointed to a darkened, cleared hill. It was somewhat further up the road that Palmerston House was on.

"Did a fire go through it?"

"Not a fire. A housing estate. Out here." The last two words were said in disgust. "What was once there succumbed to bulldozers a few months ago."

"What was there?"

"Forest. Old forest and its inhabitants, who were all displaced."

Christie turned to Martin. "That's what you wanted to show me?"

"That is what developers do."

"Why tell me to sell the cottage to them?"

Shaking his head impatiently, Martin took hold of Christie's left hand and held it up, touching her engagement ring. "Are you here to bring more destruction? Are you the scouting party now you own part of this town?"

"Me? What? How do you even know Derek is a developer?" Pulling her hand away, she unconsciously rubbed where his fingers had touched her. "Why would you even think that of me?"

"Why wouldn't I?"

Tears filled Christie's eyes and she turned her back on Martin, unwilling for him to see them. "I don't owe you an explanation."

"Why are you still here?"

"I came for my grandmother's funeral."

"That was days ago. Why are you still here?" Martin pressed.

"I don't know!"

She swung around, not expecting Martin to be so close. She took a step back, her foot slipping. Martin caught her arms with his hands and steadied her. She stared up at him with wide eyes and a racing heart. He searched her face.

"Please, may we go back now?" she ventured in a small voice.

He nodded and released her. As he walked back to the motorbike, Christie forced herself to breathe normally. Her body tingled all over and she crossly told herself it was the altitude.

"This bike used to belong to my...to someone I know. He'd bring his fiancée up here under moonlight."

Christie joined him on the bike. "Was she allowed to wear a helmet?" she grumbled.

She could have sworn she heard Martin chuckle but the roar of the engine drowned it out. Just above the horizon, Christie saw a full moon, pale in the late afternoon sky. She remembered Thomas writing of a special place where he and Martha would celebrate selling his painting. Maybe this was that place.

LET'S ELOPE

1 *967*

A full moon shone on Thomas and Martha, standing locked in a passionate kiss, their arms wrapped around each other. A night bird sailed from one of the trees, flying right next to the couple. It startled Martha, and Thomas laughed at her reaction.

"So, my fearless explorer is not so fearless."

Annoyed, Martha tried to walk away but Thomas held her fast within his arms.

"Let me go!" she pushed against his chest.

"Uh uh. Temper!" Thomas slid a hand to her behind, tapping it lightly. "That is the first thing I will work on once we marry. No more tantrums."

Martha leaned in to him and raised her face with a mischievous smile. "I can be very naughty if you like."

Thomas sighed. "You think I joke? You will see."

He pointed to the sky near the horizon. "A shooting star! Quick, make a wish."

Martha closed her eyes, smiling. Thomas watched her, his face softened by the love that sometimes threatened to overwhelm him.

She opened her eyes after a moment. "Did you make a wish?"

"No need to." He took her hand. "We should elope. Tonight."

"Thomas?"

"Yes, we should pack a small suitcase and drive to the city. Find someone to marry us tomorrow."

"But...but the wedding is less than two months away. The arrangements are nearly all complete and the guests all invited. Our engagement party is coming up and imagine how upset everyone would be!" Martha's eyes brimmed with anxiety and Thomas pulled her close to his chest.

"Sh...Sorry. No, you are right of course. Just...well, what if something should go wrong? I could not bear to lose you."

"Nothing will go wrong. I would never let it!" Martha slipped her arms around Thomas' neck and reached up on her toes to kiss him.

He returned the kiss, and held her to him, stroking her hair. Over her head, he stared off into the night, worry creasing his forehead.

JASMINE SEA

*C*hristie hung onto Martin as the motorbike hurtled along the track, apparently oblivious to any possible dangers.

"Do you have to go so fast?"

"No, but it's almost dark and there's no headlights."

"Wonderful."

"What?"

"I said—watch out for that creek!" Christie spotted a narrow, water filled dip in the track.

Without slowing, Martin ploughed the motorbike through the widest part of the dip, spraying water over them both.

"What creek?" he called innocently.

Christie gave up trying to get wet hair out of her eyes and closed them instead, hoping nobody would see her in such a waterlogged state.

Sunset approached as the motorbike rumbled up the hill to Martin's property. It slowed near Christie's car, edged through the gate and rolled over the meadow to the house. Martin parked it near the deck and Christie jumped off.

"I'll empty this into the car and bring it right back." she said, holding a hand out for the petrol can.

"Why don't you go inside and have a shower? I can fill the car." Martin held onto the petrol can. His hair and clothes were drying in the late warmth of the day, but Christie felt as though she had stepped out of the ocean. A muddy ocean.

"Shower? Well, no, I need to get home; I mean what would I wear?"

"You're going to wet that fancy car of yours. I'll loan you something. Go on."

"Um, well I wouldn't mind visiting the bathroom." Christie realised she might not make it home without a stop.

Martin was already walking away. "Through the living area, second room on the left."

Christie nodded and headed onto the deck. Randall came to greet her through the open sliding door.

"While you're in there, have a shower." Martin called over his shoulder.

Christie sighed and went inside, mentally noting it was somehow okay for his house to stay unlocked, but not hers.

It only took a glance in the mirror for Christie to change her mind about using the shower. She tried to wipe the muddy splatters off her face with tissues but only succeeded in turning them into streaks of brown.

The bathroom—a large ensuite to a guest bedroom—was a surprise with its fluffy towels, shampoo, and goat's milk soap all saying welcome. Perhaps Martin was expecting someone. Which meant she should shower and leave.

The shower itself was a delight, with much better water pressure than the cottage, and Christie had to remind herself not to linger. Wrapped in a towel and drying her hair with another, she peeked back into the bedroom. On the bed was a neatly folded T-shirt.

Finding a comb in her handbag, Christie ran it through her hair. Her makeup had washed off in the shower and all she had in her handbag was lipstick. She grimaced at her reflection.

She folded her wet pants and blouse, relieved at least her lingerie escaped the soaking. The T-shirt was long on her, stopping just below her thighs. It was plain white, like the one Martin wore the first time she visited here.

After slinging her handbag over a shoulder, she collected her wet clothes and damp shoes. The house was deserted, so she stepped onto the deck to a dramatic sunset of gold and red.

Martin stood at the railing staring out over the sea, wearing dry jeans and a dark blue T-shirt. Randall ate dinner from a stainless steel bowl, briefly lifting his head as Christie stepped out. She paused to take in the view and Martin turned around.

"Funny how things work out." she said.

"How so?"

"I'm supposed to be on Lizard Island enjoying sunsets, the ocean and cocktails."

"Would you settle for a sunset, the ocean and a local Chardonnay?" Martin picked up two glasses of white wine from the small table near the deckchairs and held one out to Christie.

Surprised, she hesitated. Was this a truce of kinds? Should she even be here, with a man who was little more than a stranger?

"Thanks." Something deep inside her wanted this to continue so she proposed a toast. "To sunsets, the ocean, and Chardonnay."

"To things working out the way they're meant to." Martin counter-proposed and they touched their glasses together with a clink.

Christie put her clothes, shoes and handbag on one of the deckchairs and joined Martin at the railing. She sipped on the wine, relaxing for the first time in oh so long. The sun dropped below the horizon, leaving a trail of fading pink and a soft golden glow across the sea. A light breeze carried the salty tang of the ocean, complementing the heady scent of jasmine along the railing.

"If ever I become a candle maker, I shall create one that smells like this evening and call it Jasmine Sea." Christie announced.

Martin turned his head to her with amusement in his eyes. It softened his features. "Do you aspire to being a candle maker?"

"I wasn't. But it's always worth having a backup plan."

Randall ran off the deck to chase a rabbit.

"Does he ever catch them?"

"Never. He wouldn't know what to do with one. He'd make friends with it and bring it back to the house as his pet."

"He's a sensational dog."

"Yes."

As the sky darkened, the pale moon Christie saw earlier from the lookout became brighter, full and white as it rose almost from where the sun set. Along the coast to the west, a storm front approached.

"Will your clothes be okay?" Martin said. "They're expensive."

"They'll be fine. Are you apologising?" she teased.

"Not at all. I've told you before—"

"Yes, yes, it weakens your position. Thing is, sometimes it takes strength to say you're sorry. When it matters."

Martin watched Christie over the rim of his glass.

Under the moonlight Martin was less intimidating...no that was not the word. Less stern and cold. His eyes were deep and mysterious black pools and the longer he gazed at her, the more they drew Christie in. Who was this man and what did he want?

Apart from my painting.

Christie turned her back on the view and leaned against the railing, not sure what to do or say. Her head told her to use this opportunity to get Martin's trust so he would help her solve at least some of the puzzles of the cottage. Her instincts told her to run as fast as she could. In between those extremes, she struggled with a need for him to understand she had no ulterior motives and no desire to harm this little town. She swallowed the rest of her wine.

Martin wandered over to the table and, without comment, brought the wine bottle back, refilling their glasses.

Randall trotted back onto the deck and sat at Christie's feet, making her laugh as he leaned against her asking for a chin scratch.

"He likes you." Martin said.

"I like him too. Never was allowed to have a dog and these days, well, I'm away too much," she leaned down to whisper to Randall, "so will you let me share you a little?"

Randall wagged his tail before dropping onto the deck with a soft grunt.

Christie straightened and glanced at Martin, who gazed into his wine glass.

"I'd never let a developer get their hands on the cottage."

"Not even your own fiancé?"

"Derek will support whatever I decide to do with it."

"Which is?"

"I'd like to keep it. Do it up and spend at least part of my home time here."

"Live here? You're a city girl through and through."

"I'm not. I live in Melbourne because of the airport. And Gran raised me there. It's not where my life started." Christie's eyes dropped to her bare feet, her toes curling at the memory of how hot the red soil of her childhood home had been.

"Rivers End has no luxuries. No beauty parlours or top end restaurants. Nothing for a woman who lives the high life."

"You do like to assume things, don't you?" Christie shook her head. "I happen to have a job which requires a certain level of presentation. I can't expect clients to engage me if I don't appear professional."

"Are there new clients here?"

"Of course not. I generally work between Hollywood and London."

"I see."

"What do you mean?"

"It doesn't matter. It's your choice how you present yourself."

The air filled with tension.

Then, Martin half smiled. "The T-shirt suits you."

Christie blushed. She never blushed, but this man who set so many alarm bells ringing in her head from their first encounter, was under her skin tonight.

"Um, thanks. Um, I like the wine. It's the same one I had the first night I stayed at the cottage. I'm going to take some home with me."

"When?"

"When what? When am I going home?"

Martin nodded.

"Derek flies back on Monday."

"From Lizard Island?"

"Yes. I'll get home just before him."

"He went without you?"

A chill shot through Christie, evaporating the warmth of the night. Her eyes filled with tears.

"You came to your grandmother's funeral and he went on holiday. You've had to deal with it all on your own?" Martin spoke with such gentleness that it was all Christie could do not to shed those tears in front of him.

She raised her chin and forced her emotions down, just as she always did. "I'm okay with it."

Martin took her left hand, as he had done at the lookout. Holding her fingers, he studied the engagement ring. "You shouldn't be okay with it."

His touch was electric. She had to leave. Her back was against the railing. Martin moved closer and Christie caught her breath. She had nowhere to go and nowhere else she wanted to be. Her hand was on fire and it was radiating through her. She had to stop this.

"He never knew Gran. He wanted this holiday so much. What would you have done?"

"It's irrelevant he didn't know your grandmother. He knows you." Martin let the words sit between them, released her fingers and turned back to the ocean. "It doesn't matter what I'd have done."

Christie rested her now empty wine glass on the railing.

Martin glanced at it. "I'm happy to refill that, but you're not driving home tonight."

"I'm fine to drive and I don't want any more wine, thanks."

"You need something to eat. I'll make something."

Martin stared intently at Christie, who somehow regained control of her emotions, forcing them below an icy weight in her stomach. Five minutes earlier she would have agreed to eat with him but now he had reminded her Derek let her down the one time she needed him. Staying here would only confuse her further.

"It's fine. I'm going now." Christie picked up her clothes and handbag and slipped on her shoes. She dug around in her handbag for her keys without success.

"I've still got them. You can stay in the guest room or you can walk, but you're not driving home." Martin crossed his arms. "Don't bother arguing, Christie. Now, which is it?"

"Why?"

"You're not serious. In your world, do you drink two full glasses of wine on an empty stomach and drive?"

"No. Of course I would never do that! Okay, I get your point. But I'd like my keys back thanks and I'll pick the car up in the morning."

"Nope. You can drop the T-shirt back to me and swap it for the keys. End of discussion. Here, give me your phone for a moment. I'll put my phone number into it."

"Why?" Christie fished the phone out of her bag and handed it to him.

He tapped away at it. "Text me when you get home please. I want to be sure you're safe." He handed her back the phone.

The wine was going to her head, or the salt air and hunger. Or all three. Christie did not know if she wanted to answer to him. She was a grown woman who travelled the world and was quite able to walk a couple of kilometres home.

"Or," he continued, "you decide to do the smart thing and stay in the guest room, which has a lock by the way. There's a storm coming…you should stay."

"I am so angry right now!"

"Then have another glass of wine and a meal with me. You can be angry but you'll be safe. I promise you, staying here tonight is a safe option."

Christie doubted that. There was nothing safe about this man, although she was unafraid of him. Just of her emotions.

"I'm sorry. I couldn't do that to Derek."

"Do what, Christie? This night isn't real to you, is it? You're meant to be on a tropical island sipping cocktails with your fiancé. I think you're with the wrong man."

"You're right about that!" Irrational feelings of rejection and disappointment powered through Christie. Without a backward glance, she ran down the steps and into the night.

Christie ran until she reached the bottom of the hill and had no more running in her. She had to stop and take deep, shuddering gulps of air to clear her head and refill her lungs. Why had she accepted that first glass of wine and followed it up with another? What on earth possessed her to get so comfortable with a man she had known for less than a week?

Somehow, ridiculously, it was as though she had known Martin all of her life. Nobody had ever spoken to her the way he did, so direct and uncompromising. It was both challenging and refreshing and he by-passed her defences as if they were mere whispers in the wind. But he did not know her, he did not understand she was happy with Derek and would mend whatever had broken. She had to get the stability back.

The road crossed the river and Christie thought about walking home along the beach. Only the knowledge she would have to go past the graveyard on the way stopped her. That was one thing too many tonight.

There was a lightning flash in the distance and Christie hurried up. All she wanted now was to get back to the cottage and close the door behind her. Shut out this day and find a way to put her life back into perspective. Tomorrow was her last full day here. Somehow, that only made her sadder.

SAFELY HOME

*M*artin stopped in the shadows of the trees over the road from the cottage, relieved Christie made it home without him having to reveal his presence. He heard the back door close and saw a light come on inside. When she'd hesitated on the bridge, he'd willed her to stay away from the beach with the incoming storm. He wasn't stalking her, but perhaps she would think that.

Maybe in her world it was normal for someone to wander around in an unfamiliar place in the dark. Not in his. From the moment she'd stepped onto the deck tonight in his T-shirt, he'd wanted to protect her. Her still-damp hair had tumbled down her shoulders, the sunset reflected in those eyes.

So vulnerable.

Except she was capable of looking after herself. Did she even know the effect she had on him?

This evening should have been different. By now, Christie should have agreed to sell him the painting. She had no need for it and he did. The opportunity had presented itself and he stuffed it up. He should have kept things light, not let his guard down and upset her by pointing out her fiancé's deficiencies. It was none of his business.

How could any man treat her that way? Why did she accept it?

It isn't your business.

Tomorrow when she came for her car keys he had another opportunity. He needed to think things through and not ruin what might be the last chance he had.

LAST LETTERS

*C*hristie stood in the middle of the kitchen. She had stripped the T-shirt off almost the minute she got home, and now wore her dressing gown. She needed to eat but only some grapes and feta remained, along with the bottles of wine. She ignored the food and took out a bottle, pouring a glass which she raised to the fridge.

"To bad decisions and poor forward planning," she said aloud, unsure whether to laugh or cry, deciding instead emotions were a dangerous waste of time and energy.

One glass down and Christie gave in and finished off the meagre offerings from the fridge. Her stomach was growling and she wondered what Martin would have cooked. She dropped onto the chair at the kitchen table and opened the next letter, dated only two days after the last one.

Her engagement ring was on her closed laptop and she wore Martha's solitaire. Somehow, it brought her closer to her great-aunt, a woman she had never met and probably never would. All she knew of Martha was the person she saw through Thomas' eyes. Someone worthy of his deep and abiding love. Someone with spirit and fire, compassion and intelligence.

Beautiful girl,

What words can I use to bring you home? I am out of ideas and it has become clear either you are not receiving my letters, or have changed your mind about us. I will not accept the latter, so write this without expecting a response. Perhaps Dorothy is keeping these from you or perhaps you refuse to open them.

Even so, it puzzles me you would not seek me out. Better than anyone, I know how strong and honest you are, and you never, ever break a promise. Not if you can help it. Why not come home and finish this properly, if that is what you want to do?

No, something is wrong beyond what happened that night. I plan to ask for time off work next week and come to find you.

I fear you may come home whilst I come to seek you, but I must take the risk. You are worth it.

I love you always,

Thomas.

Thomas had waited so long afraid he would miss Martha returning. How difficult it must have been back then, with no internet or mobile phones. There was no mention of him trying to phone Martha.

Who was stopping these letters, for surely Martha would have responded at least once to them, even if just to say goodbye? It pointed toward Gran. Christie pushed the possibility away.

She picked up the next letter. The final one.

Dear Martha,

There has been a change of plans, which I hope will not upset you. Instead of me coming to Melbourne, your best friend will bring you a letter...

A FRIEND INDEED

*1*967

Thomas and Frannie sat outside the corner café in the sun. Thomas drank black coffee and Frannie nibbled on a cupcake between sips of white tea. Thomas was uncomfortable, one finger tapping the side of the cup.

"Tom? You look so worried." Frannie ventured.

"Hm? No, not sure about your idea. Though I appreciate you wanting to help."

"You've said yourself you've not once been to Melbourne and have no idea of how to get around. What if you get lost?"

"I'll ask for directions."

"It's not like she's right in the city now. If what my contact says is true and Dorothy moved to that new part of town, well there's not even public transport there yet."

"I'd walk a hundred miles if I had to."

"But what if you go all that way and don't find her? What if she comes home at that exact time?" Frannie persisted.

Thomas nursed his coffee cup. She was making sense.

"You write that letter to Martha and I'll guard it with my life and put it into her hands and her hands alone. Cross my heart." Frannie's voice was determined.

"Are you sure? I don't want to impose on you and I know it must be hard to go and see her, after everything. What if it makes things worse for you?"

"Martha and I will always be friends. Sometimes you have to take a chance. She is not replying to your letters so either she doesn't want to come back, or she has not read them. Well, make your words special and she will remember why she loves you so much!"

Frannie reached a hand across and rested it on one of Thomas'. "You know, I care a lot about you and what happens with Martha. Let me help. Please?"

Frannie was being so kind. Such a good friend. He nodded.

"Well, I am leaving the day after tomorrow, so you had better go and write that letter. And with a bit of luck, when I come home next week, Martha will be with me."

TOO MANY QUESTIONS

I am not sure how she knows Dorothy moved, but that might explain why you have not replied to my letters. And why the phone rang out when I finally got a number.

There is no point me sending this one, but I feel I have to. Maybe Dorothy still collects her mail from her old address. At least I know there will be one letter that will find you. A letter and a painting, to remind you of your promise. Please my darling girl, please read it with an open heart and come back to me.

Love,

Thomas

That was it? Christie stood up and fruitlessly searched the shoebox for another letter. Did this mean Martha's friend succeeded in getting it to her? Or did Thomas never write it? Was that how the painting got to Dorothy?

Folding the letter thoughtfully, Christie found the whole thing mystifying. Who was this "best friend" Thomas trusted enough to act as intermediary. Would Martha's closest friend not have already spoken to her about the separation? Best friends tended to share as much as sisters did. There had been mention of a friend in other letters. Frannie, who took their photographs on the beach.

Christie flicked through the photo album to find the picture of Thomas and Martha. The love in their eyes was real. As before, Christie was struck by the similarity between Thomas and Martin, who must be his grandson. Somehow, she had to find the right way to ask him this tomorrow. She toyed with the idea of offering him the painting in exchange for a frank and honest conversation, but discarded that. The painting was staying here until she had sufficient information to make a decision.

One by one, Christie put the letters back into the shoebox. Deep in thought, she turned off the light and headed off to bed, more than ready for today to finish.

WORLDS APART

*M*artin stood on the deck in the morning sun, staring out to sea. Christie stepped lightly through the grass. He didn't know she was watching him. At this moment, hands on the railing, Martin was relaxed.

"Like boats?"

He did know!

Christie stepped up onto the deck and followed his line of vision. A sleek yacht, long and low, cut through the calm water with no effort. "Oh, I love them. Particularly yachts. So beautiful."

Martin turned to give her his attention. Under his scrutiny, she blushed. She'd worn jeans and an emerald green, short-sleeved shirt, and pulled her hair back in a ponytail. It felt natural. Nice.

"Yes. Beautiful."

"Stop flirting. I'm engaged, remember?"

"Coffee?" Martin walked into the house before she could reply, so she followed him.

Inside, Martin was in the kitchen at a coffee machine. "What can I get you?"

"Um, anything's fine."

Martin stopped with a pained expression on his face. "So, what would you like?"

"Flat white?"

"That wasn't so hard now, was it?" Martin turned to the coffee machine and Christie perched on a stool. The kitchen was spacious, with stainless steel appliances, including a double sized stand-alone oven with gas cooktop. At the end of the counter was a bowl with fresh apples, oranges and mangoes and Christie gazed at them with longing.

"Did you miss breakfast?" Martin placed coffee in front of Christie.

"Oh, thanks. Yes, ran out of food so I'll get something on the way home."

"When did you run out? No, don't answer. Do you eat eggs?"

"Love eggs."

"Drink your coffee." Martin pulled a frying pan out of a drawer and went to the fridge.

"Oh, you don't need to feed me!"

"What makes you think this is for you?" Martin placed eggs and cream on the counter, and found a bowl in another drawer. "I haven't eaten yet. If you're lucky, there may be enough for you."

"Oh."

He deftly sliced a cob loaf, then tossed two pieces into a toaster. As the frying pan heated, he cracked eggs into the bowl, added a slurp of cream and lightly whisked the mix. From an overhead cupboard, he took two plates and collected cutlery on his way past a drawer. After placing these on the counter, he took the eggs to the stove and poured them into the pan, swirling them once then walking away to get a spatula.

The toast popped and Martin glanced around from his place back at the stove.

"Can you get those, and check the fridge, should be butter and some jam if you prefer."

Christie did so, putting a piece of toast on each plate and opening the fridge. It was stocked with fresh vegetables and fruit, juice, milk, a selection of cheeses, yoghurt and seafood, plus beer and a couple of bottles of wine. She found the butter and took it back to the counter as he brought the frying pan over.

Back on her stool, Christie watched him slide half of the scrambled eggs on to one plate, then the other. Perfectly cooked, soft ribbons of yellow with flecks of pepper he added toward the end.

He pushed one plate in front of her with a no nonsense, "Eat."

She picked up a fork, waiting for him to join her. He sat beside her and took a mouthful of coffee, watching her over the rim in expectation. Christie speared a forkful of eggs. Martin nodded and started eating.

"Thanks." Christie said between mouthfuls. She stopped for a moment to butter her toast, glancing at Martin, who studied her with that same pained gaze from earlier.

"It is delicious." she said before biting into the toast.

"Are you always like this? Not looking after yourself?"

"No. I don't know. Maybe. Love your coffee. I have a thing about coffee."

He got up and took her now empty cup. "So do I. Same as wine, why drink it unless it is good quality. Applies to much of life, actually."

Christie finished every morsel, wishing she could eat it all again. Now she was done, she glanced around the living room. "Where's Randall?"

Over the grumble of the coffee machine, Martin raised his voice. "Probably in the studio."

"You have a studio?"

Martin did not answer, so Christie waited until he brought fresh coffees over.

"Where's your studio?"

"Just over there." he waved in the general direction. "He likes sleeping there in the morning. Sunny and quiet."

"So, you're an artist?"

"Sometimes."

Perhaps he was a collector as well. Maybe of local art and that's why he wanted her painting so much. She hesitated to ask in case it disturbed this pleasant truce.

"Um, last night..." she faltered.

"When do you leave?"

"What? Oh, early in the morning I think."

"When will you come back?"

Christie shook her head. "I don't know. I'd like it to be soon, but in a couple of weeks, I have a job in London so it may not be possible to come back before I go. Why?"

"Have you thought anymore about selling me the painting?" There, it was said.

"Yes. Have you thought about telling me who its rightful owner is?"

Martin put his coffee cup down and started to clear their breakfast plates. He stacked them on the side of the sink, then returned the butter to the fridge. His demeanour was not upset or angry, but nor was he forthcoming. Finally, he stopped moving around the kitchen and stood on the other side of the counter, arms crossed and expression thoughtful.

"Would you leave it with me while you're away?" he said.

"What do you mean?"

"Leave the painting here in Rivers End. It will stay safe and that way you're not transporting it all over the place."

"I'd not even thought about whether to leave it in the cottage or take it to Melbourne and get it valued."

For the third time this morning, Martin's expression showed frustration. "Its value is whatever a buyer will pay."

"Not helpful if it needs insuring. What do you think it is worth?"

"How much do you want?"

Christie rolled her eyes at Martin, who raised an eyebrow.

"How about we stop going round in circles, Martin. You tell me what you know about the painting and I'll consider selling it to you at a fair price."

"Do you roll your eyes at your fiancé?" Martin wandered around the counter and sat back on his stool whilst Christie stared at him in surprise. "You wouldn't do it if you were engaged to me."

"Why?"

"Because I'd never knowingly disrespect you and would expect the same in return."

He ran his hands over his lap, stopping with one palm on each knee, and leaned forward a fraction, dark eyes serious. "I highly value respect."

She couldn't help herself. "What would you do?"

Martin sat back and picked up his coffee cup. "That's a discussion for another day."

Christie had no idea what to make of this strange conversation. She had the oddest sensation of light-headedness and discovered she was holding her breath. Martin seemed oblivious to this and continued speaking.

"If you must know, there's someone I wish to show the painting to. I'll care for it, I promise you and when you return, if you want it I'll give it back."

"Just like that? With no arguments?" Christie forced a smile.

"More or less. Are we agreed?"

"I need to think about it."

Martin nodded and took her car keys out of a pocket.

"Oh, I forgot the T-shirt."

"Keep it."

Christie reached out with her left hand. She still wore Martha's engagement ring. Martin released the keys and glanced at her questioningly.

"Forgot I had that on. It helps me feel closer to her."

"To your grandmother?"

"Um, no, to Martha, my great-aunt. This was one of the secrets left in the cottage for me."

Instantly, Martin got up and stalked away, his face as angry as the day they first met at the graveyard. He headed for the sliding door, his body rigid.

"What's wrong, Martin?" Christie grabbed her bag and followed.

At the door, he paused. "Let it go. Nothing good can come of this, Christie, just drop it."

"But, why?" Christie reached Martin, confused.

"Please trust me about this."

"It's not about trust. Gran wanted me to find out about Martha... and others."

"Then we're on opposite sides."

"What? No, I don't understand. Please help me understand all of this."

Martin sighed and went out onto the deck, back to the same spot he was in earlier in the day. He stared out at the sea.

"Go home, Christie. Go back to Derek and your fancy life." He delivered the words in a monotone. "There's nothing here for you. Sell the cottage, the painting, the ring. Make a profit and go and find a happy life for yourself."

Why are you saying this?

Christie's heart pounded in her chest and her stomach tied up in a knot. More than ever before, she wanted to stay. With sudden clarity, it hit her. It was emotion. Raw, powerful emotions rising above anything else Christie had ever experienced and this complex, difficult man had as much to do with them as the beautiful region and the funny little cottage she already loved.

"I don't want to go." Distress choked her voice.

"There's nothing here for you. You are a Ryan, and your family aren't welcome in Rivers End. Go back to Melbourne, city girl."

Hand over her mouth, Christie turned and ran down the steps as she had the previous night. Tears blinded her as she sprinted to the gate, where she stopped, sobbing for a moment, before slipping through it.

Few minutes later Martin heard the Lotus start. Long, painful minutes where he held onto the railing so hard his hands hurt. Gripping those rails was the only thing that stopped him going after Christie when he heard her crying.

She would never understand why this was a bad idea. He was furious with himself for inviting her into his world. Her family and his could never unite.

As the car drove away, Martin remembered his words about respect. That he would never intentionally disrespect her. What he had just done was worse. Necessary, perhaps, but not fair to either of them.

LEFT BEHIND

*T*he grey light of morning and familiar sounds of traffic roused Christie from the deep sleep that, exhausted, she succumbed to in the early hours. She opened her eyes to a wet Melbourne dawn and curled back in under the covers, wishing herself back in Rivers End.

She arrived home in the middle of yesterday afternoon, packing and closing up the cottage within a couple of hours of running away from Martin's house. Her emotions were a jumbled mess, and it had taken the entire drive home to get some control back over them.

As she unpacked, her mind became calmer and more organised. She opened all of the windows and let the sounds and smells of Docklands fill the rooms. Periodically, she stopped putting her things away and watched the boats and the people below going about their business.

The bottles of wine went into the almost empty fridge. Her stomach was also empty but not from hunger. It was as though a big hole sucked all the light and colour from her life. It was too early to revisit those last moments with Martin, but his calmly delivered words had shattered some fragile part of herself.

After a while, Christie slid her feet out of bed and sat there for a moment. The city was under a cloud of hazy rain, and there was little to welcome her home. This was how her first day in Rivers End had been. She sighed and got up, longing for a shower and coffee before heading out to South Melbourne Markets to stock up for Derek's return later today.

~

A few hours later, the sky cleared and the day turned into a more pleasant late spring afternoon. The shopping trip resulted in a full fridge and pantry. Christie forced herself to eat a handful of plump strawberries but barely tasted them.

She sat on the balcony with freshly brewed coffee. Soon, Derek would be home, and her attention would turn to putting things right with him. For now, though, her mind strayed back to a decision she made yesterday.

After packing her bags, Christie had stood in front of the painting for a few moments, unsure of her next move. When Martin asked her to leave the painting with him for a while, she almost said yes on the spot. If he had not reacted the way he did to seeing Martha's ring, she would probably have gone home and got it for him.

His words still resonated, slicing into Christie like a knife but with all of her heart, she knew there was more to it than him wanting to hurt her. He was protecting himself or someone else. Maybe even just the memory of Thomas. What harm could it do to leave it with Martin while she was away? If anything, it might prove to him she was not, as he claimed, on an opposing side.

Christie took the painting off the hook and wrapped it back in the sheet. With every step, she second-guessed herself. What if he kept it? What if he was so upset he refused to take it? What would Gran think of all of this?

Christie knew she was unable to take it to him. Instead, she drove into town.

Daphne was behind the counter when Christie pushed the door open, carrying the painting in its sheet.

"Oh, Christie! How wonderful to see you, lovely." Daphne beamed as she stood up.

"Hi, Daphne. I'm going to ask a huge favour, but please say no if it doesn't suit."

"Of course, anything. I was so hoping to see you before you left."

It was impossible not to smile at Daphne's friendliness. "I'm on my way now. All packed and about to head home."

"Well, it's sad to see you go, I have to say. I hope it won't be for too long?"

"Hopefully not. Would you mind doing something for me? I get the feeling you get on pretty well with Martin?"

"Oh, yes indeed! Is that for him?"

"Sort of. He offered to keep it while I'm gone and I, well…"

Daphne rushed around the counter, delighted. "You must be hurrying off to see your young man! No time to drop it up the hill? You let me worry about that, lovely."

"Daphne, thank you. If you phone Martin, I'm sure he'll come and pick it up."

"Yes, I'll do that. I guess it's that painting you wanted to be fixed?"

"He did an amazing job."

"I told you he's a good boy! Now, give me a hug, and you head back to the city. But come back soon. You are so welcome here in our little town!" Daphne gave Christie a tight squeeze.

Driving down the main street a few moments later, Christie slowed past the bakery. Belinda was putting cakes in the window, and she wanted to weep. There were wonderful people here, people who welcomed her without judgement.

Why had Martin decided what sort of person she was before they had even spoken? Not even giving her a chance to get her bearings, he had worked it all out—wrongly of course. What had happened to the man to make him so bitter and uncompromising?

Going past the graveyard, she glanced across and whispered a silent farewell. Sorrow and grief intermingled with fear of what was ahead. A bittersweet love for the cottage and town entwined with utter confusion over the house on the hill and its complicated owner.

∾

Now, a day later, Christie wondered if she had done the right thing. Leaving the painting had been a big leap of faith and trust in a man who rattled her more than any other person in her life. The pain Derek caused with his unkind words about Gran paled compared to those parting shots from Martin.

Well, Christie decided, that was because she loved and knew Derek so well. He never set out to hurt her. He was disappointed. He was not what Christie would call an emotional man, so occasionally expressing himself might be healthy.

His temperament suited hers, helping Christie to control herself and keep a more level head when he was around.

She glanced at her reflection in the window and decided to change into something a bit more suitable than jeans.

Christie heard the front door open and close. Her heartbeat sped up and she checked the mirror. White dress, white sandals, the gold chain Derek gave her when they moved in together. Her hair was straightened and swept to one side.

Smile. It'll be fine.

Derek stood in the middle of the living room and waited for Christie to come to him, which she did, kissing his cheek. "Hi."

"You've lost weight. I like you a bit curvier."

"Coffee?" She headed for the kitchen without waiting for an answer.

I like me just as I am.

Some of the tension drained away. She did like herself. And she wasn't going to try to be someone else for anyone ever again. Derek could accept it or move on.

"Go me." She whispered with a small smile.

Coffee made, Christie found Derek sitting on the balcony, tapping on his phone. As he wrote a text message, she gazed out at the water. A yacht would be nice.

After a couple of minutes, he put the phone away and picked up his cup.

"New shirt?" It suited him, a more casual linen shirt with its two top buttons undone.

"Yeah, found it in the boutique on the island. Would have got you something but didn't know what you'd like."

Christie had no reply so sipped her coffee. On the phone the other day, Derek said he had gained weight, but there was no sign of that. He had dyed the grey out of his hair. Not that she minded it, but it always bothered him.

"Still wearing my ring."

"Of course. Why wouldn't I be?"

"Been disappointed this week, Chris. You know, we'd talked about commitment and spending more time together when you got back from L.A. unless you've forgotten."

Commitment goes two ways.

"Being up there on my own gave me plenty of time to think. To consider...options."

"What kind of options, Derek?"

"No, I'm not ready to talk about it yet."

"Okay. What would you like to talk about?"

"I thought we should host a small dinner party. You're an amazing cook when you set your mind to it, and it'd be fun to have friends over."

Thrown by the sudden change of direction the conversation had taken, Christie nodded.

"So, tomorrow night."

"Tomorrow? That might be short notice for guests."

"Not at all. Ingrid and Leon are staying in Melbourne for a few days, so I wanted to extend our hospitality."

"You already invited them?"

"Four isn't much of a party though, so you'd better ask the boys next door if they're free. Leon should get on pretty well with them." Derek said.

"Do you have anything in mind for dinner? Any likes or dislikes from Ingrid and Leon?"

"Didn't notice. Just work your magic on the food, and I'll take care of the drinks."

"If you like, use a bottle of the Chardonnay I brought home. Beautiful local wine. What?"

Derek was frowning. "I think we can manage a bit more upmarket, don't you? Like something from a decent winery that will show Victoria off to our guests."

"What better way than from an authentic small wine grower?"

"Well, you let me know by tomorrow what you're cooking, and I'll work on the right accompaniments. Okay?"

"Sure. I might go and ask Ashley and Ray if they're free tomorrow. You enjoy the view, I won't be long."

Christie took her cup into the kitchen and rinsed it, giving herself a moment to collect her thoughts. Derek was acting odd. Last minute dinner parties with pre-arranged guests. Hinting he was rethinking their relationship but refusing to discuss it. Not bringing anything home for her from what should have been their holiday, when he usually showered her with gifts.

Was Derek unsure of their relationship now? Perhaps he was afraid she might be about to leave him, so he planted a seed of doubt about his own feelings. Face-saving, just in case she called it all off. She sighed, having no intention of playing these games but somehow always backing down instead of asking the hard questions.

From the day Christie moved into the apartment, Ashley and Ray had been her neighbours. The three of them hit it off right away, particularly as Ashley was a senior manager at Docklands Studios. Christie worked on films there on occasion, and they knew quite a few of the same people in the insular industry.

Ashley was flamboyant and fun, while Ray was quieter but had a killer sense of humour. Teaching law at Melbourne University, his passion was guitar and languages. He spoke seven fluently, and he and

Ashley always chose their holiday destinations based on whatever tongue was the current favourite.

Christie tapped on the door, and when Ray opened it, his face lit up in a broad smile.

"Hello, beautiful!" He threw his arms around her.

"Derek thinks I'm too thin."

Ray stepped back to inspect Christie. "Never can be too thin or too rich, or so they say. You appear fine to me. For a woman." he added. "Come in."

"Can't, sorry. Just wanted to invite you and Ashley to dinner tomorrow night. I know this is short notice, sorry."

"You speak as though we have a life." Ray feigned mournfulness. "How shall we dress and what shall we bring?"

"The usual and nothing."

"So wear nothing and bring the usual?"

"Funny man. I missed you!"

"Well, you can tell me all about your romantic break tomorrow."

"Oh, and there'll be another couple there. Ingrid and Leon, friends of Derek. And about seven okay?"

"Seven it is. Sure you won't stay for a while? I'm finished for the year, so all I have is time."

Christie kissed Ray on the cheek. "Gotta go. See you tomorrow."

"Very well. I shall return to my solitary musings."

Christie laughed at Ray as he closed the door with a sigh. Walking back to her apartment, she remembered his comment about the romantic break. Derek must have told them about Lizard Island. Perhaps he had told all of their friends. Now, he would be embarrassed he had gone alone.

Why is everything so difficult?

Derek was in the bedroom unpacking his bag when Christie returned. Her suitcase that had gone to Queensland with Derek was open on the end of the bed, so Christie began putting her things away. As she hung a long dress in a shade of green that matched her eyes, Derek glanced over.

"Wear that tomorrow night. It's what I wanted you to wear for dinner with Ingrid and Leon. Except you never arrived."

Christie dropped onto the edge of the bed. "I was on my way to the airport when you rang. All I wanted was to be with you, Derek. Don't you know that?"

"Well, you changed your mind and stayed, that's all I know. Which gave me no confidence you wanted to come to Lizard Island." His attention stayed on his suitcase.

"Of course I wanted to be there, but you said some things that hurt me. It wasn't a road trip, it was my grandmother's funeral, and I needed to say goodbye. You told me I was selfish!" To Christie's dismay, she began to cry. Quiet tears of frustration, sadness, and probably some anger, if she was honest.

Derek stared at her in astonishment. Christie never cried. Never raised her voice or argued. She followed most of his suggestions, supported his ideas and went about her life. He disappeared into the bathroom and returned with a box of tissues, which he held out to her.

"Stop crying. There's no need, Christie, here have a tissue."

"Thanks." She took one and wiped the tears. "You called me Christie. Thanks."

The tears trickled to a stop, and she took a few deep, calming breaths. Derek left the tissues on the bedside table and kept emptying his bag, but he glanced at her a few times in concern.

After a moment or two, Christie resumed unpacking. Derek took his now empty suitcase into the spare bedroom. Christie finished by the time he returned, so he took hers and put it away. When he came back in, Christie was standing in front of the mirrored robe.

"Hey, I don't remember saying those things, but if I did, well, it would have been because I was so disappointed not to have you there. Let's put this last week behind us and move on." He put his arms around Christie and pulled her close against his chest. She leaned her head on his shoulder, wanting his strength to protect her from the world.

"I'm going to order in something for dinner, that way you can plan out tomorrow night. Okay?" He loosened his hold, and Christie stepped back a little and nodded. "I'll go open a bottle of red, and you get started on that." He kissed her on the cheek as if nothing had ever been wrong.

Once alone, Christie turned back to the mirror. Her eyes were so sad and unsure. Derek wanted to forget everything.

As though it didn't happen.

During a rare time of need, he withheld his support, his love and his understanding and forced her to take care of herself. The way she used to, growing up.

She needed more from Derek. She wanted him to be her inspiration and safe place and lover and protector. It might be an old-fashioned notion, but yes, she wanted him to watch out for her, be aware of her needs and not let harm come her way. She needed him to be her hero.

Reading the love letters from Thomas to Martha had shown her that for some people, love meant more than sharing a home and a few interests. It was about an unrelenting passion and deep, abiding love for another that defied time and circumstance. True love was putting the other person's needs above your own and being willing to see their perspective. Wanting to be with them no matter what the risks.

Christie sighed, unable to shake the sadness. She was being unfair to Derek with these unsettling thoughts. He was who he was. Unexpectedly, Martin came to mind, angry at her risky behaviour up on the ladder, his disbelief Derek had left her to go to the funeral alone, and how he followed her home to make sure she was safe. She had known he was trailing behind the whole time.

She pushed the memories away, upset with herself. Whatever was going on between herself and Derek was unrelated to Martin. She might not ever even see him again, so it was time to be real and concentrate on the problems at home.

YOU DON'T CHOOSE WHO YOU LOVE

*E*lizabeth White spent a restless night worrying about her brief encounter with Martha's great-niece. In a couple more days, her oldest friend would return to her home in Ireland. There was the check-up at the hospital first, but Martha was stronger now, and if there was one thing Elizabeth knew, it was that she had resilience.

The deep sorrow in her eyes remained, and Elizabeth believed there was more to it than the loss of Dorothy. She longed to comfort Martha but had no idea where to begin. Perhaps having a new relative in her life would provide a sense of family. She never married, although there had been men in her life from time to time.

There was little more Elizabeth knew, for Martha kept her private life private and rarely spoke of herself, other than her love of travel and long career as a primary school principal. Having been to Ireland herself, Elizabeth understood Martha's connection with the land, and in some ways, the small town she lived in was a little bit like Rivers End.

Before Martha woke, Elizabeth walked into town to get fresh milk and the paper. It was on her return trip that she saw Daphne drive in her direction and raised a hand to wave. Daphne pulled over with a cheery "Morning! Lovely day for it!"

"You're out early, Daphne."

"Yes—yes, busy day today. John's got people coming from the city again to inspect that land up near the old cottage, and I need to have morning tea all arranged."

"I see." Elizabeth could not trust herself to say more. The presence of developers around town was unwelcome.

"Good thing young Christie's gone home. Don't think she appreciated them offering to buy the old cottage the other day."

"Oh, that's the young lady with the sports car?"

"Did you meet her? Such a sweetie and I think she'll be back soon enough."

"Very soon, do you expect?"

"Hard to say. Think she rather likes it here so maybe she'll visit more often. Now, sorry to rush off but John will be expecting his cup of coffee."

"Nice to see you, Daphne." Elizabeth nodded and watched Daphne drive off.

Christie had left town and Martha would follow in a few days. No point telling her anything about her great-niece. Not yet. Elizabeth let out a deep sigh of relief.

Martha stood with her toes almost in the pond, leaning on her cane as she stared at the ripples in the water. Her ankle was improving and she was quite recovered from the incident on the jetty.

Elizabeth strolled along the path to stand at her side, holding a bowl of breadcrumbs. In companionable silence, the two women spent a few moments throwing the crumbs out to the ducks bickering over the morsels.

"Dorothy was always frightened of the ducks. They'd chase her around the pond." The words were emotionless and Elizabeth glanced at Martha's set face.

"I'm so sorry you didn't get to see her one last time."

Martha scraped the last of the crumbs from the bowl and nestled them in her hand. "Probably for the best. Some things can't be changed and now I'm the last of my generation."

"There's George."

Martha threw the crumbs as far as she could. "He was a decent man. Maybe I should have married him."

The ducks paddled away. The women turned to follow the path back to the house.

"We don't get to choose who we fall in love with, Martha."

"Someone else said that to me once."

"Oh, who?"

Martha stopped to glance back at the pond. "A man."

Unexpectedly, a memory pulled her back to this spot in 1966.

Thomas glowered at Martha. He stalked to the edge of the pond. He scooped up a handful of pebbles and skimmed them forcefully, one after another, across the surface of the water.

"You think you're so god-damned irresistible." he ground the words out.

"Sometimes I hate you!" Martha wanted to push him into the pond.

"Maybe you'll stop following me around."

Martha almost choked on her response. "Following you around? Everywhere I go, there you are. Even places you're not invited to!"

"Maybe I have to invite myself! I'm hardly suitable for the grand affairs of the Ryan family, now am I?"

"I don't care what my family thinks! I care about what I want."

Thomas tossed the last of the pebbles aside and faced Martha. With her hands on her hips and wrath in her eyes, she felt like a fireball ready to explode.

Thomas smiled.

"Don't you dare laugh at me!"

"Never. So, what is it you want, Martha Ryan, she who only cares about what she wants?"

"I want to travel the world. I want to be a famous writer. I want to..." her words trailed off as Thomas came close enough to touch Martha. She expected him to, but he did not.

"Go on."

"Um, I want the freedom to do whatever I want. With nobody telling me what to do."

"Nobody? That might be a lonely life, sweetheart."

"I'll...I'll take lovers when it suits me."

Thomas brushed the hair back from her wide-open eyes. "No, you won't."

"You can't stop me." There was no conviction in her voice.

"You don't get to choose who you fall in love with. Do you?" Thomas brushed his lips against Martha's, ever so lightly. "Do you, Martha?"

With a shuddering sigh, Martha melted against him.

Wrenching herself back to the present, Martha closed her eyes.

"Sounds like a wise man." Elizabeth remarked.

Martha opened her eyes and banged her cane on the path.

"He was a fool!" She stalked toward the house with a surprised Elizabeth hurrying behind.

DINNER FOR SIX

*A*fter an all-day blur of shopping and cooking, flower arranging and table decorating, Christie was back in front of the mirror. She critically inspected her reflection. Hair swept up and elegant in a chignon. Makeup flawless. The dress followed her shape, and her shoes were almost flat leather sandals.

"Baby, I need some help here!" Derek called from the kitchen.

"Just stir it. I'll only be a minute!"

Derek had offered to help while Christie got ready, so she gave him the task of occasionally stirring the pasta sauce. Last seen, he had a glass of wine in one hand and a wooden spoon in the other, standing as far from the sauce as he could, in case any splattered on him.

After dabbing on some perfume, Christie hurried to the kitchen, the dress swishing against her bare legs. The day had been hot and humid, still sticky in spite of a light breeze coming through the open French doors.

Derek poked at the large skillet. His wine glass was empty, and the sauce was bubbling a bit too high. "I think it's going to burn. Just as well you got here in time."

Christie lowered the heat and the sauce settled to a gentle simmer. She stirred it once and turned it off.

"No, it's fine honey. Just needed to keep it a bit lower."

"Well, you're the cook, not me. I need to refill my glass. I'll get you a drink."

As he passed Christie, he kissed her cheek. "Very pretty."

"Thank you. I'd like a glass of white?"

Christie took a teaspoon and tasted the sauce. It was rich and delicious, made from her own recipe with over-ripe tomatoes, fresh basil, garlic, and a tiny touch of chilli. She had taken a homemade loaf of bread from the oven before changing and still warm, it mingled with the herbs to fill the kitchen with beautiful aromas.

Derek wandered back with two glasses of red wine and put one on the side of the stove before heading back to the dining table.

"Um, white?" Christie called after him.

"Red's better for you."

Christie rolled her eyes at his back and immediately put a hand over her mouth. She did do that! It was as though she was back in Martin's house and could almost hear him telling her how disrespectful she was being.

Off to the naughty corner!

She giggled, but that lightheaded sensation returned, and she drank a mouthful of wine. The doorbell rang, and she silently scolded herself for allowing ridiculous thoughts in.

Derek opened the front door with a flourish. "Gentlemen! Welcome to an Italian night in Docklands."

He shook hands with Ashley and Ray as Christie came out of the kitchen.

"Bella!" Ashley embraced Christie in a bear hug that left her breathless. He kissed her on both cheeks, and she laughed. Ashley was younger than Ray, well-groomed with short-cropped platinum blonde hair, a perpetual tan and a contagious laugh.

Ray inserted himself between Ashley and Christie and did over the top air kisses on either side of her face. "No Bella about it! It's more ragazza più bella del mondo! Green suits you, darling."

"Show off," Ashley commented as Ray disappeared into the kitchen.

"Now, Derek will get you a drink, and I'm going to get Ray out of my sauce!"

In the kitchen, Ray tasted the sauce with a tablespoon he had taken from the drawer, his eyes closed as he savoured the big mouthful. Christie took the spoon away from him, and he opened his eyes in mock outrage.

"We should go into business. I know someone who bottles stuff, and you don't want to be running all over the world for the rest of your life!" He thought about it for a moment. "Scrap that, you get the best of both worlds already."

"Go get a drink." Christie grinned.

"Well I will, but first, tell me about Lizard Island. It's always been on my radar. What's wrong?"

With a frown, Christie opened the fridge. "Um, I didn't go. There was a last minute change of plans, and I had to attend my Gran's funeral."

"Oh, darling, that's awful. About your Nanna."

"Thanks. We weren't close, but going there was the right thing to do."

"Well of course it was. But, you both went away afterwards?"

Christie closed the fridge, keeping an eye out for Derek.

"Derek went alone. He didn't know Gran, and I found out literally as we were leaving. No time to talk it through. I'd planned on meeting him there the next day."

"Oh-kay."

"Um, Gran left me a cottage and a painting and stuff. It was a big week."

Ray opened his mouth to speak then closed it again. Instead, he gave her a hug. "You worry about dinner, and I'll go entertain."

He disappeared out of the kitchen, and Christie sighed. People would ask. She opened the fridge again and removed two platters of antipasto. These could go out as soon as the other guests arrived and later, it would only take a few minutes to cook her pasta and reheat the sauce for mains.

The doorbell rang, and Christie took a sip of wine, nervous about meeting these people, unsure of what they might know of the problems she and Derek had experienced over the past few days. However, they were guests, so she forced a smile and went out to meet them.

The couple coming in through the door were nothing like Christie expected. Leon was around sixty, a tall, bald, overweight man with a small grey beard. He wore a jacket just a little bit too tight and had gold rings on four fingers.

Ingrid was tiny by comparison. About five feet tall, her short gold dress showed off a curvy body and gorgeous legs accentuated by gold stilettos. Her hair was short, and the same platinum blonde Ashley sported. Christie guessed she was about thirty.

"Ah, there she is...Chris come and meet our other guests." Derek held his hand out for Christie's and took it in his for a moment when she was close enough.

"These are my friends, Ingrid and Leon. And this is Chris," he announced.

Christie slipped her hand from his and held it out to Ingrid. "Welcome to our home, Ingrid."

Ingrid's handshake was like jelly. Her hand was cold, and her smile did not reach her eyes. Leon took Christie's hand and shook it firmly, before pulling her close for a kiss on the lips.

"What would you like to drink?" Derek addressed Ingrid.

"Do you have sweet white wine?" Her voice was Australian, soft and educated. "Leon will have a beer or red wine. Whatever you're drinking."

Leon caught Christie's eye and winked. She smiled back, liking him immediately and surprised at how different the couple were from each other. Oh well, each to their own.

For a few moments, the three couples mingled, punctuated by Ashley's laugh and a smattering of German between Ray and Leon. Christie brought out the platters.

The table was inviting with white linen, crystal, and silver cutlery. Purple and white camellias floated in bowls, and two purple candles gave an intimate and soft atmosphere.

"Christie, my love, you can decorate my table anytime." Ray admired.

Seated opposite Ray, her fingers playing with the stem of her wine glass, Ingrid smiled faintly. "Yes, you have talent. But you do makeup, don't you?"

Ray answered for Christie. "If by "do makeup" you mean be one of the film industry's most talented specialists, then yes. You should see some of her work. Oh and not just on humans—there was an alien once I thought had to be real. So lifelike!"

"It wasn't an alien, silly. Just a politician." Ashley interjected.

"Alien. Politician. Who can tell the difference?" Ray lifted both hands up in a confused gesture, and everyone laughed.

THE PARTY

*T*he conversation moved from aliens to corporate law, selling luxury cars—Leon owned a European distributorship—to land development. After mains, Ingrid steered the conversation to her own work in London, and she and Derek swapped a few stories about their achievements. Christie used the opportunity to finish two cheeseboards.

She placed them on the table, happy with the mix of Victorian hard and soft cheeses, locally made crackers and sticks, and beautiful quince paste from the Barossa Valley. Complementing these were grapes, sliced figs and Victorian olives. She poured six glasses of fortified wine from the Rutherglen wine region in the north of the state.

Ashley lifted his glass and tipped it toward Christie. "To a gracious hostess and a beautiful menu."

The others all raised their own glasses and said cheers. As people began selecting from the cheeseboard, Ashley leaned back in his seat, his face curious.

"So Christie, I believe you inherited a cottage! Do tell us all about it."

"What do you want to know?"

"Everything! Where, what it is like. Value ha-ha!"

"Well, it's a little old cottage in a tiny town called Rivers End. It was built over a hundred years ago for the stationmasters to live in when the town was booming with timber production. Um, the cottage has been uninhabited for some years so is pretty rundown, but it has an orchard and a vegetable garden still growing heritage plants."

"And you've been staying there this past week, I understand?" Ingrid said.

"I have. Gran left me a box full of mysteries. A painting, wedding rings, old love letters. She wanted me to find some hidden family secret, and those are a few of the pieces of the puzzle."

Leon's face lit up. "Ah, a secret! Have you worked out who did what to who? Or whom?"

"Bits. But it will take more time and research to see what I can find."

"And what of this cottage? Are you keeping it?" Leon asked.

"Of course not." Derek dismissed the concept. "It'll cost more in rates and repairs than it's probably worth. Best thing is to get what you can and move on."

"Maybe. Although the local area is a hot spot for developers. New estates popping up and I even had a visit by one of the agents who liked the land attached to the cottage."

"What land?" Derek leaned toward Christie, expression intent. She went to get her phone.

"I'll show you. Here, from this pic onwards."

Derek shared the images with Ingrid.

"Me next," Ashley said. "You mentioned rings? And letters...what's the story there?"

"Well, I found out I have a great-aunt Martha. Nobody seems to know where she is, but it's been years since she was home in Rivers End. She was engaged to a local boy named Thomas Blake, and just before their wedding, something happened that not only drove Martha away but also destroyed the relationship. Love letters that he sent to her were intercepted by a third party. Or at least, that's what I've found out."

"Oh my, a real love story! In addition, a painting? Where's that now?" Ray was as interested as Ashley and Leon.

"Um, I left it with someone. It needed some repairs and a frame."

"So it's in safe hands. Thanks." Ashley took the phone from Ingrid.

"Yes. Safe hands."

A STRANGE PHONE CALL

The dinner party wound up near midnight, after coffee out on the balcony. The air was still thick with humidity, and before long Ray and Ashley made their farewells. Leon and Ingrid followed soon after.

Leon gave Christie a big hug and wished her the best with her cottage and the mystery. Ingrid shook hands again, her fingers still limp and cold. She gave Derek a kiss on the cheek and whispered something that made him laugh. Christie kept smiling until the door closed and then she sat on the sofa with a sigh.

"Another drink?" Derek poured himself a glass of red. He was a bit tipsy. Christie shook her head, but he poured her one and sat beside her.

"That was fun. We should invite them over more often."

"Ray and Ashley?"

"Ingrid and Leo."

"Leon. Might be a bit hard if they live in England." Christie took the glass and sipped it with a smile.

"Didn't I mention? Ingrid is going to work here in Melbourne for a while. Leon probably will stay at home though."

Christie decided she had enough of Ingrid tonight and got back to her feet. "I might pack the dishwasher."

"I'll go sit on the balcony for a bit."

Christie dropped a kiss on Derek's cheek and wandered into the kitchen. She peered around the corner to make sure he had gone outside and took her sandals off. The tiles were cool under her bare feet.

After cleaning up, she went in search of Derek, carrying a small plate of leftover cheese and fruit. As she approached the balcony, she realised he was on his phone, back turned to her. She stopped, not wanting to interrupt, but it was impossible not to hear him.

"I agree. It's worth looking into and if so..." he listened for a moment, nodding. "Let me try first, that's the easier way of handling it." He laughed at something the other person said. "Trust you to think of that, but yes, it might be that important. The opportunity we wanted."

He hung up the call and stretched his legs out. Christie tiptoed back to get her sandals, making sure Derek heard her walk out onto the balcony.

"More cheese?"

"I'm pretty tired baby, so might call it a night."

"Who was on the phone so late?"

"Phone? Oh, Ingrid and Leo wanted to say thanks and let you know what a delightful meal you cooked."

"Leon. That was sweet of them to call."

Derek took Christie's hand and unexpectedly kissed it.

"I'll lock up. You head off." Christie picked up the plate and Derek got to his feet a bit unsteadily.

Something was going on between Derek and Ingrid. It probably was only business, but that cryptic phone call made her wonder if there was more to it.

A lightning flash lit up the water below, followed by a loud crack of thunder that made Christie jump. The air smelt of incoming rain and it reminded her of the night she walked home, so distressed, from Martin's house.

She wanted things to work out with Derek. She was sure she did, in spite of his increasingly poor communication and strange friends. So why was she thinking about that night? Why did Martin keep intruding on her thoughts and clouding her feelings?

The rain arrived in a torrent, cooling the evening air. Christie watched it for a while, curled up in a chair, her mind in Rivers End.

WOOING HER AGAIN

$\mathcal{F}$or a few days, Derek spent close to every waking moment with Christie. He was like the man she had first met, attentive, caring, and respectful. They went to the movies and wandered along the river under moonlight. Derek brought her flowers and paid her compliments.

Until Derek, she'd been so lonely. Angus was her rock at home, but he was Gran's employee and not there to entertain Christie. So Gran often said. When she left home she made friends, but her job took her away so much it was hard to stay close. She liked her own company, but longed for more. For love. And one day he was there.

She started to enjoy his company again instead of being on guard. He mentioned setting a wedding date in passing, suggesting they make time for a honeymoon in the Greek Islands. It had Christie thinking about life as his wife. Her career would continue for now, but one day they would want children. Before that happened, she would change direction—opening her own beauty salon or pursuing her interest in remedial make-up. Whichever it was, her family would come first.

Exactly a week from the day Christie got home from Rivers End, Derek cooked dinner for them both. It was such a rare event Christie could not help but hover around the kitchen, much to his amusement.

"You don't trust me in here!"

"No. I just thought I could help." she lied, giggling at his disbelieving expression.

"Alright, seeing as you've told me how fantastic it is, get a bottle of that Chardonnay out and pour us both a glass. That should keep you busy."

"Oh, goodie!"

Christie opened a bottle and poured two glasses.

Derek held his glass up to inspect the clear gold liquid. "A toast," he said, "to life working out the way it should."

He offered his glass to Christie to clink hers against, and she did, murmuring "Cheers".

His words had been uncannily like Martin's counter-toast on his deck overlooking the ocean. She could almost smell the jasmine and sea air and had to turn away. Her heart rate had gone up a bit, and she took a long sip of the lovely wine.

Derek made a big deal about setting the table and sitting Christie with a refilled glass before placing her plate in front of her.

"It smells wonderful!" Christie saw his smile widen and reached across to squeeze his hand. He turned his hand over and held hers, playing with the engagement ring.

"Time to think about adding a wedding ring, don't you agree?"

She nodded, wondering if now was the time to mention her ideas about changing direction with her career.

"Wine's alright," he commented, piling salad on Christie's plate. "Where did you say you got it?"

"Thanks, that's plenty! Oh, there's a little wine shop in Rivers End, part of a pub. This comes from a family winery a bit further west."

"One thing about small towns is there's always a pub. Or four."

"True." Christie sliced into the pie.

"And what else is there? How big is this place?"

"Not big. A couple of streets of shops. You know the sort of thing, real estate agents, hairdresser, small supermarket, a couple of clothing shops. The most divine bakery." Christie smiled to herself, thinking about Belinda.

"So not much at all. Not your thing I imagine, no real substance to the town."

"I quite like it there."

"But it won't suit you for any length of time. I mean, no spas or boutiques or a decent hairdresser. After all, at heart, you're a city girl." Derek speared some tomato and feta.

"So I've been told," Christie commented.

"Who told you that?"

Christie filled her mouth with pie and shrugged. Derek let it go, more interested in the wine bottle.

He read the label. "What else do they make?"

"We should google it. I told you it was lovely."

"Let's take a drive tomorrow." Derek topped up the glasses.

"What? Where?"

"Well, to the winery, silly. And you can show me that cottage on the way back."

Christie could not believe her ears. All she wanted when she was there was for him to show any kind of interest in her inheritance. Instead, he had made her feel awful about staying there and had shown no interest. Until now. She picked up her glass but only played with the stem as he continued.

"We can leave after breakfast and find somewhere for lunch. Maybe this winery does lunches. Or that bakery you mentioned."

All of a sudden, the idea of Derek in Rivers End was disturbing. Christie did not want him meeting Belinda. He could be such a snob about people in service jobs he would likely dismiss her as just a shop assistant. He would hate the condition the cottage was in and miss its charm and heritage.

What if we run into Martin?

She kept her tone neutral. "I'd rather not. Not until after London, if that's okay?"

"I'd like to see this place. Why wait?" Derek pressed her, his eyes cold.

"There's a lot I need to do before London. It's less than a week away. Why don't we plan to have a weekend there once I'm back?"

"It's one day, Chris. Then I'll be back in the office, and I can't count on having a spare weekend when it suits you." He pushed his plate away.

There it was. The side of Derek he showed when she attended Gran's funeral. The familiar cold stone dropped into her stomach as she gazed into her wine glass. The silence dragged on.

Hold your ground.

Christie dug deep for words.

"This week has been wonderful, Derek. It means a lot to me that you've taken time off to spend together, it does. I'd rather stay in Melbourne though. I'll be back before Christmas, and we always talked about staying by the sea around that time, so why not stay in the cottage this year? We can choose a wedding date then if you like. Please, honey?"

Derek finished his glass of wine. "So, you're saying no to me?"

"Well, you did suggest I should on occasion."

"Yes, I did. All right, let's do what you want. See how that pans out."

As if nothing happened, he pulled his plate back and continued eating, leaving Christie confused and unsure. Something was terribly wrong.

The following morning, Christie woke up uncharacteristically late to an empty apartment. Near the coffee machine, she found a note from Derek. He was going to the office for a few hours and would take her out tonight to Crown Casino for dinner.

She sighed, knowing dinner at Crown meant several hours afterwards in one of the Casino rooms playing any number of the games he enjoyed.

Give and take.

He'd backed down over going to see the cottage so she would go with him tonight.

Over breakfast, Christie planned her morning. First, she wanted to check her emails to see if her final arrangements for London were here. She would see if Angus was free for coffee. It was time to find out how he was and whether he could help her decipher Gran's note.

THE FORBIDDEN ROOM

A tight band squeezed Christie's chest as she drove through the wrought iron gates to Gran's home. Not her home, for despite many years living there she'd never once been truly welcome.

Except by Angus.

It was Angus who'd driven her here from the airport as a small girl. She'd had one little suitcase and the clothes on her back. The formal, perfectly kept outside of the huge house had scared her. But not as much as the woman inside.

She parked in front of the house, all the old feelings vanishing when Angus threw the door open and held his arms wide.

"Oh, let me look at you!" he laughed, and she stepped back from his bear hug.

"What, in jeans and T-shirt? No heels or designer stuff." She did a small twirl. "Don't tell Derek."

"Why would your young man object? Although, if I might say, you are a little on the thin side."

"That's what Derek said too. And I don't know why. I ate so much gorgeous produce in Rivers End!" She put her arm through his. "There's so much to tell you. But first, how are you doing?"

"I'm well, just tired. But, nearly everything is done now."

He paused at the doorway to let her go in first. She took a step inside and stopped. The furnishings had gone, and paintings no longer graced the walls. The floor was bare boards instead of the expensive Persian rugs with their intriguing patterns Christie had been afraid to drop anything on.

"So, the contents are sold? Then the house will be?"

"Not quite. There'll be a couple of boxes of photographs and trinkets you should have, but Miss Dorothy wanted the antiques, the quality furnishings and artwork to be sold by an auction house with the proceeds to go to charity."

"That's wonderful. I always wondered...I mean, she never said anything..."

"Your Gran could be gruff and fiercely private, but deep down she had a warm heart that led her to deep generosity. Secretly, of course. She supported two worthy causes for a long time. Surf Lifesavers and the Royal Flying Doctors."

Christie's hand flew to her mouth as her eyes filled with a sudden rush of tears.

1993.

Just seven years old, Christie baked under the heat of a late morning sun as she squinted up at a single winged plane overhead. It circled once and now prepared to land over at the airfield, only a couple of hundred metres from their house. In minutes, the ambulance would meet it and transport some sick or injured person from the plane to the small clinic where Dad would care for them. Mum might be there too, to help any family that travelled with the patient.

Christie had been on the plane a few times with Dad, not to fly but to sit in one of the few seats in the small plane as he replaced emergency supplies and talked to the pilot, who was also a doctor. The smell of disinfectant and diesel mingled together.

Other times Dad and Mum would fill the old Jeep with supplies to drop off to even more remote settlements, do health checks and attend to minor ailments. Before leaving, Dad would squeeze her so tightly in a hug that she would squeal and wiggle as he reminded her to behave for Trishi while she stayed there. Mum would wave until they rounded the furthest corner. It might be a few hours or a few days, but they always came home with stories and little gifts sent by the communities they serviced.

Except one day, they did not come home. Everyone tried to pretend it was just taking a bit longer than usual, but as the hours dragged on, Christie knew something terrible and beyond her understanding had happened to her Mum and Dad. It had. Trishi said to take comfort knowing they were doing what they loved and they had not suffered. All Christie knew was they left her all alone.

"Miss Christie?"

Christie snapped back to the present to find her face wet with tears. Angus held out a perfectly folded white handkerchief.

"I wish I'd known. I mean, everything Gran had must be worth enough to make a difference. To save a life?"

"It will make a difference. Come on; let's not dwell on all of that. The kettle just boiled so what about a cuppa and catch up?"

On a bench under an old elm, Christie updated Angus on the events following the funeral. At least, an edited version. There was no reason for Angus to know how cruel Derek had been.

She smiled though as she described her discovery of the orchard and vegetable garden, of the growing love she had for the cottage. She told Angus about the painting.

"So you think this Thomas Blake was the artist?" he asked.

Christie nodded, playing with her empty coffee cup.

"And you've left it in Rivers End, with the man you believe is his grandson?"

"Yes, and I'm not certain it was the right thing to do. I mean, what if he refuses to return it. He wants to show it to someone, so perhaps it will disappear."

"Yet you left it there."

"Yes. Well, he seems to think there is some reason why the Ryans aren't welcome in Rivers End, and that includes me. Funny how his dog loves me though." Christie missed Randall. That gentle, friendly dog had wiggled into her heart.

"Your great-grandparents' grandparents virtually founded Rivers End. Who knows, maybe the Blake family settled around that time as well, but it seems to me something a lot more is in play than who is welcome or not. It sounds like bad blood."

"That's what I think. And those letters, oh Angus, the love Thomas had for Martha! Saving her from drowning in the middle of a storm and waiting months for her to come home but she didn't. Not ever, I think, although…"

"Although what?"

"I'm being silly. It's just I thought maybe Martha had come home. Just after Gran's funeral, I found a pendant on Thomas Blake's head-stone that was T and M with a love heart. And there was an inscrip-tion in the limestone cliff almost the same. But I've searched everywhere I can think of. There was a newspaper report of an elderly lady found on the jetty—I even went to the hospital, but they'd only say she was released and wouldn't tell me her name."

"Did you read the note Miss Dorothy left?"

"Oh! Yes, and I need your help because some of the writing is quite hard to decipher. Something about a box. I think."

Christie found the note in her handbag and passed it to Angus. He read aloud. "Dearest Christabel, my last request is you find my sister and give her the diary. In the box. It is… in…" he hesitated, caught on the same words as Christie had been. "Maybe inside? Yes, it is inside the dwelling? Not dwelling, but a d to start. And that is a double s. Inside the dress? Oh! Inside the dresser! Yes, come on, I know what she means."

Face animated, Angus almost leapt to his feet.

At the doorway of the attic, Christie baulked. Angus had unlocked the door and gone straight in, but Christie's feet would not follow. It was a forbidden room, and the consequences of being caught in there by Gran were etched in her memory. Gran might be gone, but the little girl in Christie remembered the anger on Gran's face and the fury in her voice as she dragged her by the arm out of the attic and downstairs to her bedroom.

"It's quite safe now. She was protective of her past. Come in." Angus held a hand out to Christie, and with a gulp, she stepped inside.

Not much remained of the mix of old furniture and knick-knacks that intrigued Christie so long ago. Just a few packing boxes and an ornate dressing table. It was white with gold handles, gold coloured inserts and its mirror was a perfect oval in a gold frame.

"This belonged to your Gran when she was a child and is the only piece of furniture I was instructed to keep. To be honest, I'd begun to wonder what to do with it, but perhaps we shall find out?"

Angus opened the single drawer and there, inside, was a box. About the size of a book, it was made of timber and etched into the lid was a tulip. Painted white.

Christie and Angus turned to stare at each other in silent recognition of the white tulips at the funeral. Unsure of herself, Christie hesitated to pick up the box, so Angus did, placing it onto the dresser. A tiny padlock kept it secure.

"Oh, it needs a key," Christie said.

"You have it. On the keyring from the cottage." Angus prompted.

Christie found the keyring in her bag and slid the smallest key into the padlock. It turned and released the lock.

Inside was a small diary with "1968" on its leather cover. Underneath were two envelopes. The top one was in that familiar hand Christie recognised as Thomas Blake's, and her heart skipped a beat. Her instincts had been right!

The second envelope was addressed to Thomas at the cottage. With trembling hands, Christie turned it over. From Miss M Ryan. It was a letter from Martha.

MARTHA'S LETTER

*B*ack at the apartment, Christie fought her compulsion to
read Martha's letter. Gran had explicitly requested
Christie to get the diary to Martha. If she read those two letters and
found Martha, how would she explain herself?

Sitting cross-legged on the bed, the tulip box open and the diary to
one side, she stared at Thomas' letter. Addressed to "Martha", with no
return address or postmark, this must be the one Thomas sent with
the friend. She started to open the letter but realised its seal was
unbroken.

Had Martha refused to read it? Or, had Gran somehow got it first
and kept it from her for some unknown reason? Perhaps the friend
had not given it to her. So many questions filled Christie's mind, and
she had no stomach to find out. She put the envelope down, shattered
that all of Thomas' attempts to bring his girl home had failed.

So, what was Martha's part in all of this? Christie picked up her
envelope to find the postmark, but there was none. Just a stamp. Its
seal was also unbroken. Another unread letter but this one had not
even been posted.

Christie opened Martha's letter before she had time to stop
herself. With shaking hands, she slipped out a single piece of paper.

Dear Thomas,

You promised you would wait! You forced me to promise to return! And I would have, once I had a chance to calm down and be able to speak with you rationally. Yet, there was not one word from you, nothing.

Just a phone call or a letter would have done. Anything at all to reassure me you still wanted me to keep my side of the promise. That you still love me and meant what you said that night. Instead, there was only silence. Now I know why.

She told me all about it. Gloated in fact. By the time you read this letter, you will be just days away from getting married to someone else.

I want you to be happy, I do. But Tom, it should be our wedding. It should have been us together, forever. My heart is broken. Truly broken. I shall love you until I die.

Martha

Christie read it twice, then a third time. How could Thomas Blake have married someone else so soon? Who had gloated—Gran or the friend who had been the go-between? Had Martha ever known Thomas waited for her or understood the depth of his love and determination to have a life with her? Who interfered?

Poor Martha. Waiting and hoping for a sign Thomas still wanted her to come home. After whatever happened between them that night, Martha needed something more to believe in than a promise he possibly may have regretted in the light of day.

Why was love so complicated? Christie's mind wandered as she returned the letter to its envelope. Thomas and Martha loved each other deeply, passionately, in a way Christie thought possible only between the covers of a romance novel.

The little snippets she remembered of her parents were of a couple who held hands and laughed a lot, but their love died when they did.

Gran married four times. Rebecca's father died young, and Gran divorced her last husband not long before Christie came to live with her. There were no more husbands after that, and the only time Gran ever referred to her marriages was in a tone of contempt for the men involved. No true love there, if any love at all.

Christie always believed she would fall in love with someone who loved her just as much. She had thought Derek was that man.

This past week, Derek had tried so hard to make up for his unkindness, but now Christie knew he was capable of being quite cruel. The pain of his selfishness and lack of empathy were a stark contrast to the sense of peace and belonging found in her cottage.

Rivers End was always in the back of her mind these days. The smell of the garden when it rained, the warm crunch of sand under her feet on the beach. Randall's soft eyes and the sheer glory of the sunset the night she stood, barefoot, on Martin's deck, dressed in his T-shirt and sipping the local wine as she inhaled the heady scent of jasmine and sea spray.

Those moments were magic. Etched in her memory. Martin had said to her the evening was not real and she was with the wrong man. Strangely, that made things even more chaotic. It occurred to her she may be living with the wrong man.

SOLE SURVIVOR

*P*erched on a stool, Derek impatiently checked his watch as Christie spotted him in the Atrium Bar. As she crossed the floor to meet him, Christie glanced in a wall mirror, happy with how she looked. Hair braided to one side, she wore a short, body-hugging silk dress in ruby red. Derek saw her and stood up to kiss her cheek.

"Fashionably late?"

Christie calmly smiled.

Without asking, Derek ordered two glasses of Champagne. "Sexy dress. Appropriate, as always."

"Um, thanks." Christie assumed it was a compliment. "So, what's the occasion?"

"Do we need one? Seeing as you didn't want to leave Melbourne before you head off to London, I thought this would be a fun way to spend an evening instead."

The Champagne arrived, and Derek handed one glass to Christie before picking his up and offering a toast. "To us."

Christie clinked her glass against his. "To us."

"I made reservations for Rosetta."

"Oh, yum. Perfect choice, honey." Christie put her hand on

Derek's, and he squeezed her fingers before letting go to pick up his glass again.

"There's a bit to talk about. Something happened today which I think you'll find interesting. Well, you will because it affects you."

That got Christie's attention.

"So, I told you Ingrid is opening an office here in Melbourne?"

Best news all year. Not.

Christie nodded.

"Well, we're considering a merger."

"Wow. That's a big move. I thought you preferred full control?"

"I do. But this way, I can grow the business faster, and Ingrid will buy me out when I want to retire. Until then, I'll still be the boss, but she brings experience in carving out new regions, not just estates. It'll open up ventures beyond anything I've done before."

"New regions?"

"There's so much need for housing." he laughed. "Got a call from some developer about Rivers End. He's already put one estate in and wants more."

Christie's heart sank. "Bryce, by any chance?"

"That's him. Told him it is yours, not mine, and if you said no, it is no."

"You said that?"

"Sure did."

Christie leaned across to kiss Derek. "Thank you, honey. You've no idea how that makes me feel."

"Nah, don't worry about dealing with his type. I want to see your cottage. I really do, baby. The way you talked about it at dinner the other night made me realise how much it means to you."

"I'll be back before Christmas."

After emptying his glass, Derek glanced at his watch again. "Need to get going."

～

Dinner was delightful. Rosetta was a sophisticated Italian restaurant owned by iconic chef Neil Perry. With an enchanting smile, Christie absorbed the stunning city views, white scalloped curtains, marble flooring and hand-blown chandeliers.

She and Derek had eaten at Rosetta a few times in the past, and tonight she had her favourite main, the pan-fried snapper, accompanied by a glass of Italian red wine and followed by refreshing lemon gelati.

Derek directed the conversation to the time they met and their early days together, reminding Christie how much he loved her. There were no more mentions of his planned merger again, nor Rivers End. Christie believed at last he understood. The way he resisted what must have been an enticing approach by Bryce was impressive and gave Christie hope for their future again.

Hand in hand, they left Rosetta and wandered through the complex. Instead of heading to the VIP gaming room that Derek frequented, he led her through the Palladium and to the River Room, one of many function areas of Crown. Outside the door was a banner advising an art exhibition "Coastal Splendour".

"Shall we go in?" Derek said.

"Sure. But I thought you didn't like art galleries?"

"Not really. Just want to find something to put in the foyer at work. To mark the merger. New beginnings and all that."

Christie loved art but could not remember ever seeing any with Derek. He said once that apart from the masters, artists were only a step up from beggars. She pushed that memory aside as she drank in the beautiful offerings on display. Most were traditional oils depicting Victorian coastal scenes, with a few watercolours and charcoal sketches.

"What about this one?" She paused in front of a sunset over St Kilda Beach, the long pier silhouetted against a red sky.

"Sunsets are so yesterday, don't you think?" A female voice behind them interrupted, and Christie closed her eyes for a moment in recognition.

"What a pleasant surprise!" Derek spun around to Ingrid. Christie opened her eyes and forced a smile.

"Hello, Ingrid," Christie said. If Derek wanted to meet up with Ingrid, why not say so?

"How...pleasant to see you again." Ingrid turned to Derek. "I saw a rather intriguing piece that might fit the bill. Perhaps a little large though."

"Well, let's go and see. Are you coming?" Derek included Christie almost as an afterthought. Ingrid hooked her arm through his. Her long silver dress was split right up to her left thigh and wearing high stilettos, she exuded a confidence Christie found quite intimidating.

"Oh, that's okay. I'll browse."

Almost before she finished the sentence, they hurried off together. A waiter with a tray of drinks paused near Christie, and she gratefully accepted a glass of white wine with shaking hands.

She wandered along a row of abstract artwork, her stomach churning. Was this what their future would be? Ingrid appearing without notice and taking Derek's attention? If so, what hope did they have of moving forward to a marriage?

One painting caught Christie's eye, and she stopped directly in front of it. Incredible use of colour turned a simple beach scene into a fantasy world. The sky was emerald and the sea its darker reflection, but with streaks of red and the hulking remnants of a misshapen shipwreck near land. A silver sun melted like a puddle into the horizon. A misshaped man dragged an anchor twice his size to an amethyst shore.

It was a fascinating, multifaceted painting with the initials MB in one corner. Below the painting was a brief on the artist.

SOLE SURVIVOR

Martin Blake is a reclusive artist living on the Victorian west coast. Specialising in abstract visions of the sea and creations using locally sourced sustainable timber, he rarely offers pieces for public sale. He recently spent over a month travelling to regional and remote Victorian youth centres teaching basic art and woodwork skills to disadvantaged teens at risk. Sole Survivor represents the human ability to rise above tragedy.

Christie did not realise she was reading aloud until noticing the couple at the next painting cast her odd glances. This confirmed Martin was indeed one of the Blake family and he was an accomplished and even exceptional artist. What she kept rereading was the information about his other work. Helping troubled youth.

Her mind went back to the first time she had seen him. At Gran's funeral, in the drizzly misty rain, he stood watching her. There had been an underlying emotion about him she thought was anger, and when she said that to Daphne, the response had been, "I imagine he is, dear. Today of all days."

Christie had taken that to mean he had an issue with Gran and her family, and time had proven that. Daphne also said he was "back", so perhaps he had returned from his month away and had come to the graveyard expecting to work uninterrupted on tidying Thomas' grave. Finding a funeral party in attendance may have caused the reaction. After all, if he had just returned, how would he know it was Gran's?

She sighed. This artist, this man—Martin Blake—was as complex and compelling as the painting in front of her. Now another layer revealed itself, showing compassion and care that rarely made it to his eyes.

"Do you like this?" Derek was right beside Christie, and she jumped. He stared at the painting as if it was graffiti on the side of a building. Ingrid still had her arm through his and her eyes on Christie, as if waiting for a reaction.

"Yes, I do."

"Too...weird. But the colours are pretty." Derek was bored.

"It's so typical of abstract art which I think is merely the work of a disorganised mind." Ingrid declared, and Derek nodded in agreement.

"Well, clearly neither of you have met the artist if you think that!" It came out more forcefully than Christie intended, but as Derek and Ingrid turned as one in surprise, she did not care how she sounded.

"And you have? Met the artist?" Derek's voice had a hard edge.

"I have. And he has one of the most logical, intelligent minds I've encountered. The word disorganised is the opposite of this artist."

Christie finished her glass of wine as Derek stared at her. She gazed back at the painting, not sure what to do now. Over the music and talk in the room, she heard Derek speak to Ingrid, who stalked away. Derek put an arm around Christie's waist as if contemplating the artwork, but his embrace was too tight for comfort.

"Why don't you have an early night? I know you don't gamble so there's no point hanging around for a few hours to keep me company."

It was on the tip of Christie's tongue to ask if Ingrid would keep him company instead but she controlled herself. It was clear Ingrid would spend the evening with Derek and that the two women were not about to become friends.

"That way you can do the rest of your preparations for London." Derek continued. "You have your e-ticket now?"

"No. In fact, I still have no confirmation of this job. It is strange as everything was on track."

"Odd. Maybe you should chase it up." He glanced at his watch. "It's lunchtime in London. Go home and sort it out."

"You're not coming with me?"

"Clearly you're not yourself tonight. I'm going to go buy a painting and spend some time at the poker table. Give me a call once you know about London if you want."

You're dismissing me!

As if she was an employee, not the woman he wanted to marry. She didn't move when he kissed her cheek before heading off after Ingrid.

A LINE CROSSED

*A*s if in a dream, Christie got herself home. She was numb
inside. Even the Uber driver asked if she was okay and she
had only been able to nod.

Leaving the apartment in darkness, she kicked off her shoes near
the front door and went straight to the kitchen to make coffee.
Nursing the hot cup in both hands, she stared out of the window at
the city lights in the direction of Crown Casino.

Somewhere in there, her fiancé was enjoying the company of
another woman. If she had gone to Lizard Island, would this have
happened? Would his re-acquaintance with Ingrid have blossomed
into this merger, not to mention the relationship that apparently was
more interesting than the one he had with Christie? Or was it
inevitable?

She turned on her computer and opened her emails. Before going
out for the evening, Christie had emailed the director's personal
assistant to let her know no itinerary, e-ticket or schedule had arrived.
This was the first time working for this particular company, but they
had come well recommended and by referral.

With a soft beep, a reply email arrived. Christie read it without understanding. It was short, stating that—as requested—the contract had been cancelled.

Christie dialled the phone number at the bottom of the email, wondering how such a mistake could happen. She had signed the contract some months ago, and although the only contact since then had been via email, all had seemed normal. The other end answered.

"Mr Kennedy's office, Janet Green speaking."

"Hello, Janet. It's Christie Ryan here. How are you?"

There was a silence, before, "Ms Ryan. I'm surprised to hear from you."

"Janet, there seems to be some misunderstanding about my contract. I've not requested it be cancelled."

"No, another lady did. On your behalf. She explained you were quite ill, too ill to speak to me yourself."

"I'm not ill." Christie was stunned.

"Well, I'm pleased you've recovered so fast, but it did leave us in a difficult position. Changing your availability so close to the beginning of a commercial shoot. I had everything ready to send you, and we've had to find a replacement at short notice." Janet's words were clipped.

"What I'm saying is I've not been ill at all! Nobody was authorised to speak on my behalf, and you should have confirmed the situation with me. Who phoned you?"

"I have no idea. Don't blame me, I have enough to do without worrying about chasing up people who can't decide if they want to work or not. I do have to work." Janet hung up.

Christie jumped to her feet in agitation. What had gone on? Who would do such a thing as pretend to represent another person? Why would anyone want her to lose this contract?

She paced around the lounge room. This evening started well but was turning into one of the worst nights of her life. Derek's support about Bryce warmed her heart. Then, in an instant, he turned the tables and left her to find her own way home.

He was so hot and cold she struggled to keep up. Did he want to marry her or not? Where did Ingrid fit into all of this? Janet Green told Christie another woman phoned and cancelled the contract. Was it Ingrid? Surely, having Christie on the other side of the world was more advantageous if she wanted Derek herself.

Or, was it more about what Christie owned? Christie stopped pacing and gazed at the balcony, remembering the overheard phone conversation between Derek and Ingrid after the dinner party.

"I agree. It's worth looking into and if so..." then, *"let me try first, that's the easy way of handling it,"* a laugh and, *"trust you to think of that, but yes, it might be that important. The opportunity we wanted."*

Try what? Derek had begun to press Christie about going to visit the cottage after that dinner party. He mentioned Ingrid's special ability to move into new markets, ones he could not reach. That excited him. He was all about pushing the boundaries and growing his wealth.

Christie picked up her phone and dialled Derek.

"Hi, baby."

"I made it home okay."

"Well, why wouldn't you? You travel all the time on your own so I wouldn't think a couple of kilometres in the same city is a concern."

Martin Blake, who barely knew her, ensured she made it home safely. Her own fiancé did not care.

"I phoned London. There'd been some sort of mix up with my contract."

"So, you're not going?" Derek could not even sound surprised. "Sorry, baby. How about we head to that cottage of yours in the morning. That should cheer you up."

The numbness inside Christie vanished, replaced by slow-burning anger. She took a moment to gather her self-control before replying in a light tone.

"You misunderstood. Of course I am still going! In fact, I'm starting to pack now as my departure day has changed."

The stunned silence on the other end of the phone was enough to force a disappointed smile from Christie. It was true. She was about to start packing. Just not for London.

"I'll head straight home."

"Goodness, no need. You and Ingrid enjoy your evening. I'm quite capable of packing."

"Chris, what's wrong? You sound a bit strange."

"It's Christie. Not that it matters now, but my name is Christie."

She hung up and tossed the phone onto the sofa. Derek's ringtone began, and she stood with her hands clenched, willing it to stop. It did but started again.

Scooping the phone up, she hurled it at the wall.

LIE UPON LIE

*D*erek fumbled at the front door and stumbled over Christie's abandoned shoes. Cursing, he turned on the light and kicked the shoes to one side.

Christie was asleep in bed. The lamp on his side of the bed was on, the way Christie always left it if he was last home. He stood and watched her for a moment, still drawn to her natural beauty.

Such a shame.

Neatly stacked on the floor at the end of the bed were several suitcases. Much more than she usually took on a job. He glanced into her robe. Empty.

In the bathroom, only his things and a small makeup bag remained.

She wouldn't.

He crept out of the bedroom and into the small study down the hall. Christie kept a small selection of novels, some photos, and her business files in here. All were gone. Derek swore. He dropped onto a seat and phoned Ingrid.

~

Christie opened her eyes when she heard Derek swear. Earlier, after picking up the pieces of her shattered phone—keeping the sim card and throwing the rest away—Christie wasted no time in packing. She only wanted her personal items. He could have the kitchen utensils and furnishings she bought when she first moved in.

She slipped out of bed and put her dressing gown on before padding, barefoot, down the hallway. Outside the study she stopped, leaning against the wall while she listened to Derek speak on the phone.

"Yes, everything! I don't know if she's moving to London or back to that damned cottage or somewhere else, but it won't be without a fight."

Without making out what the words were, Christie could hear Ingrid's voice on the other end. An angry voice.

"Calm down. Seriously, calm down and leave it to me. I'll find a way to change her mind."

How are you going to do that?

Every word he said ripped away another layer of trust.

"She'll calm down. Whatever she thinks she knows, I'll persuade her otherwise. By this time tomorrow, everything will be back on track. Just trust me. Okay?"

Ingrid's voice was quieter when she said something that made Derek laugh.

"Of course I will. Our interests come first, and you know that."

Christie stepped into the room and Derek swung around.

"Christie. Sorry, did I wake you?" He hung up on Ingrid without a word.

"What interests, Derek?"

"Huh? Oh, just that our family interests must come before work. I was saying to Ingrid I should have come home with you tonight. You know, making sure you were safe and spent the rest of the evening here."

"Right. That's what you were saying." Christie stared steadily at Derek. He avoided her eyes.

"Sure baby. Particularly if you're about to go to London." There was a question beneath his words.

"If?"

"I mean, earlier than expected. What exactly did London say when you rang?"

Christie smiled. What else could she do? If he believed she was so naïve and stupid that he could deny all knowledge, what was the point?

"Derek, I'm tired, and I'm going back to bed. I suggest you do the same and when you come home tomorrow, the place will be all yours. No mess, no shoes by the front door. Nobody you feel obliged to come home to."

She needed water. In the dark, she padded to the kitchen and filled a glass. Her hands shook with the effort of keeping the anger under tight control.

Derek followed, turning on all the lights and then standing in the middle of the doorway. "We need to talk about this. It feels as though you're leaving me. Like, really leaving me."

"Does it? Well, you're right."

"But why, baby? Maybe I was a bit dismissive earlier, but that didn't mean anything. I had my head somewhere else and didn't think you needed me to hold your hand getting home."

"You told me to come home. Quite dismissively. There's nothing more to say unless you want to explain about my London contract?"

Christie put her now empty glass on the counter and watched Derek closely. He swayed a bit then stepped into the kitchen. "I had nothing to do with that."

"Oh, come on, Derek. How stupid do you think I am?"

Christie pushed past him, pausing in the lounge room, unsure of where to go.

Derek was right behind her. "Hey, I love you."

"You are drunk."

"Sure as hell not enough to let you leave me! We're getting married, so stop the hysterics and calm down."

"I am calm. But we're not getting married. We're not." Christie took off her engagement ring. He ignored her outstretched hand and flopped onto the sofa.

"Here, sit down and let's talk. Come on, give me that much!"

Christie put the engagement ring on the coffee table. Derek dropped his head into his hands.

"I've been such a fool." His words were muffled. "I can't lose you, baby. I can't. Please don't go. I love you so much."

Christie sat next to him. Exhausted.

"I got greedy. You know I want a prosperous life for us. Early retirement and the world at our feet. I want to give you the world." Derek reached for the engagement ring, playing with it in his fingers. "I chose this 'cos it's like you, baby. Beautiful and perfect. Somehow, I let business overshadow that. This whole thing was Ingrid's idea, and I've terminated our planned merger."

"What? You've done that?" A flicker of hope rose in Christie.

He took her hand. "I can't have Ingrid or anyone else telling me how to run my life. Your cottage, your land. Yes, I'd like you to trust me with it because it represents our future, but then again, without you in the picture, what's the point?"

Christie slipped her hand from his. "To be honest, I don't want to be away so much. One day soon, I want to take a step back. Have a family."

"Family? You mean children?" Derek almost recoiled from Christie as he got to his feet.

"And a dog. A house with a garden. Yes, all of that." The flicker of hope went out.

Derek spoke through an expression of revulsion. "Sounds fun, baby. Let's set a date and work toward that."

"You misunderstand." Christie clasped her arms protectively around herself. "That is my future. After everything you have done, who you have shown me you are, well, that future doesn't include you. I'm sorry. I am."

"Everything I've done? Tell me what!"

"You want me to spell it out?" Christie jumped up. "You messed with my career. You and Ingrid. If you want to buy the cottage, why not ask?"

"Okay. Will you sell it?"

"No."

Derek threw his arms up in the air. "See? What you want is more important than our relationship."

"That's almost funny, coming from you."

"I don't understand."

"I know you don't and that's what's sad about all of this."

"If you're leaving, why haven't you gone? Why are you still here?"

"I'll be driving."

"So?"

"I had a few glasses of wine tonight."

"Oh for goodness sake. Why would that stop you?"

Christie remembered the moment when Martin crossed his arms and told her firmly, "You can stay in the guest room, or you can walk, but you're not driving home." He refused to let her be in danger, or be a danger.

"I'll leave my keys on the table. Keep whatever else is here. The apartment is yours so let's call it quits and move on."

In a swift move, Derek was right in her face. "You'll regret this, and it won't be the last you see of me, Chris."

She held her ground, and after a moment, Derek spun around and stalked out of the apartment, slamming the door behind him.

UNBEARABLE LONELINESS

Martha was drowning. The water was crystal-clear, perfectly still, and icy cold as it filled her lungs. Tiny bubbles escaped from her parted lips, and she watched them ascend to a surface only inches above her but impossible to reach.

There was no pain, and that was as strange as the warm sand imprisoning her feet. How could the water be so cold and yet the sand so warm? Streams of sunlight piercing the surface, straight into the seabed like tiny columns of solar heating.

Thomas swam toward her, his hands reaching for hers. She leaned forward, smiling at his handsome face. She wanted to tell him she was okay, but the words would not come out. She stretched her own hands out, and their fingers almost touched.

Almost.

Someone else, their back facing Martha, swam between them. A woman wearing a red dress who put her hand up to stop Thomas. He swam away.

Martha tried to follow him but remembered she was drowning. She reached down to tug helplessly at her feet in the sand, and when she glanced up again, he was gone. The woman was gone. She was alone.

"Martha, wake up dear. Martha!"

An insistent voice intruded, and with a start, Martha awoke. Disoriented, she struggled to sit.

Elizabeth sat on the side of the bed, her arm on Martha's. "You were dreaming, dear." She reached over and turned on a lamp.

Martha took a deep breath, recognising the bedroom in Palmerston House and clearing the nightmare away. "Oh my," she said. "Did I wake you?"

"Not at all. I was reading and heard you call out."

"What did I say?"

"I'm sure it was nothing important. Now, shall I get you some water?"

Elizabeth stood up to go, and Martha put her hand on her arm.

"Please, what did I say?"

"Wait, Thomas. Please wait for me."

Tears flooded Martha's eyes.

Elizabeth sat again. "I know you wished to go home earlier and although I'm sorry staying wasn't your choice, my selfish side is still thankful."

The doctor at the hospital had insisted Martha stay in Rivers End after her check-up. The old ankle injury from Egypt had always been troublesome and only weeks before Dorothy's death Martha underwent corrective surgery. She was partway through rehabilitation when the letter arrived, begging her to come to Rivers End. Now, a small blood clot had her grounded until medication resolved it.

"So, shall I fetch some water or some tea?" Elizabeth said.

"Neither thank you. I'll try to sleep, and hopefully no more dreams!" Martha put her arms around Elizabeth and hugged her. Sleep might evade her, but she was not about to burden anyone else with her silly thoughts.

Once Elizabeth left, Martha lay on her side, the lamp still on. The dream haunted her. The image of the faceless woman nagged at her. She knew enough about dream psychology to understand the woman might represent any one of a number of things. Herself, a manifestation of the loss of Thomas, or simply a memory of the woman who stepped in so quickly to take her place.

She had called out for Thomas. For him to wait for her. Well, in real life he had not waited. Certainly not long enough for them to have found each other again, and now, five decades on, it was only a matter of time before she followed him to his resting place.

Martha was so tired. So sad and so lost without Thomas. Even apart, he had always been there in her heart and in the back of her mind. Now, he was gone, and that left an emptiness nothing in this life was going to fill.

TALK OF THE TOWN

*C*hristie drove with the radio off, taking the twists and turns on the Great Ocean Road a little slower than usual. If she allowed her mind to drift, it hurt too much.

Don't think, just drive.

Before leaving, she'd tapped on Ashley and Ray's door. When there was no answer, she wrote a note with her new contact details. Slipping it under their door, the realisation she was leaving more than Derek behind almost brought her to tears. These two men were friends she wanted to keep in her life.

As she drove through Green Bay, Christie thought about Martha. Just like her great-aunt, she had left her relationship. Gran had not maintained a relationship for any length of time. Were the Ryan women destined to be alone?

∼

Martin tended the grave of Thomas Blake. Close by, Randall lay flat on his side, fast asleep in the sun. When he was finished, Martin sat back on his heels to check his work. It was the third in a row of graves he had worked on today, and it left him melancholy.

Randall woke and sat bolt upright, listening intently to a sound in the direction of the road back up the hill.

"What's up?" Martin said, getting to his feet. He got a wag in response, but Randall's focus was on something only he could hear, his head tilting from side to side.

A moment later, the unmistakable rumble of the Lotus came into earshot, and a few seconds later, the car rounded the corner. As she went past, Christie glanced across. She slowed, as though she was going to turn into the carpark, accelerated again and disappeared toward town.

Randall trotted a few steps toward the road, his tail madly wagging. Martin watched in the direction the car had gone.

Why are you back so soon?

What about London? This was the last thing he expected.

"Let's go." The dog didn't move. "Home, Randall. Come on."

Martin collected his tools and headed to the steps. Randall followed a minute later, running to catch up by the time Martin reached the beach. From the moment Christie had come into their lives, the dog loved her. Martin had only ever seen him respond to someone like that once before. It said a lot about her.

As they followed the tideline, water lapping at feet and paws, Martin knew he couldn't give the painting back yet.

He'd told Christie he wanted to show the painting to someone. In spite of the subsequent discord between them—mostly of his making —Christie had kept her side of the agreement. He could not keep his. Not yet, as he was still waiting for his visitor to arrive.

If Christie came to his house asking for it, he would have to stall her, and he had no idea how to do that. If only she were not Dorothy's grandchild.

∽

Christie's heart had skipped a beat when she saw Martin and Randall at the graveyard. Her instinct was to go to them. Even as her foot touched the brake, Martin's harsh last words resurfaced, and she sped up, unwilling to let him hurt her again.

Too much pain lately.

Pulling into the driveway half an hour earlier, there had been no doubt in Christie's mind this was the right decision. In her absence, flowers bloomed, bringing the garden to life. She longed to start working on it.

The cottage itself had reverted to that musty, stale smell and as Christie wrote a shopping list, she added scented candles and WD40. The stubborn windows were going to open one way or another, and this little place will be filled with fresh air.

In her hurry to leave for the city, she had left the mind map here. It still took up much of the kitchen table, asking for Christie's attention. There would be plenty of time.

Now, in town, her first stop was the supermarket. This time, when she approached the register, the woman behind it smiled. Christie smiled back.

"Thought you'd left." The woman said.

"I did, but I think I'll be staying a while this time."

"Lot of people moving in now."

"You mean with the new estate?"

The woman nodded.

"I'm not in the estate," Christie mentioned.

"I know."

Did everyone know everything here or just assume?

"Are you the owner?"

"With my husband. Why?" The woman answered suspiciously.

"You have the best fruit and vegetables. I guess they're local?"

"Mostly. My husband also goes to the market in the city once a week."

"South Melbourne markets?"

"That's it."

"Oh, I live close by and shop there all the time. Well, I did live there."

"I'm Marilyn. If there's anything you need, let me know."

"Oh, thank you. I'm Christie."

"I know."

Of course you do.

Box of groceries in the car, Christie went to the bakery. She pushed the door open, greeted with a warm smile from Belinda as she carried a tray of steaming scrolls from the kitchen. The smell of cinnamon was mouth-watering.

"Hello! You're back! You couldn't stay away from our croissants, could you?"

"Hi, Belinda. Well, that had been my intention, but those scrolls smell incredible!"

"So they should! These very scrolls won 1st place at our agricultural show. Best in the region."

"These scrolls? So, did you keep them from the show and heat them up now?" Christie watched the humour light up Belinda's face.

"Absolutely. They are three months old, but you'd never know it. We make them so fresh that they are only just ready for eating now. How many?"

Belinda grinned as she slid the scrolls into the display cabinet. Christie was starving. She had not eaten since dinner at Rosetta, and it was all she could do not to buy out the bakery.

"Two, please. And a loaf of that fantastic sourdough."

"Coming right up." Belinda picked up a brown paper bag. "You're famous."

"Me?"

"But you are. You have a Wikipedia page and everything."

"I do?"

"You're funny. Yes, you do. But no Facebook?"

"Okay, now how exactly do you know all of this?" Christie tried to sound stern, but Belinda laughed.

"I stalked you. Well, I was hoping to be your Facebook friend, but when I couldn't find you there, I searched and got hits on your movies. You've worked with some amazing people!"

"That I have. And no, I don't do Facebook. I do have a profile on LinkedIn though. For business."

"Well, you should have a Facebook account. That way your fans can stay in touch. Like me! I saw some of your work and wow, I mean, just wow!"

Belinda put the bag with the scrolls on top of the counter and got the bread.

"Do you do normal people's makeup?"

"Normal? As opposed to actors and aliens? Of course."

"Your Wiki page said you do stuff at hospitals. For accident victims?"

Christie handed Belinda some cash, thinking she was going to have to check out this Wiki page about herself to see what else it said. "It's the most satisfying job. Being able to help people regain their confidence."

"I was wondering. Well, it's just..." Belinda went shy.

"Come on. I'm not famous, just a person."

"There's an end of year dance coming up."

"I'm happy to do your makeup."

"Not me. It's a school dance."

"Oh, for your sister? Of course, I'll do it. I'd love to, in fact, I'd intended to see if she'd like a couple of tips because that birthmark can be easily hidden."

"You'd help Jess?" Belinda had tears in her eyes and Christie wanted to hug her.

"Tell me when and we'll set it up. I'll need about an hour. I can do hair as well if she'd like? Shall I come to you or would you both like to come to the cottage?"

"Yes please to the hair! She won't go to the hairdresser or anything and wants to go to the dance but lets the mark spoil things. It is tomorrow night so can we come up to you?"

"You know where I am?"

Belinda laughed. "Everyone does. You've been the talk of the town since you arrived the first time. Brightened our little village up no end."

How funny. Christie remembered her mother once saying small towns are like big families and Rivers End certainly fitted that description. Moreover, half the town seemed related so an outsider like Christie, with a flashy car and inherited cottage, might well offer a lot to discuss.

Elizabeth White drove down the hill to Rivers End, having left Martha at Green Bay Hospital for some rehabilitation on her ankle. Martha had insisted she not wait, wanting to spend some time in the town after her appointment, so they agreed on a mid-afternoon pick up.

Last night, Martha had cried out for Thomas. The only Thomas that Elizabeth knew of was the artist. He had married and had a family so if he was the man in her dream, they must have known each other when quite young. Whatever happened had broken Martha's heart.

Elizabeth sighed at her musings and was about to take the turnoff to Palmerston House when she saw a white sports car approaching. She slowed to be sure, but yes, it was Dorothy's grandchild at the wheel. Now what would she do?

It was almost dark by the time Christie pried open every window in the cottage. Pouring a glass of wine, she wandered to the lounge room to unplug her new phone from its charger. On her drive here, she stopped in Geelong and bought a new phone, installing the sim card from her shattered one.

The last remnants of the sunset gave an eerie glow to the room. The old curtains were still heaped on the floor where they had dropped, almost hitting Martin on the way down. The anger in his eyes had been enough to get Christie off the ladder, and the scent of sea on his skin, his muscular arms on the ladder either side of her had made her pulse race.

Even now.

She shook her head. Better to remember how he tried to force her to sell the painting and stormed off when she refused. Better to think about how harsh his words had been on his deck that morning. Might be better, but her mind preferred to wander back to sitting beside him eating breakfast. Or cuddling Randall. None of which was helpful and did nothing for her state of mind.

Cross with herself, Christie closed the window, unplugged her phone, and went back to the kitchen. Sooner or later, she would have to go and see him to retrieve the painting. Her heart lightened. She'd be able to cuddle Randall. That was why she smiled.

Yes. That was why.

Next morning, Christie woke with the first light. Coffee in hand, she wandered around the garden, letting the tranquil beauty fill her empty heart. Today she would make a start on weeding and see what was under the overgrowth, and later on, transform Jess.

Belinda's desire to reach out to Christie via Facebook was touching. Asking her to help Jess even more so. Christie hoped Jess would like the experience, having seen how shy she was. This part of her work she loved the most, being able to use makeup to bring positive changes to others. Film had served her well, but she had been honest with Derek. She did not want to be travelling forever.

Perhaps now was the right time to find some stability. A home of her own, maybe even a dog. If she stayed here, there was the room and the perfect lifestyle, with the beach so close and winding country roads to explore.

Utter bliss.

Maybe her dog and Randall could have play-dates and chase a Frisbee along the shoreline.

In spite of what brought her back, the turmoil and betrayal and hurt, Christie knew it was for the best. As long as she kept busy, she was fine. Otherwise, a little voice taunted her about losing the only real relationship she had had. That little voice cared little that Derek had risked damaging her reputation in the industry, had chosen Ingrid's company over hers, and had been a controlling narcissist.

Christie found herself staring at a tree. She had no recollection of stopping in front of it and decided she'd done enough thinking for now.

THE PRINCESS INSIDE

$\mathcal{C}$hristie added to the mind map with a black marker. There had to be answers here.

She drew a new line out from *Cottage* under Thomas's name, then wrote—*Thomas' wife*. She connected the two and added—*Believed married 1968*.

So, who had Thomas married? Christie reached for Martha's letter. Rereading it, there was no name mentioned.

She told me all about it. Gloated in fact. By the time you read this letter, you will be just days away from getting married. To someone else.

Was "she", the friend entrusted with Thomas' final letter to Martha, the same person he married? Or just a messenger? There had been mention of Frannie taking their photo on the beach. Frannie could be anyone in their circle of friends, not necessarily Thomas' future wife.

What made absolutely no sense to Christie was the fact she had Thomas' letter here, unopened. Presumably the one he wrote to send with this friend to give to Martha. The same friend who told Martha that Thomas was to marry another. Someone who would gloat was clearly not a true friend.

Christie gazed around the kitchen. Once, a family lived here. More than one family over many years. Children raised here, meals prepared and eaten at this table. Laughter and tears, joy and sorrow. The last of the stationmasters was Thomas' father, who retired around the time Thomas and Martha broke up. Had Thomas and his new wife lived here? If his future wife was the one he entrusted with the letter and painting, maybe she had gone one step further than withholding them from Martha, by keeping them.

But Gran had them!

It was the shoebox with its rings and letters hidden in the attic. Half a puzzle in one house and half in another. Almost as though there was some conspiracy between two parties to stop Martha and Thomas from reuniting. Presumably, Thomas' wife was one party, but it was inconceivable Gran was the other.

Christie placed the pendant from the graveyard on the table and scrolled through her phone to find the photo of the engraving on the cliff face. Of course, it was not there because throwing her other phone at the wall destroyed everything not on the sim.

This had to stop. She could not just run from one place to another, breaking things. Relationships, jobs, phones, who knows what else. Losing Gran, losing Derek, losing her last contract—it all added up to a whole lot of unrest. Regardless, getting emotional enough to throw a phone at a wall or run away from Martin when he upset her was not Christie.

After Jess had been this afternoon, she would return to the beach and take some more photos. At least being near the sea would help calm her soul.

～

Belinda and Jess arrived at four. They walked up from the town, Belinda carrying a suit bag and backpack. Christie opened the door with a smile.

"Come on in, ladies. The kettle just boiled and there is tea, coffee and some rather yummy hot chocolate to help yourselves to."

Jess scurried in with her head dropped, but Belinda beamed. "Well, that's perfect because I have some of our world famous eclairs in this backpack!"

"There goes that diet again!" Christie sighed.

"As if you need it." Belinda laughed. "You two get to work, and I'll make afternoon tea."

"Yes, ma'am." Christie kept a straight face as she turned to Jess. "She's bossy, isn't she?"

Earlier, Christie set up an area in the kitchen to work from. The big kitchen table was ideal to spread out makeup, hair products, and her laptop, ready with photographs Christie wanted Jess to see.

"Okay Jess, sit here and go through these first." Christie passed the mouse to Jess, whose eyes darted from product to product, her mouth open. "I can do any of those styles on the laptop. You have lovely hair!"

Jess's hair was just below shoulder length with a hint of a wave in it. The colour was a true golden blonde, healthy and glossy.

"Oh?" Jess touched her hair in surprise. "You can do that. To me?"

"Sure. Part of my original beauty course included special occasion hairdressing, you know, weddings, deb balls, that kind of thing."

"How many courses have you done?" Belinda plugged the kettle in.

"Two. I started by doing a Diploma of Beauty Therapy and went on to a Bachelor of Health Services, specialising in Dermal Therapies. I've also done one on one training with an industry expert. So, I can do stuff to help burns victims, or change the colour of someone's skin for a movie, or even," she lifted Jess' chin to scrutinise her cheek, "disguise birthmarks."

"Mum says I shouldn't hide it. Mum says it is part of me and I shouldn't let other people upset me about it."

"Well, I think your Mum is right about that. It is part of you and what other people think shouldn't matter. But, sometimes it does, hmm?"

Jess nodded, her eyes fixed on Christie.

"So, what if I show you some simple tricks to cover it a bit and will also protect your skin against the sun. That way, if you have a special occasion, like tonight, you can cover it up if you choose to."

Christie sat near Jess. "Sweetie, you have beautiful, clear skin.

Pretty eyes and a gorgeous smile. But you need to let people see that smile more often. Your birthmark isn't who you are, it's a patch of different coloured pigment. A tiny part of you. What matters is that lovely person inside the skin, and I'll bet anyone who knows you doesn't see anything but your smile and eyes."

Jess' lips quivered and flickered up on the corners. Taking the mouse, she scrolled through the images. Christie glanced over her head to Belinda, who stood with a cup in one hand, a teaspoon in the other and had tears streaming down her face.

Christie took a tissue box to Belinda. "She'll be fine, you know that?"

Belinda took a few tissues and wiped the tears away, nodding.

"Where're those eclairs?" Christie grinned.

At almost six o'clock, there was a soft tap on the back door. Christie had finished packing up everything off the table. She opened the door to find Belinda and Jess's mother standing back near the steps.

"Hello, good timing, Jess is almost ready." Christie held the door open, but the other woman did not move. Her expression was stern.

"Would you like to come in?"

"No. Thank you. I'd rather speak outside for a moment."

"Sure." Christie stepped onto the small porch and closed the door behind her. "I'm sorry, we've never been introduced. I'm Christie." Christie held her hand out, and after a moment, the other woman took it and shook it without surprising pressure.

"I'm Sylvia. Sylvia Crossman."

"You have two wonderful daughters in there! Belinda adores Jess and Jess—"

"That's what I want to talk about." Sylvia interrupted. "I know you think you're helping and it's generous of you to put some makeup on Jess, but she can't start believing things will be different. She'll end up sad and disappointed."

Sylvia's eyes filled with worry and her fingers twisted around each other.

"You've raised her so well if you don't mind me saying. Jess said you've told her the birthmark is part of her and not to let others upset her. Wise words."

"She said that?"

"She did. The way I view covering up scars and blemishes and the like is that it doesn't change you, it gives you a bit more control and confidence. Don't know about you, but when I was about Jess' age, I thought everyone was staring at me and whispering about me."

"Because you're so beautiful! And rich. People stare at what they don't understand."

"Oh Sylvia, if only you'd seen me! Gangly and awkward and shy and not at all what you think. But what you said hits the nail on the head. People do stare if they don't understand. So, Jess now knows a couple of simple tricks that not only make the birthmark less obvious but will protect her skin. Just having that ability will give her a bit of confidence and every teen needs that."

Sylvia listened, unconvinced.

"Why don't you come and wait inside? Belinda is helping Jess with her dress."

Before Sylvia could answer, Belinda opened the back door. "There you are! Okay, now stand back, well don't fall down the steps or anything. May I present..." she glanced over her shoulder. "Mum's here! Come on. So, as I was saying, may I present Miss Jessica Crossman, ready to dance!"

Sylvia gasped and put a hand over her mouth. Wearing a short blue dress and matching shoes, Jess could have been dressed for a school dance in any city. Her hair was in a sleek high bun with loosely waved tendrils around her face.

"Jess? Darling, you..." Sylvia shook her head, not able to go on.

"Oh, Mum, don't get all soppy." Belinda laughed. "She doesn't look that amazing!"

"Hey! Mum. Is this okay? The dress?"

Sylvia took a deep breath. "It's lovely. You're lovely."

Jess' makeup was natural, her eyes highlighted to match her dress and her lipstick a soft pink. There was no sign of the birthmark at all. But it was the smile in her eyes that made her beautiful.

"Is it time to go?"

"Yes. If you're all ready?"

"I need my bag thingy."

"Clutch." Belinda reminded her. "I'll get it."

Jess hugged Christie. "Thanks. Thanks, lots, Christie."

"My pleasure. Make sure you have the best time tonight. Remember what we talked about, okay?"

"Every girl is a princess. Sometimes they look like one and sometimes they are a mess, but they are still princesses inside."

"Hmm. Don't remember saying a mess, but you've got the gist of it."

"Come on, Belinda! I'll be late!" Jess called out, and everyone laughed.

SANDALS IN THE SEA

*C*hristie stood at the top of the stone steps; breathing in the ocean air. Those couple of hours with Belinda and Jess had been rewarding, but hard work. Mostly with Jess, who took convincing almost every step of the way. The difference in self-confidence between the girl who had been almost afraid to walk into the kitchen and the one who virtually dragged her sister back out was incredible.

Even Sylvia changed. Christie had walked with them to their car and Sylvia grabbed her hand. Not to shake, but to hold it for a moment and squeeze the appreciation she could not vocalise. Belinda's earlier tears reinforced Christie's love of this side of her work.

The sun was low in the sky as Christie made her way to the beach. The air was balmy, and she was pleased she had changed into shorts and a T-shirt. As soon as she reached the bottom, she slipped her sandals off and dug her toes into the sand, grinning in almost childish pleasure.

She found the engraving in the cliff face and traced it with her finger. So much had happened since finding this poignant symbol of the love-that-was-no-more. T loves M. There for eons in the limestone until natural erosion took it forever. How often had Thomas stood at this spot, remembering the day he carved it for Martha?

Christie took a few photos, and afraid of losing them, emailed them to herself. She turned her attention to the jetty, capturing its image from near the cliff, and right at the waterline. The tide was rising, and as she stood on the edge of the wet sand, her attention on the photos she was taking, warm water unexpectedly rushed over her feet.

She jumped back, dropping her sandals—and almost the phone— into the waves. Up on dry sand, she buried the phone in a pocket, heart racing. As she stood there, chiding herself for such a ridiculous response and rechecking the phone, her sandals began to disappear into the sea. Another wave scooped them up and carried them further away from Christie.

She watched the water recede, trying to judge whether she could reach them between waves. It was a battle between woman and ocean. Or, her logical side corrected, woman and a woman's phobia. Christie ventured back to the wet sand. She counted the seconds between waves. One-one-thousand. Two-one-thousand. Three-one-thousand. The waves were quick and coming up the beach a fraction higher every time.

As she hesitated, the sandals drifted further away with each onslaught of water. She wanted to get them, to prove to herself she could. A wave rushed in, almost to her toes. She watched the foam sparkle on the sand as the water retracted. There was no way she was following that wave back out. Tears of frustration and despair filled her eyes.

"Do you intend on polluting the sea?"

Martin was at her side, watching the sandals float in and out again with the surf. "I would imagine a sea creature might become entangled in those."

Panic overwhelmed Christie, replacing a whole other set of feelings that bombarded her when she heard Martin's voice. She had to get those sandals. In her mind, she was running into the surf and getting them.

Unable to speak, she turned to Martin. He must have understood the fear in her face, for his own expression softened. Without a word, he strode into the ocean and scooped the sandals up in one motion. There he remained.

"Christie, it's safe. The tide's still pretty low."

She stared at him with wide eyes. He held a hand out. "I won't let anything happen to you. Come here."

She wanted to. Martin knew the sea. He knew the area and the tides, and he was only in knee-deep water. She was being crazy. His hand stayed outstretched as he watched the struggle in her face.

Christie shook her head.

Martin dropped his hand and waded back out of the sea. He stopped in front of Christie with the sandals. She took them, her head down to escape Martin's puzzled scrutiny.

Randall raced across the sand and Christie dropped to her knees to throw her arms around him, burying her face into his coat, loving his wet dog smell. Randall licked her face, and she laughed.

After a moment, Martin wandered away in the direction of his house. He called, "Are you coming?"

Christie thought he meant Randall.

Martin stopped. He half-smiled at his dog and Christie, still cuddling on the sand. "We need to talk. Walk with me."

It was a command, not an invitation. It took all of two seconds for Christie to get back to her feet and jog after him, Randall in tow.

BUYING TIME

Martin seemed content to walk in silence, so Christie fell into step with him, Randall trotting alongside. She kept checking her pocket to reassure herself the phone was still there. Apart from the photos, she kept most of her contacts in the phone, including Angus' number and she could not bear to lose touch with him again.

At the edge of the shallow lagoon, they stopped. Randall happily plunged in, splashing around like a puppy.

Martin stared into the clear water. "The river that feeds into this lagoon starts right up in the mountain range. There's a lake, several hours hike into the bush. It's in a valley that barely sees the sun, so steep are its sides and so dense its growth of old forest."

Wondering where this was leading, Christie watched Martin, who was still intent on the lagoon.

"In the scorching heat of summer, when you finally reach the lake, it is utter bliss to dive into its icy waters."

"Sounds wonderful."

"I did say several hours' hike. In pretty rough conditions."

"Are you inviting me to go hiking?"

"Could you keep up?" Martin only now raised his eyes to meet Christie's.

She unconsciously rechecked her phone.

"Must be an important phone," Martin commented. "Expensive. New?"

"Oh. I'm a spy. It has classified information."

"You almost dropped it in the ocean. What sort of spy are you?"

"Pretty bad one. You're right though, it is new and has a couple of phone numbers on it I don't want to lose."

Martin stared at Christie. Did he really believe she was only interested in expensive toys, as he once put it? He needed to stop thinking that.

Her words blurted out. "I destroyed the last one. I threw it at a wall, and it shattered. Shall we walk on the jetty?"

"No. Don't change the subject. Why did you throw it at a wall, Christie?"

"To stop it ringing, if you must know."

Christie stepped into the lagoon and waded across to the other side. She laughed when Randall followed and shook himself, spraying water all over her. She tried to brush the droplets from her hair, all the while talking to Randall.

After a moment, Martin crossed the lagoon and continued along the beach. Christie joined him again, squeezing water out of the bottom of her T-shirt.

"You're not afraid of water." It was a statement with a question behind it.

Christie sighed. "I can even swim. Quite well. The ocean thing is a childhood fear, and I want so much to get over it."

"I'll help you," Martin said. "When the tide is low."

"Oh. It's okay; I can sort it out myself. Thanks."

Martin gave her a sceptical glance. "Yeah. That's been working so well."

Christie went quiet. Inside, the fear bubbled away. Fear of the waves, fear of failing in front of Martin. The only way he would get her in the ocean was to carry her, and she would never let him do that. She needed to get his mind off her phobia.

She stopped. "Martin? You said we need to talk."

Martin checked his watch, and dropped onto the sand, stretching his legs out.

"Sit," he said.

With a small, bemused sigh, she joined him. Randall flopped beside them.

"Who was calling?" He glanced at her ring-less left hand.

"What?"

"When you threw the phone at the wall?"

"Derek."

"I see."

"I left him."

Silence fell again. Christie was puzzled. That was all he had to say. No more questions or probing stares?

"So, what did you want to talk about?"

"Are you staying for a while?"

"Yes."

"No London?"

"No. I don't want to talk about this right now."

"You only ever need to tell me what you want to, Christie. Just because I ask a question, doesn't mean you have to answer."

Christie stared out at the beautiful early evening sky over the sea. It was still quite light. Part of her longed to unburden herself onto him. To share what happened and listen to his perspective and uncanny insight into the situation.

"I hadn't expected you back so soon."

"This is about the painting, isn't it? You want to hold onto it for longer?"

"I'd like to. Just for a day or so, then we can talk again about its future."

Randall rolled onto his back, and Martin scratched the underside of his chest, his eyes on the dog. Christie's heart tugged at the strong connection between man and dog.

"Let me ask you one question. And give me a straight answer." This was her chance,

"One question and you'll leave the painting with me?"

Christie nodded as Martin turned his attention back to her.

"I saw one of your own paintings at Crown Casino. Sole Survivor."

Uncertainty crossed Martin's face.

"It is an incredible work. You are so talented."

"Is there a question in there?"

"No. While I'd suspected it, the description with the painting confirmed you are one of the Blake family."

"I could have told you that. Anyone in town would have."

"So, my question is this. Are you Thomas Blake's grandson?"

"That's the question?" Martin raised an eyebrow.

"Yes."

"I am."

Christie remembered the first time she had seen a photo of Thomas Blake. His strong features, intense gaze and undeniable good looks. So similar to Martin. Now, the resemblance was even more apparent. Particularly the eyes. So expressive and so quick to bring the shutters down when challenged. Was that one of Thomas' traits as well?

"You realise you're staring at me?" Martin sounded amused.

"Oh. Sorry." Christie's mind worked overtime. "So, if you're his grandson, you would know if he ever lived in my cottage?"

Martin's amusement disappeared, and he got to his feet. "I answered your one question."

Christie gazed up at him. "I know, but I have so many more. Please?"

He held his hand out, and she took it, standing in one fluid motion. He kept a gentle hold on her fingers. A current blazed through Christie, and she prayed it did not show on her face as she tried to focus on his words. "I'll keep the painting safe. Thank you."

"But no more answers?"

"I have to go. Stay away from the sea. We'll work on that fear of yours another day."

Martin released her hand and strode away toward his house.

"I think I said I could manage," Christie called after him.

"Perhaps I'll be the judge of that. Low tide is late morning."

Randall realised his master was leaving and took off after him. Martin reached to pat the dog's head, and Randall's tail went crazy. Their sense of belonging to each other was tangible, and Christie longed to run after them.

Instead, she turned back toward her end of the beach. She could not, must not become attached to them. She rubbed her fingers, troubled by her reaction to his touch. Martin had made it abundantly clear in the past he was only interested in the painting, and while his view of her may not be as cynical as in the beginning, he was every bit as guarded. He had been quick enough to shut her down after answering her question.

Why had she asked about his relationship with Thomas rather than a hundred other questions? She answered herself. Knowing Martin was Thomas' grandson was the closest she would ever get to meeting Thomas Blake.

Randall bounded up the road to the house ahead of Martin. Parked outside the gate was an old Land Rover, caked with dried mud and dust. Randall ran around it in excitement. Martin kept going, straight through the open gate and to the house.

The sliding glass door was wide open as usual, and Martin had to step aside as Randall, like a bullet, rushed past him, straight to a man sitting in an armchair near the window, a glass of whiskey in his hand.

"Well, well, Randall. Good thing it's only me, not some thief, the way your master leaves the place open." The man put his glass on a table beside the chair so he could scratch under Randall's chin. The dog lay at his feet adoringly, his tail thumping the ground.

"It's a peaceful community. No thieves around here." Martin stopped in the middle of the living room.

"Growing community. Since when were there houses up past Palmerston?"

"Not long."

"Not happy about it."

The other man used his hands to push himself up from the chair and stepped over Randall. He extended his hand. When Martin took it, he pulled him in for a hug and patted him heartily on the back. "Pleased to see you, my boy."

Martin stepped back. "And you too, Thomas."

WHAT WE WISH TO FORGET

"Well, at least you lock this door!" Thomas had brought his glass of whiskey into the studio.

"The contents of the house are more replaceable than in here."

Thomas stood in front of one, and then another of his paintings. From a young age, Martin learned how to paint from his grandfather, sat at his knee with his own small easel and palette at their home high in the nearby mountains. Growing bored with landscapes, Martin experimented with abstracts and developed his own style from there.

"You're welcome to comment," Martin said.

"No need. You know your strengths and your flaws. I've always admired your boldness. The intellect you weave through the art."

"Some would call it madness." Martin poured himself a whiskey from the bar and topped up Thomas' glass.

"Not worth your time. If someone understands you, they—they are worth your time."

Randall padded in and after getting a pat from Thomas, settled himself in his bed.

"You going away again soon?" Thomas watched the dog, and Martin laughed.

"Did you enjoy his company that much?"

"He's a fine dog."

"So I've been told."

Something about Martin's tone alerted Thomas. "And who told you that?"

"Someone."

"Ah. Someone."

"The same someone who loaned me what I need to show you. Why I called you."

"Well, show me." Thomas put his glass onto the top of the bar.

"It's over here, Granddad." Martin walked to the central easel, covered with a sheet.

"Uh oh. You only call me that when there's a problem. Did you buy something you shouldn't have?"

"Oh, I tried to buy it. I'm still trying to buy it."

"For goodness sake, Martin, show me the thing!"

In one quick action, Martin pulled the sheet off.

Thomas' face went as white as the sheet and walked away. Back to the bar where he grabbed his glass and drained it in one long gulp.

Martin folded the sheet, keeping an eye on Thomas. Moments passed as Thomas refilled his glass but ignored the contents, finally walking back to stand in front of his own painting.

With shaking hands, he touched the image of the jetty. "Where?" His voice was so quiet, Martin had to move closer to him. "Where did you find it?"

"It's a long story, and I think we need to be sitting down for it."

"You said you've tried to buy it. Who, Martin? Who from?" He turned to Martin, his eyes filled with tears and his expression halfway between hope and fear.

Elizabeth paused in the doorway of the living room, watching Martha stare at a white envelope in her hands. Her friend had been introspective all through dinner, worrying Elizabeth she may have received bad news at today's hospital visit. She drew a deep breath as she walked in.

"Well, how about a sherry to finish the evening?" she headed straight to a tray on the sideboard.

"Never say no to a sherry."

"I shall miss these evenings when you go home." Elizabeth prompted as she poured sherry into two crystal glasses. There was no reply. Martha was distracted and only glanced up when Elizabeth placed the glass on the table beside her.

"Oh, thank you, dear." Martha smiled. "I'm alright, Elizabeth. It's positive news."

Elizabeth sighed in relief and sat opposite Martha, taking a sip of sherry.

"Turns out that young doctor wasn't so difficult. He's written me a letter of clearance to fly." Martha placed the envelope on the table and picked up her glass. "I can go home, Elizabeth."

"That's what you want?"

"I do want to go back to Ireland, to my little house and garden," Martha stared at her drink, "but I shall miss you terribly."

"Why not stay? Come and live here, with me. There's more than enough room, or we could find you a place of your own? You've already said how much you love the summer here and after all, this is where you grew up."

"You shouldn't tempt me," Martha said. "I would soon become a boring companion and drive your patrons away!"

Elizabeth laughed. "Boring is something that would never describe Martha Ryan so that is a risk I would take. So, what would make you stay?"

Martha shook her head, deep again in her own thoughts. The silence stretched out before Elizabeth decided it was now or never to talk about Christie.

"What about family?"

"Family?"

"What about Dorothy's children?"

"I lost contact with my sister many years ago. Apart from when our parents died, we've not communicated."

"So, you don't know of any children. Grandchildren?"

"My sister was not the nurturing kind. I can't imagine her with small children running everywhere, spoiling her garden and muddying her floors." Her tone was bitter.

"But she did have a child, darling. A daughter."

"A daughter?" Shock filled Martha's face. "She never told me!"

"You did say you lost contact with Dorothy a long time ago."

"She managed to find me when it suited her! Why wouldn't she tell me about a child?"

Martha got to her feet, agitated.

"Oh, I didn't mean to distress you."

"No, I'm glad you told me. It reinforces I need to go home. To my own home."

Elizabeth stood. "Please, darling. Please sit again. There's more to tell you, and it might change your mind."

"Don't tell me. No more, Elizabeth. I shouldn't have come back."

Martha hobbled to the doorway. Tears coursed down her cheeks.

"Martha, please wait, dear. I won't mention it again."

Something in Elizabeth's voice made Martha stop. "You are my dearest friend. I wish things were different, but they're not and staying here just...it just hurts too much. Too many memories."

It had been a mistake to mention Martha's family, or maybe, the mistake had been waiting too long.

Night had fallen hours ago, and the moon shone brightly above a glassy ocean. Martin stood alone, motionless at the edge of the cliff, not seeing the beauty in front of him.

Thomas had reacted badly. Shock, followed by sharp anger and bitterness.

"Why? Why would this be in her estate?"

Martin had no answers. After throwing the sheet over the painting, Thomas stormed out of the studio. An hour of silent drinking later, replacing emotions with whiskey, Thomas staggered to the guest room. Randall went with him, curling up on the floor at the end of the bed.

For a while, Martin watched Thomas sleep, his heart broken for the man who raised him. A man who lived for the colours he transformed into paintings.

The passion this painting ignited in Thomas made Martin even more determined to buy it. Perhaps not for its artist anymore, but for him. As a reminder some things are not meant to be. That some things are best left alone.

Martin turned his attention to the opposite cliff. Not far from there, Christie was no doubt asleep. She was the one thing he knew he had to leave alone.

TOO MANY SECRETS

*C*hristie was far from asleep. Laid out on the kitchen table were all the clues. The laptop displayed a montage of photos from the beach—the love heart in the cliff face, the ocean, and the jetty. Thomas' letters were in a neat pile, with the final one unopened at the top, Martha's letter beside them. The rings and pendant lay alongside each other on a silk scarf from Christie's wardrobe. Gran's diary remained in the open tulip box next to the photo album. Only the painting was missing.

How do the pieces fit?

Secrets kept by Gran and others. For what purpose? To protect or to harm? Everything kept coming back to this cottage.

Keys to both the cottage and the trunk in the attic.

The shoebox in the trunk with unopened love letters and unused wedding rings.

Why did Gran have the keys to the trunk? That implied Gran knew what was inside. Why would she hide the property of Thomas Blake? Was it possible whoever last lived here left the trunk key by accident?

That was a promising theory. Until Christie picked up the keyring and saw the one that opened the tulip box. No, Gran knew. The keys were all linked.

There was the painting. Kept for too long inside a cylinder, concealed from the world, from its artist. Frustrated, Christie picked up the pendant. She should have taken it to the police station. It was valuable, at least to its owner. Yet here it was, in her hands. That day, at the graveyard, she learned Thomas Blake was dead. It was ridiculous to believe this pendant, on his headstone, could be coincidental, so who left it there?

Christie closed her eyes, searching her memory. She found the pendant the day after the funeral. At the time, she had other worries, so let it go. Now, she forced her mind further back.

When she had driven out of Rivers End to go to the airport, something caught her eye in the graveyard. The earthmoving machinery had gone, as had all signs of the funeral. Someone was there. A woman. Yes, an elderly woman, standing before the headstone of Thomas Blake.

Christie's eyes flew open.

Martha.

Who else would have been there except Martha, saying goodbye to her own sister and visiting Thomas' grave?

There was a single tulip placed on Gran's grave. After the funeral.

Why didn't I stop?

She would have prevented Martha coming to harm that day and found her only relative in the world. How would she find her now?

Christie's head dropped with tiredness. All she craved was sleep. She systematically turned off the kettle, computer and lights. Sinking onto her bed a few moments later, she was barely awake enough to take off her dressing gown and slip under the sheets. As she wrapped her arms around a pillow, Derek's face flashed into her mind. Except it was a goodbye. Her love for him disappeared overnight. Perhaps she never loved him.

Christie did not mind being alone, but as she drifted into sleep, her mind played tricks on her. Strong arms held her close against a rock hard chest. In steady unison, his heart beat in time with hers as he watched over her, keeping her safe while she rested. Smiling, Christie slept.

Derek stood in the foyer of his building, a takeaway coffee cup in one hand and briefcase in the other. As usual, he was the first to arrive, his day already planned out until evening. Yet he was wasting time here again. Staring at the painting.

Over Ingrid's objection, he had chosen this one. Clients already commented on it. He had no idea what it was about, but Christie had educated art sense, which made this a worthy investment.

The fact Christie knew the artist was interesting. That she had defended him even more so. This painting, Sole Survivor, or its artist, meant something to her and Derek intended to find out what.

Martin woke to Thomas talking to Randall on the deck. The sun was rising when he took two cups of coffee out a few moments later.

Thomas accepted the coffee with a grunt. Randall came over for a pat before dashing down the steps, and Martin sat on the other deck chair.

Martin noticed the deep lines in his grandfather's face were more visible than usual. Thomas was miles away, his eyes on the distant horizon. They drank their coffee in silence, each in their own thoughts.

"Your grandmother was a good woman," Thomas announced.

Martin looked at him in surprise.

"Nobody's perfect. Just remember that."

"Okay, I will."

"So, tell me about her."

"Who?"

Thomas turned to Martin. "This mystery someone who is smart enough to know that Randall is a fine dog."

"Hmm."

"Not an answer."

"There's nothing to tell you."

"Martin James Blake," Thomas warned.

Martin sighed. "The painting."

"What about it?"

"I should have left things alone. I'm sorry, Granddad."

"Are you changing the subject, son?"

There was a long silence, and Thomas narrowed his eyes as he worked out what Martin was not saying. "She's one of them."

"Dorothy's granddaughter, Christie."

"Well, that's not going to work now, is it?"

"I know. God, Thomas, don't you think I know?"

Martin stood and held his hand out for Thomas' coffee cup. Thomas stared at him.

"You're trying to buy it from her. Don't, son. I don't want it."

"But I do."

Handing his cup over, Thomas got to his feet.

"Some things are best left in the past. I might get some more sleep."

He squeezed Martin's shoulder before heading inside. Martin shook his head and muttered to himself, "and some things can't be left alone."

A BARGAIN...OF SORTS

The tide was low when Christie, in shorts and tank-top, reached the shore. As soon as her feet touched the sand, she took off her sandals, holding them aloft in one hand. Nobody else was around as she wandered to the jetty. At its end, she stood for a while, consumed with peace. Nothing matched this serenity and natural beauty, and she hoped it stayed this way for a long time.

After a while, she realised she was not alone. Martin was in the sea, swimming alongside the jetty. When he reached the end, he trod water, smiling. Christie dropped onto the timber boards and let her legs dangle over the edge.

"Where's Randall?"

"At home."

"All alone?"

"I didn't say that." Martin climbed up the side of the jetty and sat next to Christie.

Unsuccessfully, she tried not to stare at him. Water droplets trickled down his torso. He ran a hand through his hair, slicking it back, which made him look younger. He smelt of the sea.

"So, who's looking after him?"

"You love asking questions, don't you?"

"The issue is you don't like answering them!" Her tone was sharper than intended, spoken out of frustration.

Martin gave her a long, concentrated stare, reminding Christie of the day she rolled her eyes at him. A shiver shot through Christie. It wasn't unpleasant. She dropped her eyes.

As if he could read her mind, Martin half smiled. "Relax. Today is about conquering fears, and you need to focus on that."

Christie glanced at him, her voice soft. "I said I could manage."

"How do you propose to do that? You were frozen in place yesterday. Waves frighten you, or maybe open water, but you love the ocean. I see it in your eyes."

Not knowing how to respond, Christie stood. Martin joined her, pointing to the clear, calm water a few feet below them.

"See the fish?"

Christie peered down and was enthralled with a school of spotted fish darting in and out of graceful seaweed. "What are they?"

"King George Whiting. No doubt you've eaten this species, but these are babies. Too young to catch."

"The water is virtually transparent!"

"It's calm and safe. Walk with me." Martin wandered back to the beach leaving Christie on the jetty, hands on her hips. He was so bossy. Before he could turn around, she dropped her arms, not wanting him to see the defiant gesture.

She caught up with him on the sand where he waited. Christie shuffled her feet, playing with the sand, uncomfortable thoughts about him throwing her in the sea racing through her mind.

He grinned, then held out his hand. "Come with me."

Almost as afraid to take his hand as go in the water, Christie hesitated.

Stop it. He isn't interested in you.

Christie grabbed his hand to convince herself, catching her breath as electricity surged through her.

Martin led her to the edge of the ocean, the hard sand cool and firm below their bare feet. Christie turned and tossed her sandals high up onto the soft sand, and Martin chuckled. She laughed in response, her eyes sparkling.

"Where is that new phone of yours?"

"At home."

"And your house keys?"

"And you say I love questions!" Christie grumbled. "Here. Inside a zipped pocket." She patted the seat of her shorts.

He waded into the sea. A few feet in, with water lapping his ankles, he turned to Christie.

"Tell me why you're afraid."

"Of the ocean?"

"How many fears do you have?" He crossed his arms.

"I told you, it's a childhood thing. That's it."

"Did you nearly drown? Get taken by a rip?"

"No. It will sound silly, but Gran forbade me from going into the ocean. She once caught me swimming at St Kilda Beach and…"

"Your Gran's not here now, and you're a woman, not a child. Don't allow her reasons to be your reasons." Martin held his hand out. "Come to me."

Christie took a couple of steps forward, stalling when her feet sank a little, and her toes got wet. Exasperated with herself, she clenched her hands

"Ask me a question," Martin suggested.

"What?"

"Ask me a question, and when you're close enough to take my hand, I'll answer it."

"Any question?"

"Give it a go, and we'll see."

This was what Christie wanted since their first conversation. Now he was handing it to her. On his terms.

"How much do you want it, Christie? The answers you seek?"

How much indeed.

Christie's mind went into overdrive at the possibilities. This might be the only chance to ask the questions that haunted her. She focussed on Martin's eyes, using him as an invisible lifeline.

"Okay. Did Thomas ever live in the Stationmaster's Cottage?"

"Come here and find out."

Shivering as if in the snow, Christie waded to him. It was only a few feet, but each step sent a flight response to her brain. Her eyes never left his and then, he had her hand in his again.

"Good girl. Yes, Thomas did live there."

"Oh! How long for?"

"Is that the next question, Christie? Choose carefully because there will be a limit."

Martin let go of her hand before she could react and stepped back a few more paces. Now alone, with the water halfway to her knees, Christie had to fight the instinct to wade back to the safety of the beach.

"Next?" Martin prompted.

"Did Thomas paint the seascape and if so, how did it get to my grandmother's estate?"

"That's two questions."

Christie was sure a glimmer of amusement flicked into his eyes.

"It's a two-part question," she retorted, "but fine, I'm pretty sure he did paint it, so how did it become part of my grandmother's estate?"

Martin offered his hand. This time, Christie had to draw more deeply on her resolve to get to him. The water was above her knees when she did. There was approval in his eyes now, and she began to be a bit proud of herself.

"The water is inviting, isn't it? Just warm enough to make you want to slip into it and become one with the current."

"I'm asking the questions today."

"That's a tricky question because I don't know."

Disappointment drooped Christie's shoulders. A wasted question.

But Martin surprised her. "I'll expand on this one because there's no answer. That painting disappeared when Thomas was in his early twenties. That's all I can tell you."

This tied in with the letter when Thomas described sending a painting with Martha's friend. A friend who delivered a different message, one that shattered Martha's heart and had driven her away from Rivers End for a lifetime. Somehow, between writing his final letter and sending it to Martha with the painting, he changed his mind.

Martin tried to release Christie's hand, but she clung to him. The next steps would take her waist high, and her eyes widened in alarm.

"You're doing well." He squeezed her hand, and she reluctantly let go.

"Next question?" He trailed his fingers in the water as he retreated. When the water was just over his hips, he stopped. He planted his feet apart to let him balance as a mild undertow rippled beneath the surface.

Just get to him.

"Who did Thomas marry?"

A flash of reluctance crossed Martin's face before he controlled it. This must be getting closer to home. It was a moment before he held his hand out.

Trying to imagine the sea was a swimming pool, Christie somehow covered the distance between them. It was more than the need for an answer that drove her, she wanted his respect.

"I don't understand why it matters who Thomas married."

"It does."

Martin sighed. "Frances Williams."

"Frannie."

"That's what Thomas called her. Now, we need to move down the beach a bit. Away from the jetty. Let's swim."

"Swim? No, I couldn't!"

"Sure you can." Martin pulled both of her hands up around his neck and slid backwards into the sea, drawing her with him, so his body supported hers.

Shocked, Christie clasped her fingers together, eyes wide and body rigid.

"That won't work," Martin said. "Relax, oh, and feel free to kick. We'll get there faster."

Christie giggled, and her fears evaporated. She was safe. Protected. Despite his suggestion, he needed no help from her. His strength made her feel invincible. They drifted through the ocean as one, their bodies moulded to each other.

I wish time would stop. Just for a while.

Martin slowed and put a foot down to test the depth. He let a small wave carry them a little further in, and stood up in waist deep water. Christie braced herself against the tug of the tide.

"You should be proud, Christie. I'm proud of you." He steadied her with an arm around her waist. Her hands rested on his arms, and he tightened his hold. She swayed but not from the current, from a need to be against him again.

"Thank you." Christie's lips stayed half-open.

"For showing you the ocean is safe or for answering some questions?"

"Both. I just wish…"

Martin shook his head. "No more questions today."

"It's sad Thomas never saw his painting again."

"Why would you say that?"

"Because he's dead."

Martin released Christie in surprise. "Thomas most certainly is not dead!"

But, she'd seen his gravestone. Without thinking, she spun around and started swimming for shore.

"So, now you can swim in the ocean." Martin's words followed her.

A TRUTH REVEALED

How could Martin say his grandfather was alive when Christie had seen his grave with her own eyes?

Once on the sand, she took off at a sprint. Martin must think her crazy, but she had to find out for herself. If Thomas was alive, everything changed. Everything.

She raced up the steps. It was only at the top she stopped, desperate for air. For a few seconds, she stood with hands on her knees, gulping in oxygen, clothes and hair soaking wet. She straightened and scanned the graveyard.

At Gran's funeral, Martin had started tidying the overgrown grave. But he'd walked away. She'd seen from the carpark, his back rigid as he'd left the graveyard.

Now, the grass was short, there were no weeds, just a small row of newly planted, brilliant blue lobelia at the base of the headstone. Christie read the inscription.

Thomas Blake
Son of Thomas and Frances
Husband of Anna
Beloved Father of Martin

Christie gasped. This belonged to Martin's father, not his grandfather. How could she have misunderstood?

The next grave had a similar headstone, with white lobelia adorning its base. Christie reluctantly read the inscription, afraid of what it would reveal.

Anna Blake (nee Crossman)

Adored wife of Thomas and sister of Sylvia

Deeply loved Mother of Martin

Oh my God, both of Martin's parents are dead.

Like hers.

Christie stumbled to the last grave. There was purple lobelia at the base of the headstone.

Frances Blake (nee Williams)

Loving Mother of Thomas Jnr and Wife of Thomas

Tears poured down her cheeks as Christie returned to the first grave and sank to her knees.

How had she missed this? Long grass had hidden enough of the inscription to let her jump to incorrect conclusions. Instead of checking properly, perhaps via public records or local knowledge, she assumed Thomas was dead.

"Are you satisfied?" Martin's voice was tense as he stood behind Christie. "Thomas is alive but his son, his daughter-in-law and his wife all rest here. Killed by a driver who'd had one or two drinks too many."

"Oh, no. I'm so sorry, Martin."

No wonder he had been so adamant about taking her car keys away that night. He could have lost it entirely with her but instead calmly insisted she not drive. To lose nearly all of your family in one terrible accident was something she understood.

"How old were you?"

"It doesn't matter. It happened." His voice choked with long-buried emotions.

"My parents died in a car accident when I was seven." Christie volunteered. "They were travelling to a remote town to deliver medical supplies, and I never saw them again."

"I didn't know that."

Christie turned glistening eyes to him.

"Why are you crying?" he asked curiously. "For your parents?"

"Yes. And for your parents and your grandmother. For Thomas. For you."

"Don't. It was a long time ago, and we're both adults now."

Christie went to Martin. She rested her palm flat against his chest, where his heart was.

"Inside, we're always their children. This pain you and I hide from the world...it keeps us connected to their smiles, their voices and love. That way, we never forget them."

Grief flooded Martin's face, and he gathered Christie in his arms, holding her close. She heard the steady beat of his heart and wrapped her arms around his waist. He tightened his embrace, and they stood for a while in silent understanding.

"I left your sandals at the top of the steps," Martin said.

"Thank you."

Martin released Christie, and reluctantly, she dropped her arms. He went to his father's grave. Christie wanted his arms back around her. Instead, she followed him.

"I thought this belonged to your grandfather."

"Clearly."

"Is that who you wanted to show the painting to? Is Thomas here?"

"No more questions, Christie. Go home and put some dry clothes on."

Christie only half heard him, thinking instead about the pendant. Had Martha drawn the same wrong conclusion about Thomas? "Why did he change his mind?"

"What do you mean?"

Christie failed to register the sharp edge to Martin's voice.

"Why did he marry Frannie?"

"Why do you call her that? Thomas was the only one who did."

"Just from the letters. Her name is mentioned as Frannie."

Martin turned to Christie, arms folded and his expression hard. She gazed at him. He was shutting her out again.

"He had such love for Martha—"

"You have his letters?" His words cut across hers, demanding an answer.

"I told you that, ages ago. Well, that I had love letters. I thought you knew they were his! I have other things. Rings. Photos he may want."

"You read his letters? His private letters."

"I thought...I didn't know who he was. Martin, I would never..." Christie almost wept at the contempt on Martin's face.

"You really are a Ryan."

"You don't understand, Martin, I'm trying to help!"

"Then help us both and go back to the city."

The words hung between them.

"I'm sorry." Her voice was little more than a whisper.

"Don't say it if you don't mean it."

"I do mean it. But I also have to finish what I started."

Christie took a hesitant step toward Martin, who put up his hand and shook his head. "I'm so angry with you right now. So disappointed."

Without another word or glance, he spun away and stalked back to the steps. Christie sank back onto the grass. With heart-wrenching understanding, Christie knew why this man affected her so much.

Somewhere between their disagreements and tenderness, the understanding and misunderstanding, the secrecy and honesty, somehow Christie had fallen in love. Totally, irrevocably in love with Martin Blake.

PLANS, NEWS, ARRIVALS

artha was rather impressed with herself. Not accustomed to modern forms of communication, she nevertheless managed to book her flight home to Ireland using Elizabeth's computer. Now, the printed ticket was in her bag.

"I don't mind driving you all the way to the airport." Elizabeth arrived with a plate of sandwiches and put them on the coffee table near Martha.

"It isn't necessary, dear. The bus trip from Green Bay is pleasant, and it connects with the bus to Tullamarine Airport. It will give me a chance to watch the scenery one final time."

Elizabeth sat opposite. "This is farewell."

"There's always a spare room in my little home."

"And I may take you up on that." Elizabeth looked sad. "I have enjoyed your company so much."

Martha helped herself to a sandwich. It would be so easy to stay here in Rivers End for the remainder of her days. The town had only changed a little, and still had the charm she loved as a young woman. As her ankle mended, the desire to walk along the beach or even up the hill to the clifftop had increased. To sit in that meadow again in springtime, the flowers tickling her legs and breeze ruffling her hair… it was a bittersweet thought.

What would her life have been, had she controlled her temper that night? Marriage, children. Grandchildren now. The home Thomas once promised to build her would stand upon that cliff where he painted her portrait. But there was no Thomas, and besides, he had chosen another. Frannie.

"Martha? Are you okay?"

"Yes, just lost in thoughts. Memories."

"Would you like to talk about them?"

"Some things are better left in the past."

"Perhaps. I see your sadness though and can't help but think I can tell you things that would make you happy again. If you'll let me."

Martha knew what Elizabeth meant. Something about Dorothy's daughter. In this day of computers and the internet, if anyone wanted to find her, they would.

"Let's have dinner in town tonight. My treat." Martha changed the subject with a forced smile. "I can't recall the last time I had a pub meal."

"And I don't believe I've ever had one here!"

"Well, about time. A counter meal and glass of local wine to toast our last evening?"

Thomas was making lunch when Martin stormed in. "Have a shower, boy. You're dripping water from that long hair of yours."

"My hair is just fine, thanks, Thomas."

"Then have one to cool you off."

Thomas piled ingredients onto thick chunks of bread, tossing a piece of meat to Randall, who sat at his feet.

"Granddad?"

"Oh dear, there's that granddad thing again." Thomas started cutting the sandwiches.

"After my shower, we need to talk."

"No, first we'll need to eat. Not getting any younger, you know. Every meal counts."

Martin shook his head and stalked off to his bedroom. Thomas stared after him, wondering what else Martin could say that would shake his world. Seeing his painting had been enough, but somehow it seemed that was only the tip of the iceberg.

~

Christie straightened her hair in front of the bathroom mirror still patchy with condensation from her shower. The repetitive task of segmenting her hair, brushing then running the hot tongs through it was soothing. Every so often, she stopped and stared at her reflection.

She could not have fallen for Martin. His firm gentleness in the ocean obviously affected her judgement. By giving her courage, he had taken her heart. His harsh words in the graveyard were a sharp reminder of the other side of his nature. Now though, she understood he had been protecting his grandfather this whole time.

Thomas Blake was alive. If the pendant meant anything to him, he should have it, along with his own letters and the rings intended for his wedding day.

What will I say to Thomas?

Once her questions would have filled a book, yet now she just wanted to apologise for reading his private letters. All she longed for was Martin to respect her, to forgive her, to trust her.

She sighed as she unplugged the tongs. She would pack up all of Thomas' belongings and return them to him, even if it meant angering Martin further.

~

Derek pushed open the door to Rivers End Real Estate, wrinkling his nose at the overpowering floral scent from a plugin freshener.

Daphne pushed her lunch to one side, trying to swallow the mouthful she had just taken. She stared at him as though she'd never seen a well-dressed, handsome man.

Poor love. Probably never has.

"Don't rush." Derek flashed a smile which he dropped when he turned away to peruse the wall of properties for sale. His practised eye discarded most of them, only finding a new estate of interest.

"Please forgive me, on my own, so lunch is between clients!" Daphne stood up and came around the counter to offer Derek her hand. "I'm Daphne Jones and my husband John is the principal here."

Derek shook her hand. "Yes, I've heard decent things about him."

Daphne beamed. "You have?"

"He's well regarded in the industry. I'm Derek Hobbs from Hobbs Development International."

"Oh, a developer! Well, there's plenty of opportunities around here. Is there something, in particular, you're interested in?"

"More a someone." Derek winked. "My fiancée is here, staying in her newly inherited cottage and I've come to make a surprise visit."

"You're Christie's young man! Well, it is lovely to meet you. I didn't know she was back in town."

"I'm hoping you can help with directions."

"To the cottage?"

"Yes."

"Easy. Head straight back toward Melbourne and turn left after the cemetery. Then, on the right a little way past the railway line."

"Thanks. Is there a florist nearby? Can't go there empty-handed."

"Just over the road. What a lucky girl Christie is."

"Appreciate your help. Will have to have a chat with John once Christie agrees to sell."

"He'll love that! You give Christie my best now." The woman had an odd expression on her face. As if she knew what he was up to.

Ignore her.

He nodded and left. The sooner he fixed this problem, the better.

❧

Christie finished packing the last of Thomas' belongings into the shoebox. All of his letters were in the bottom, then, the rings in their box. The pendant was inside one of Christie's own ring boxes. She did not know what to do with the photo album. Perhaps she could send him copies of them once she had some made.

She put the lid on and tied it up with the velvet ribbon. Even though the box was a bit soft, it held together well enough with the ribbon in place. Thomas already had the painting, presumably, so that was everything. Now, she had to find the nerve to drive to Martin's house once again.

Last time she was there, Martin called her a city girl and told her to go home. This morning, on the beach, he virtually repeated himself.

"Anyone would think you're trying to get rid of me." She murmured aloud, trying to push down the jumbled emotions threatening to spill over all the time. At least she might get to see Randall again which was almost worth the angst.

Christie went to her bedroom to find her sandals. She'd picked them up from the top of the stone steps earlier in the day where Martin left them.

She was not in love with him. She had only just broken up with Derek. Except, the love for Derek had long gone, pushed away by his narcissistic personality and interest in Ingrid. What she felt for Martin was different.

Not that it matters, she thought as she went back to the kitchen.

Martin doesn't even like you. He thinks you're terrible for reading private letters and he might be right.

Even if Thomas Blake had been dead, he still probably would hate her for reading his grandfather's writings.

Before she could pick up the shoebox, there was a sharp tap on the door, and she hurried to open it, worried. What if it was Martin? Maybe he wanted to talk or tell her off some more.

Thomas Blake stood on the porch. Resting against the wall beside him was the seascape.

He stared at Christie for a long moment.

She gazed back, not believing her eyes.

When he spoke, his voice was exactly as she imagined it would be. "I've come to get what's mine."

TOO MANY VISITORS

*T*homas stood inside the door, the painting in his hands. His eyes darted around the kitchen, but his face was expressionless.

"Please, sit down Mr Blake," Christie said.

"It's Thomas, and I'd rather stand, thank you."

"Oh, okay. Would you like coffee?"

"No, but I'll have a whiskey if you have any."

"I wish I did. Not one trace of alcohol, I'm afraid."

"You don't drink."

"I didn't say that. All I have is a sadly empty wine bottle at the moment."

Thomas glanced at the bottle next to the sink. "You've got good taste."

He crossed to the kitchen table and placed the seascape on it. "I don't want this. Your grandmother left it to you, so here it is."

"I think she meant for me to return it. To you, Thomas."

"Martin told me you won't sell it to him."

"It was never for sale. And besides, he refused to tell me why he wanted it."

Thomas chuckled, his whole face relaxing.

"I thought you were…" Christie stopped, not knowing how to phrase it.

"Dead? Not yet, young lady. You're not much of a detective."

"I never set out to be one. I didn't even know about this place or you or my great-aunt until Gran died and I've done the best I could to uncover these secrets she so desperately wanted to be known."

"There are no secrets. Just terrible mistakes. I'd like my letters please."

"They're here. Back in the shoebox I found them in." Christie straightened the ribbon before picking up the shoebox. "This was inside a trunk in the attic."

"Here? They were in this cottage?"

"Yes. And there's more you need to know." Christie held out the shoebox.

"No. Not another word about it." Thomas took the shoebox and tucked it under his arm. "This is none of your concern so leave it be."

He headed straight for the door. As he opened it, he glanced back at Christie. "You're so like her."

"Do you mean Martha?"

She saw Thomas flinch. Christie watched him curiously, not understanding how after all these years, and after he had broken Martha's heart, her name would elicit such a response. Thomas gathered himself and nodded to Christie, before stepping outside and closing the door with a firm click.

Christie gazed at the seascape, hanging again over the fireplace in the lounge room. Her short meeting with Thomas taught her a lot about Martin. The same expression that shut out the world. The determination to keep information to themselves. Even the same engaging laugh and glimpse of humour in their eyes.

The back door opened and there was a footstep in the kitchen. Christie froze. Thomas must have returned. Perhaps he checked inside the shoebox and wanted to ask Christie questions. His knock must have been too quiet for her to hear.

Almost running into the kitchen, a smile on her face, Christie skidded to a stop.

"Hello, baby," Derek dropped a bunch of orange lilies on the table. "So this is where you've been hiding."

Shock reverberated through Christie and the smile vanished.

"No welcome kiss? Never mind, soon you'll be back where you belong."

"You let yourself in," Christie said. "This is my home, Derek."

"The door was unlocked. Besides, you're my fiancé."

"Not any more. Why are you here?"

"Why are you so hostile? I'm here to make amends. See, expensive flowers and I have your ring with me. I spoke to a celebrant, and we can be married before Christmas."

He glanced around the kitchen, unable to disguise his disdain. "This place is a dump. Thank goodness the land is worth so much. Kind of makes up for all the chaos you left behind. Friends asking where you are. Bills arriving that need paying."

"Just send me any bills, Derek. I'll get everything redirected."

"You didn't bother to leave an address. All I ever wanted was to look after you." He changed his tone, smiling as he held his hand out. "I'm sorry I messed up."

Christie shook her head and took a step backwards.

"Don't be afraid to admit you've made a mistake. I forgive you for leaving. Look, here's your ring." Derek took the ring from his pocket and lunged forward, grabbing Christie's hand.

"Stop it!" Christie cried out. "I want you to leave!"

"You're going to wear my ring and marry me, Chris." Derek held her wrist and tried to unclasp the fist she instinctively formed. Christie struggled to pull away from him with all her weight, but he was far too strong, and her feet slipped from under her. She fell to her knees.

Derek loomed over her, his face enraged in a way she had never seen. One by one, he forced her fingers to unclench.

"Just go, Derek," she sobbed. "Get out of my home!"

"What's yours is mine, baby."

"She said get out!"

Swinging around at the voice behind him, Derek released Christie.

Martin stood in the open doorway, fury radiating from every inch of his body.

"Who the hell are you?" Derek postured.

Ignoring him, Martin strode to Christie and lifted her onto her feet, his touch gentle. He pulled out a chair.

"Are you okay here for a minute?"

She nodded and sank onto the chair as her legs shook. Christie could have sworn Martin winked at her before turning back to Derek.

"You're still here," Martin said with surprise. "Don't let me reach zero."

"What the hell are you—"

"Five." Martin interrupted, taking a menacing step toward Derek.

"Now, just you listen! Do you have any idea who I am?" Derek stepped backwards.

"A bully?" Martin suggested. "Four."

"I own one of your paintings if you call them that. Christie liked it, so I bought it for my office."

"The money goes to disadvantaged kids, so you've done something worthwhile with your investment."

"So you're the reason she's here instead of with me. You'll find she's ordinary without the makeup. Pity, her dinner parties were something special. Doesn't matter, we lived together long enough for me to get half of this place."

Martin moved swiftly into Derek's personal space, towering over the other man but not touching him. "Three. Time to leave."

Derek glowered at Christie. "This won't be the last time we meet."

"Two. Get out, Derek." Martin's voice was like steel and Derek tore out with Martin on his heels.

"One."

Christie heard Martin's footsteps hard on the ground behind

Derek and a moment later, the roar of a car engine. Her heart pounded out of control, and her stomach was tied up in knots.

Martin rushed back inside, closing and locking the door behind him.

"Breathe, Christie." He took her left hand and extended each finger out, caressing them ever so tenderly. "He's gone. He'd be a fool to come back."

Christie stared at her hand in his, still shocked by the past few moments and so relieved he was here. "He can't have some claim over the cottage?"

"Only if he's happy to give up half of his empire in return." There was almost humour in Martin's reply, but he sighed. "Christie."

Christie raised her eyes to meet his.

"Did you let him in, or did he let himself in?" His tone was stern.

"The door was unlocked."

Martin tightened his hand in frustration. "What have I told you about that?"

"You were right." Christie's voice was almost inaudible.

"Yes, I was right. He could have harmed you."

Tears rolled down her cheeks.

Martin dropped her hand. "How can you have any tears left?" He spotted a box of tissues. "Here. Have a dozen."

Christie pulled some out and wiped her face. "Why are you here? I mean I'm so glad you are...I don't know what I mean."

"Derek went to see Daphne, and she was suspicious about his intentions. She rang me."

"Why?"

"Because she knew I'd come and check on you."

"Thank you."

"Thank Daphne."

"I will. So, about what happened earlier today...?" Christie stared at the floor.

"Nothing's changed. I'm still angry with you. But I know Thomas is not, which may count for something."

Christie's eyes flew up to his. She wanted to say so much, but some wise part of her brain told her to stay quiet.

Martin offered her his hand and when she stood, he held it for a moment, his eyes unfathomable.

Heat rushed to Christie's cheeks and she slipped her hand from his. She busied herself filling the kettle, wondering why her legs were still unsteady.

"Would you like a coffee?"

Before he could answer, there was a knock on the door, and Christie almost dropped the kettle in panic. She spun around as Martin went to open it. But it was Sylvia, who stared at Martin with surprise. He held the door open, and she cautiously came in.

"Hello!" Christie plugged the kettle in. "You're just in time for a coffee."

"I can't stay. Shouldn't you be checking on George?" Sylvia directed this to Martin.

"Yes." He turned to Christie. "Lock the door behind me."

Sylvia waited until Martin left, closing the door behind himself.

"It's about Belinda." Sylvia was upset. "She's coming to see you, and you mustn't do what she asks."

"What do you mean? Won't you sit down?"

"You've put all sorts of ideas into Belinda's head, and now she wants to enrol in some fancy school in Melbourne! You have no idea what you've done!"

"We talked a bit about how I got my qualifications, but that's all. I've not spoken to her since Friday night."

"I think you've done more than that! She wants you to help with her application, and I'm telling you not to. Her place is here, in Rivers End, not Melbourne!"

Sylvia raised her voice, and she twisted her hands around each other as she had the other night, showing her anxiety over Jess. Christie's heart went out to her.

"Sylvia, if that's what Belinda wants to do, I'm most happy to help her. It won't be as bad as you think."

"No, I told you not to help! You should go back to where you came from instead of upsetting people and giving them ideas above their place in life!"

The door swung open, and Martin stepped back in with a now familiar pained expression.

"Okay, enough. I could hear you from the driveway."

"You're defending her?" Sylvia put her hands on her hips.

"Christie won't lead Belinda astray, and it's about time you loosened those apron strings."

"You don't understand!" Sylvia almost cried in anguish.

"Probably not, but attacking Christie isn't dealing with the problem. Please, shelve this for a day when you are not upset, Auntie. Say bye and walk away."

Sylvia glanced at Christie without a word, before hurrying out.

"Come here, please." Martin was still by the door, and from his tone, Christie knew exactly what he was about to say. It took all of her willpower to make those few steps.

"I'm not coming to your rescue anymore today. What are you going to do when I leave?"

"Lock the door."

"Lock the door. Didn't I ask you to do that last time I left?"

Wide-eyed, Christie nodded. Martin slipped an arm around her waist and pulled her close against his body, forcing her to look up at him. His hand ran down her back.

"If anything should happen to you..." his voice broke and he looked away. "Don't put yourself at risk, sweetheart."

Was Martin getting emotional? "I'll be more careful."

"Lock the door." Martin dropped a careless kiss onto her forehead and then released her. Closing the door behind himself, he left without another word.

Christie turned the lock. A few seconds later, the door handle rattled, and she heard Martin chuckle.

A STORM BREWING

*A*s night fell, Martin left the house to find Thomas. In the oven a seafood lasagne bubbled away, so he poured a couple of glasses of wine.

Thomas was in the shed beside the house. The motorbike was in pieces, and Thomas was bemused.

"Is that how you tune one of these?" Martin held a glass out for Thomas.

"I think it's the valve heads. Or pistons. Either way, I need some tools and parts, and those are back home." He wiped his hands on a rag before accepting the wine.

"It didn't sound that bad to me." Martin hoped Thomas knew where all the pieces belonged.

"That's because you don't listen! This old beauty was trying to tell you she needs some attention with that little cough she developed. How long since you did anything other than ride her?"

"I hardly even do that, Thomas. So, it'll be fixed soon?"

"If I have the parts, it might be done tomorrow night. I'll go home in the morning and see. Maybe I should take the dog and spend a week at home?"

"Maybe I should buy you a dog? Dinner in twenty minutes."

Martin headed back to the house, and after closing the shed door, Thomas followed.

Randall wagged his tail without lifting his head from his food bowl as Thomas climbed onto the deck. He stared out at the last glimpse of light on the horizon, breathing in the humid air.

"We should eat out here tonight." Martin carried the bottle of wine over and topped up Thomas' glass.

"Storm coming."

"We'll be done before then. Why don't you move back?"

"And live where?"

"Here of course."

Thomas glanced at Martin with his eyebrows raised. "Don't know if your young lady would appreciate that, son."

Martin busied himself tidying the small table.

"Unless you intend to move over her way." Thomas grinned to himself.

"You made it clear the Blakes and Ryans don't mix." Martin retorted, not amused.

"Well, I formally withdraw that statement and release you from any obligation to please me above your own happiness."

"Why?" Martin picked up his glass, eyes on Thomas.

"She's good for you. Makes you happy."

"She makes me cross."

"Same thing. Don't make the mistakes I did. Is dinner ready? Meals matter at my age."

"Did Christie talk to you about her theories?"

"You can't change the past and whatever Dorothy Ryan thought she knew went to her grave with her." His tone of voice warned Martin not to pursue it.

In the distance, a flash of lightning briefly lit up the sky.

Christie wandered aimlessly about, wearing boy leg panties and Martin's T-shirt. The soft fabric soothed her as if he was close.

The humidity was oppressive, and open windows made little difference.

The events of the day filled her mind. She was exhausted, and her hand still hurt where Derek tried to force the ring on. If Martin had not arrived when he did... Christie shut the thoughts away. He had got there in time to throw Derek out.

She opened the wine she had picked up earlier this evening. Going into the bottle shop, the welcoming sounds of the pub next door almost drew her in and she hesitated before buying the wine and coming home. Now, staring into the almost-empty fridge, she wondered if she should go back tonight.

There was only some bread, cheese and olives left. Although the sourdough was a few days old, it still smelt inviting, so Christie sliced cheese and melted it, with the olives, over the bread.

The small meal was gone too soon, and Christie sadly played with the crumbs. After cleaning up, Christie checked the back door was locked. Twice. She giggled and refilled the glass. She read the label on the wine bottle, remembering Thomas' approval of her choice and later, Martin saying Thomas wasn't angry she'd read his letters.

Of course, Martin might only have told Thomas she had them. It was odd how he said there were no secrets, just terrible mistakes. Did he mean marrying Frannie so soon? The way he recoiled when hearing Martha's name was puzzling. As though Martha hurt him, not the other way around.

Christie moved into the bedroom, which was marginally cooler than the kitchen. The tulip box was on the bed. She lifted the diary out and saw to her dismay the final letter from Thomas to Martha was there. She had forgotten to add it to the shoebox.

Was this last letter another declaration of love, or an admission of Thomas' feelings for another woman? Perhaps Frannie was the reason Martha had run away in the first place. Something happened that night so distressing to Martha she left her ring and her plans to wed Thomas behind.

None of this made sense. Every single letter penned by Thomas reinforced his love for Martha. He spoke of their plans and his determination to bring his girl home. To send her a painting of the night they separated was a bold move.

Christie picked up the other letter, the one from Martha to Thomas. Yet another lost letter. Lost? No, hidden. She read it. Then reread the words that still confused her.

Just a phone call or a letter would have done. Anything at all to reassure me you still wanted me to keep my side of the promise. That you still love me and meant what you said that night. Instead, there was only silence. Now I know why.

Thomas had tried to contact Martha. He had written letter after letter. He even phoned, but Dorothy had moved. In desperation, he agreed to allow a friend to take the painting and one last letter to hand to Martha.

Instead, the friend told Martha Thomas was about to marry another woman. Frannie.

Before she could stop herself, Christie swapped the letter for Gran's diary. Gran was definitely not returning from the grave and had made it clear she wanted this information to go to her sister. Well, short of finding Martha, Christie was the closest thing to anyone who cared now.

1st January 1968. Martha is still here with me. Still fussing about Thomas and what happened that night and fretting he has not been in touch. If I had given her even one of the letters he has written, no doubt she would have gone running back to Rivers End. Every time one arrives, I remind myself this is for her own benefit. In spite of his actions that saved her life, the man is not suited to Martha, and one day she will understand. She cried at Christmas time but is otherwise beginning to cheer up and even came out with me last night to celebrate the New Year.

Christie dropped the diary and stood up. No. It was inconceivable Gran was responsible for this! For keeping Thomas' letters from Martha and deliberately steering her into a new life? *Oh my God, how could she do this?* Upset, Christie retrieved the wine bottle and glass from the kitchen. There was lightning in the sky now, far away and silent.

After pouring a fresh glass of wine, Christie picked up the diary again. Almost a month of entries went past without mention of anything other than Gran's boyfriend and her work. Martha's name appeared again.

21st January 1968. I almost gave in. Yesterday, Martha and Thomas should have been married. She would not get out of bed until last night and sat by the window with tears going down her face for hours. Why she has not got on a train and gone back to talk to the boy is beyond me. Pride and probably fear of rejection I suppose. It made me think about what I have done to her.

Christie had to walk back to the kitchen again to get the box of tissues Martin offered her earlier in the day. Why would Gran have done this to her own sister? Even if she believed Thomas was the wrong man, how could she have justified this to herself?

20th February 1968. I am getting frustrated with Martha. In spite of my encouragement for her to find a job or study anything she likes, her heart stays with Thomas Blake. There must be a way to break this bond and free Martha to find a new future. Frances has insisted on meeting with me this week, and although I cannot stand the girl, she helped before and might help again.

Christie was unable to digest what she was reading. She and Frannie had some kind of relationship, and with a deep sense of foreboding, Christie flicked through the diary for the next entry about Martha.

26th February 1968. Frances has a suggestion I struggle to agree to. Keeping letters from my sister is one thing, but to be party to an outright lie? It is clear Frances has strong feelings herself for Thomas Blake, but she refused to reply when I asked if he returns them. I suspect he does not.

What would make Thomas marry Frannie if he did not even love her? Something was missing from this diary. There had to be more to the story.

28th March 1968. It is done. Martha never wants to see Thomas again, and I stood by and let that happen. I thought I would be happy this day has finally come, but the light has gone out of my sister's eyes. The hope, the love and her irrepressible joy of living have been extinguished. I cannot repair this, and I can never, ever let her know the truth. All I hope is one day she understands I do love her so much.

Christie burst into fresh tears, her heart broken anew for Martha and Thomas, and her love for Gran shattered.

~

Sleep evaded Thomas. It was the incoming storm making him restless. In the foot-well of his car was the shoebox Christie had given him, and although he planned to keep it shut, its existence burned a trail of questions through his mind. Thomas had been shaken by Christie's resemblance to Martha. But she was not Martha, and Martha had chosen another over him.

The pain tonight was almost as raw as on that stormy night nearly fifty years ago. He had seen Martha come within seconds of drowning, and then she left. Not dead, but dead to him nevertheless. The shoebox with its letters was a stark reminder of the anguish left behind after she had gone. Always expecting her back, but not able to make it happen.

He stood at the edge of the cliff, remembering another time close to this spot. A day when he was mixing colours to paint a seascape and Martha had come up behind him, summer in her eyes and her long hair glistening in the sun. He painted her instead. A portrait crafted by the hands of a young man who was deeply in love.

Thunder rumbled low and long. In moments, it would rain, but for now, Thomas wanted to stare out over the sea. From here, he could see the jetty, its end already covered in waves. So like that other night.

Those letters. The rings. How had they got there? Unless Dorothy brought them with her before dying, he could not imagine how they made it into the attic.

~

So tired of crying, Christie sadly flicked through the rest of the diary, right up to the end of December. There was no further mention of

Martha. About to return it to the box, Christie noticed a slight bulge at the back. There, taped between two pages, was another letter. Not even sure she wished to find out more about Gran's duplicity, Christie opened one page filled with Dorothy's neat writing.

This is not for you to read, Martha, should you find this. However, if you do, understand as your big sister I have certain obligations to protect and guide you. Mother is not strong enough, and Father loves you regardless, so it is up to me to ensure you take every opportunity they worked so hard to provide.

That night, I made some poor decisions. I anguish over those choices now but months have passed, and the future is set in stone. If only you had not sent your friend to entertain me. This might not have all occurred, and instead, you would have wed Thomas, and your life would not be my responsibility. The night was almost over when your friend came back to speak with me, this time with an idea...

A DREADFUL PLAN

*1*967

Guests began to trickle out, and the music changed to slower songs. Martha and Thomas kept dancing, their arms around each other. Wanting to leave but not sure whether to slip away or wait for a break in the music, Dorothy's heart sank when she saw Frannie head her way again. She was not interested in more commentary about how unsuitable a match Thomas and Martha were, even if it did echo her own thoughts. Frannie sat beside Dorothy and leaned in to her as if part of a conspiracy.

"I made a decision." Frannie had an air of excitement. "I can't let Thomas marry Martha without him knowing how I feel! I just can't."

"I see." Dorothy wondered whether it was alcohol speaking or if the girl was mad. Thomas was clearly smitten with Martha and barely noticed Frannie this evening even with her too tight dress and impressive cleavage.

"Yes, so after the party I'm meant to be going to Green Bay with some of the girls, but I intend to miss the bus."

"Bus? You mean train."

"You haven't heard? The line is closing and buses are replacing passenger trains for now."

Dorothy could not imagine the town without trains. It allowed her family to flourish and now, what would happen to Patrick and his business?

Frannie prattled on. "The station is right next door to Tom's place, and I happen to know his parents left an hour ago to visit friends in the city so he will be all alone."

"You plan to tell him tonight? After his own engagement party? What if Martha is there?"

"Well, that's where you come in. I was hoping you might make sure Martha is well away from the cottage tonight to give me a chance."

"You want me to help you break up my own sister's engagement?"

"Don't sound so outraged. I know you don't like Tom and besides, all you'll be doing is stopping her see something that might upset her more than needed. She is my friend, you know!"

It was at this moment Dorothy saw an opportunity. Frances was unlikely to make a difference to Thomas' feelings for Martha. If anything, he would reject the girl's half-drunken advances and send her home. Nothing would come of it, and this one chance to change things would slip away.

Back at Palmerston House, after the party, Martha was at a loose end. The air was thick with humidity, and she sat out on the verandah for a while, playing with her engagement ring. Dorothy brought them both a glass of iced tea, joining her on the timber seat.

"I am so glad you're staying tonight. We can all have breakfast together. I'll make pancakes."

"You must be so tired though. Such a big day today!" Dorothy kept an eye on her watch.

"Yes, but it's a happy kind of tired. I miss Thomas already."

Dorothy took a deep breath. "You two did not get much time to say goodnight, did you?"

"No. There were so many people all leaving at the same time and somehow we only managed a quick kiss."

"Do you think he will still be up?"

"Of course! But if I walk all that way at night he'll be cross with me."

"Why not let me drive you?"

Martha's eyes widened. "Would you? I thought you don't approve of Thomas?"

"I shall have to get used to him if you plan to marry him. Go freshen up, and we can leave in a few minutes."

It took so little to persuade Martha to go to the cottage. When Dorothy stopped the car outside, Martha was puzzled by the lack of house lights and speculated Thomas may not be home. She walked up the driveway and suddenly stop as a light came on in a room. It seemed as though she was going to tap on the window, but froze.

Martha stared through the window into Thomas' bedroom, her hand raised to tap on the glass, her face alight with anticipation. The colour drained from her face, and her hand dropped to her side. She stood, unmoving, for more than a minute.

She gasped, "No!" and backed away, onto the driveway. She turned to run, unaware Thomas had flung the window open.

"Martha?"

Martha ran past Dorothy's car, toward the railway line. Dorothy put her hand on the ignition then stopped. She needed to know what happened.

The back door slammed and Thomas, his shirt open, raced onto the road. With barely a pause, he gave chase.

Dorothy slipped out of the car. She needed to follow them, but first, she had to speak with Frannie.

The back door was unlocked, and Dorothy made her way straight to the bedroom. Frannie sat on Thomas' bed, wrapped in a sheet. Wailing sobs made her face red and blotchy.

"Oh my, whatever did you do?"

"Nothing. I didn't get a chance to!"

"Stop carrying on! What did Martha see?"

Frannie found a handkerchief and blew her nose noisily. "I came to see Thomas and told him I'd missed the bus and could I please stay the night. I asked him for a glass of something, and he told me I could use his bedroom."

"And?"

"Um, and I got undressed. You know, I waited until I heard him coming down the hallway and I took my dress off and undid my... well, you know. And he walked in."

Dorothy wanted to slap the girl. "I thought you were going to tell him you cared, not turn into a little tart! No, don't start crying again, tell me what happened next."

"He told me to put my clothes back on and then saw Martha outside and ran off after her. Now he hates me!"

Dorothy had no sympathy whatsoever for Frannie and did not bother to wait around to hear any more. By the time she turned onto the main road, she saw Thomas at the top of the stone steps. Lightning flashed as she drove into the graveyard carpark.

MANIPULATED

*C*hristie threw the diary across the room and burst into tears.
How could you?

Even Frannie didn't deserve what Gran did. Infatuated with Thomas, there was nothing to hint she'd ever crossed the line with him.

"She was Martha's friend!" Christie brushed the tears away and collected the diary.

What kind of family did Christie come from? Clearly one where status mattered more than love. And where deceit and lies were acceptable, as long as the outcome was favourable.

She stomped to the kitchen and filled the kettle. There'd been more in the diary. Gran had documented her horror seeing Martha fall into the sea.

No wonder she forbade me from swimming in it!

And the promise. Thomas fully expected Martha to come back. She was hot-headed and impetuous and he knew her so well. Let her go and cool off. So, what kept them apart?

She opened the back door and stood on the porch for a while. The air was thick with humidity as the storm drew closer. Like the night Thomas lost Martha.

The conspiracy between Gran and Frannie left Christie cold inside. She locked the door behind herself and finished making coffee. It was time to finish this.

She opened Gran's diary on the next page.

Frannie returned from Melbourne, where she'd delivered Thomas' letter to me, not Martha. She found him on the jetty, sunburnt and confused from a day in the heat.

LOCK AND KEY

*1*968.

Frannie couldn't believe Thomas cared so much for Martha that he'd risk his health on the chance of her coming home. Always the jetty. She hurried along it.

"Martha?"

"No, darling. It's Frannie." She sat at his side.

"You're back. I thought…"

"I know. And I wish I had better news." Frannie crossed the fingers of one hand, hiding it behind her back.

"You couldn't find her?" Thomas dropped his head.

"Tom, I spoke with her."

The sudden lift of his head and spark in his eyes almost undid Frannie's resolve, but she had come too far to back down now.

"Tom… the thing is Martha is marrying someone else. Someone she met when she was at that rich school in the city years ago. They kept in touch, and she's been seeing him since she went to stay with Dorothy."

Thomas stared at Frannie. He didn't seem to understand what she was saying.

"Um, and she's getting married soon. She wanted me to say how sorry she is and she hopes you'll remember her kindly." Frannie rushed the words.

"No. She promised. Frannie, she promised to come home."

"I know you loved her, but she's not like us. Tom, she is rich, and she wants to be with a rich man. You need someone who cares about you for who you are."

Thomas staggered to his feet, shaking his head.

"Tom? I'm so sorry to have been the one to tell you." Frannie put every ounce of emotion into her voice.

Thomas held out his hand. "You've been a loyal friend to me, Frannie. It isn't your fault."

She leapt up and took his hand, squeezing it as they left the jetty. "I'll always be here for you."

UNFORGIVEABLE

Christie stood at Frannie's grave. The storm was overhead; thunder boomed across the beach and shook the ground. Lightning snaked into the sea, its waves whipped up by a fierce wind.

Only wearing Martin's T-shirt, a pair of shorts and sandals, Christie was drenched in seconds when the rain descended in sheets.

With the light from a torch, she stared at the headstone.

Frannie Blake (nee Williams)

Loving Mother of Thomas Jnr and Wife of Thomas

This woman lied her way into Thomas' life. Lied to him and lied to Martha, supposedly her friend. Yet, Thomas loved her. She had intended to marry Thomas, and she wilfully destroyed true love to make it happen.

Christie pushed soaking wet hair from her eyes and fought against the wind to reach Gran's grave. It did not matter Gran had loved Martha and wanted the best for her. Or that she had not foreseen the terrible damage she would do. It meant nothing she paid for it her whole life with failed marriages and estranged family.

"How could you have done it?" Christie cried. "I will never forgive you. Never!"

THE TRUTH WILL OUT

*M*artha willed the time to pass. Through her bedroom window in Palmerston House, the clear blue sky might have been hand painted, so vivid was its colour, refreshed by the storm so similar to the night so long ago. She should have listened to Thomas, given him the chance to explain what happened. Instead, her mind refused to let go of what she had seen.

Thomas' bedroom, lit only by his bedside lamp. Beside his bed was Frannie, slipping out of her dress and undoing her bra as Thomas—carrying two glasses—entered the room. Mesmerised, he stopped as Frannie tossed her bra onto the bed and stood before him, almost naked.

Later, on the beach when Thomas told her it was not what she thought, instead of trusting him and letting him speak, she had thrown her ring on the ground and run away. He deserved better, and in time, he had chosen Frannie as his wife.

She missed him. Oh God, how she missed Thomas. Should he miraculously appear in front of her now, she would beg his forgiveness and promise him anything if only he would give her a second chance. Except, he was dead. There were no second chances.

Thomas had struggled to sleep. Before the driving rain forced him back inside, he could have sworn he saw someone at the graveyard. A light moved around for a while, but it was too far to see who was there. The remainder of the night had been about "what ifs".

What if he had insisted Martha listen to him about his innocent agreement to let Frannie stay the night? What if he had told her how shocked he had been at seeing Frannie undressed? What if the argument changed direction and Martha had forgiven his poor judgement?

He kept coming back to the same answer. No matter how deeply he loved Martha, time and circumstance changed him forever. Raising his son, seeing him marry and have his own small family were the happiest years of his life.

A drunk driver took it all away. His son, daughter-in-law and wife all killed instantly on a trip to the city. Only three-year-old Martin survived the accident, somehow unscathed in his booster seat. The devastating loss was almost too much to bear. Except he had a little boy who needed him. His creative, compassionate, stubborn grandson.

No, he would not change one thing. Martin was only here because of that night, and it made the whole tragedy tolerable. Martha had made her choice, marrying a boy from her past. No wonder she had not bothered to reply to his letters. He had glanced inside the box and found they were all opened. She had read them but ignored his heartfelt pleas.

Drenched to the skin, Christie had dragged herself back after more than an hour in the graveyard. At one point, she sat at the top of the stone steps, waiting for flashes of lightning to illuminate the jetty. Over and over, she imagined Martha falling into the wild ocean and Thomas diving in to save her.

Under a hot shower, she gradually stopped shivering and crying. Gran had done something unimaginably cruel to her own sister in the name of love, and in volumes, she paid for it. Her guilt and regret interfered with every relationship she forged, from husbands to her own daughter and even with Christie. Lie after lie compounded until it was beyond her to tell Martha what happened that night and instead, she let her sister believe Thomas had not loved her.

It was all a hopeless, tragic story and Christie would never forgive Gran. Tossing and turning through the night it was early hours when she fell asleep, her arms wrapped around herself.

Now mid-morning, she parked the Lotus outside the bakery, so hungry she felt ill. She had woken late, exhausted and lethargic from the events of the night and previous day. Totally drained, she did not think she even had any more tears left in her body.

Christie was relieved only Belinda was there when she entered the bakery. She hurried to Christie, glancing behind her.

"Mum's upset with me," she said.

"I know, but she's just afraid to lose you," Christie explained. "She loves you lots and children leaving home is scary sometimes."

"I want to do something useful with my life! What you did for Jess was amazing, and I love makeup and stuff. It's time I did something for me."

"So, come and see me and I'll run through all the pros and cons of the beauty industry. I can talk to your mum as well to reassure her. Just give me a day or two, okay?" Christie got a smile from Belinda. "Now, I haven't eaten properly in ages, so what shall I get?"

"Well, there's no croissants left because Mrs White phoned a few minutes ago to put the last couple of them on hold. So, what about a scroll?"

"Yes, please. How was the dance? Did Jess enjoy herself?"

"Hmm?" Belinda concentrated on selecting the biggest cinnamon scroll. "Oh, yes she did! The thing is she's got lots of friends who don't even care about that silly birthmark, but looking so darned awesome made her shine." Belinda secretly added an apple slice to the bag before scrunching the ends and putting it on the top of the counter.

"I'm so glad. Jess has a natural beauty, and she's easy to work with, once you get past the shyness." Christie hid a smile, having seen Belinda's generosity.

The door opened, and Elizabeth slipped in.

"Hello Mrs White, I'll be right with you."

Christie turned to Elizabeth. "Hello, I keep meaning to phone to see if you'd let me drop by."

"Of course. Maybe...how about tomorrow some time?" Elizabeth averted her eyes.

"Thank you. I might bring a photo album to see if you recognise the person I mentioned. Martha Ryan. My great-aunt?"

Elizabeth's hand covered her mouth and her eyes glistened.

"What is it?" Christie prompted. "Are you alright?"

All she got in response was a shake of her head.

You know something!

There had been too many secrets, too many lies.

"Mrs White, I don't mean to sound rude, but if you know anything at all about Martha, you need to tell me now." Her tone was abrupt enough to send Belinda hurrying to find the croissants she had put aside.

Almost in relief, Elizabeth grasped Christie's hand, her words rushing out. "I wasn't honest with you, and I am so sorry. I was trying to protect her, but it isn't my place to do so, and she will leave without ever knowing you exist if you don't go and find her now!"

Goosebumps covered Christie. "Do you mean Martha?"

"Yes. Martha, your great-aunt, is here in Rivers End."

Martha was here! This changed everything.

Thomas is alive and in Rivers End. Martha is here.

She could reunite them!

Belinda came back with the croissants. "Do either of you want some water? Maybe to sit for a while?"

"Was Martha there when I came to Palmerston House?" Christie kept her voice even.

"She was upstairs. You surprised me as I thought I knew everything about Martha after all these years, yet there you were. A great-niece. And you need to understand she was terribly fragile. Just home from the hospital." Elizabeth dropped her gaze. "I should have told you, and I certainly should have told her."

Christie agreed. People kept making decisions for other people, all in the name of misguided love. "You've known her for a long time?"

"We've been friends forever. We met when both of us were sad as I could never have children and she would never marry. It was what bonded us."

"Where is she?"

"Saying goodbye to Dorothy."

"Goodbye?"

"She's going home to Ireland and has a bus to catch."

"I have to go." Christie took off for the door.

"Wait! What about these? You need to eat!" Belinda was uncannily like Martin, and Christie almost laughed.

"I'll be back. I've got to find her!"

As the door jangled behind Christie, Belinda picked up the bag. "Fine. Just go. I'll stay here with your delicious food. Now, Mrs White, I have your lovely croissants."

Martha paused at Dorothy's grave after Elizabeth dropped her off, waiting until the car disappeared. She had time to visit the grave later before her friend returned.

Now her ankle was improved, the stone steps were much easier to navigate. The morning was beautiful with a higher than usual tide-mark and ocean debris the only reminder a massive storm swept through last night.

Once on the sand, Martha turned to the cliff face. Her hand reached instinctively to the carved love heart as her mind went back to 1966.

SAYING GOODBYE

*1*966
Thomas chipped out the last of the engraving and stood back, happy with the result.

Martha was more critical. "Why does T heart M?" she reached out to touch.

Thomas lightly smacked her hand, and she grinned at him, not at all affronted.

"Don't annoy the artist!" He tried to sound stern.

It was hard to do when Martha snuggled into him. Thomas dropped a kiss onto her head. "It will take millennia before this cliff erodes. This way, only time itself can erase our love."

Now

How those words taunted Martha.

If only she'd turned around that night. Better still, if only she'd planted her feet at the cottage and demanded an explanation on the spot.

But you didn't. You let your pride drive you away.

She'd let Dorothy persuade her to stay in Melbourne at her apartment. For weeks she'd moped around, letting hurt feelings stop her from phoning Tom. And he hadn't tried to fix things. No letters or calls. Nothing until Frannie turned up with her barely contained joy at taking Thomas away from her so-called best friend.

Martha turned her back on the love heart.

In a few hours she'd board a plane back to Ireland, and there she'd see out the rest of her life. No more gadding about on pyramids or sailing the Nile. No looking for lost Inca temples, or seeing the Northern lights over Norway.

Her life had been good. Productive. Full.

Soon, Rivers End would once again be a memory. But for now she wanted to watch the whiting swim around the seabed from the end of the jetty and think one last time about the man who she would love beyond eternity.

A PLEA FOR HELP

*C*hristie's tiredness and hunger vanished the minute she got behind the wheel. Her mind was in overdrive. She had to find Martha first and introduce herself, then work the rest out.

As she drove to the corner to head around the block, she recognised a dirty four-wheel drive coming toward her. Sure enough, Thomas was driving along the road to the mountains.

She almost did a U-turn to follow him but knew she had to find Martha first. Without another thought, she dialled Martin's number. As it rang, she hoped somehow he was past his disappointment in her, remembering the last thing he had done was kiss her forehead.

He answered with a curious tone. "So, you do have my number."

"What do you mean?" Christie's mind was on Martha.

"I recall asking you to text me when you got home that night. When I confiscated your car keys."

"Oh. Yes."

"But you didn't."

"No, but that has to wait. I need to ask about Thomas."

"Thomas?"

"I passed him leaving town. Would you go and bring him back please?"

There was a long pause as Christie pulled into the carpark. The graveyard was empty.

Where are you?

"Thomas will be back this afternoon."

"That's too late! Martha is here, Martin! Here in Rivers End and she's leaving soon to go home to Ireland forever."

"This isn't our business, Christie. Leave things alone."

"Please, please help me." Her words tumbled over each other. "Both of them were lied to. My grandmother was behind it, and other people helped. If we don't tell them, we're no better than anyone else who kept them apart."

"Calm down. How do you know this?"

Christie took a deep breath to settle herself. "I read Gran's diary, and there is a full account in there of what she did the night they broke up, and what was later done to keep them apart. They need to know the truth and make their own decisions."

She was desperate to get out of the car and sprint to the beach.

"I can't get Thomas. My bike is in a million pieces thanks to him dissecting it so you'll have to find him."

Christie turned the motor on and started nosing out of the carpark. "You need to locate Martha."

"No."

"Yes. I think she's on the beach so, please find her for me. Keep her there until I bring him back."

"You're being rather bossy," Martin said.

Christie laughed. "No doubt you'll sort that out too."

"I wouldn't be laughing about it though."

He hung up, and Christie grinned. She was being bossy, in her own quiet way. It was about time she stood up for herself and what she believed in. She turned the car toward the cottage.

A STAND FOR THE TRUTH

There were juvenile whiting darting around the seaweed below the jetty. Martha watched them with a smile, remembering beach barbeques with fresh fish purchased for cents from the fishermen. Her friends were all ghosts now, but their laughter lingered on this jetty.

Its familiar creaks and groans changed a little. There were footsteps on the old timber boards, and Martha hoped it was not that poor man who found her in the rain. The footsteps came closer and then stopped.

"Martha?"

Martha froze at the familiar voice.

~

"I can't believe you stopped me for this!" Thomas was furious. Christie caught up with him not far out of town and after tooting her horn and flashing her lights at him without result, found a safe passing point. As she had gone past, she gestured for him to stop and he had, concern flooding his face.

They met halfway between the two vehicles.

"Is something wrong with Martin?" Thomas demanded.

"No. Of course not. Oh, I'm so sorry if that's what you thought." Christie realised she must have driven like a mad woman and made him think it was an emergency.

When Christie said she needed him to come and see Martha, he had gone white and stormed back to his car. Christie grabbed the tulip box, which she had rushed to get from the cottage, and followed.

"Thomas you don't understand—" Christie started, but he cut her off.

"Nothing to understand. Stay out of my business. Not one more word."

Christie held out the box.

"What's that?"

"It's the truth. You were lied to."

"I know. She never loved me."

"You were her one true love. Other people lied, Gran for a start. It was all one big set up, Thomas! Other people created the catalyst for your separation and other people kept you apart."

Thomas stared at the box. "But why didn't she come home when she read my letters? It doesn't make sense."

"Gran hid them from her. She never read them."

"But they're open."

"That was me, and I'm so sorry, but I thought…" She faltered.

"Even dead people have rights, young lady. Besides, there was another letter hand delivered to her. She knew how I felt." Thomas got back into his car.

He closed the door and spoke through the open window. "What other people?"

"I'm sorry Thomas…who took the last letter to Martha?" Christie's heart broke a little as he worked out who she meant.

His face went hard and his eyes cold. "You dare to stand there and tell me my late wife did this thing?"

Christie pushed the tulip box through the window and onto his lap. "You won't even say Martha's name! She stayed true to you her whole life."

"She married another boy months after leaving me." Thomas snapped through gritted teeth as he threw the tulip box onto the passenger seat. He started the motor.

"She never married. And if you open the box, you'll see your last letter is unopened, and you can even read Gran's diary, if it's not too much below your principles! Sometimes somebody needs to make a stand for the truth, and I think I've just about done all I can."

With a glare, Thomas wound up the window and drove away, leaving a cloud of dust as he sped off the shoulder. Christie stood helpless, unable to believe he would turn his back on Martha again.

Thomas only made it over the next hill before pulling over again. The tremor in his hands was from anger. It had to be. That young woman had no idea what she was doing, bringing all these things to the surface.

But what if she is right?

He closed his eyes. That night on the beach, in the midst of a storm, he'd pointed to the jetty.

"I'll wait for you. There, at the end of the jetty, I will wait. Every day I will be there to meet the dawn, as we have done so many times. Promise you'll come back."

She had promised. And he wasn't there for her when she returned.

His eyes opened to stare at the empty road ahead. She was here in Rivers End. His girl.

Foot hard on the accelerator, he did a U-turn. And stalled. 'Not now, dammit!' The engine spluttered as he coasted to a halt.

Afraid to turn around and find herself confronted by a ghost, Martha stoically stared out to sea. Being here played with her mind and now she was hearing the voice of a man long dead. If she ignored it, the moment would pass.

Instead, someone sat next to her, long male legs dangling over the end of the jetty. Heart pounding, she stole a sideways glance. No, not Thomas. Just someone like him who was gazing at the fish below the jetty without seeming to notice her.

For a while, the only sounds were the soft sploshing of the water against the pylons and ever-present cawing of seagulls. Martha's mind raced with questions she would not ask. The possible answers scared her too much.

A small gust of wind blew Martha's handbag onto its side, and her airline ticket slid out.

The stranger picked it up. "When do you leave?"

Looking straight at him now, Martha saw the relationship to Thomas. Strong features, those intense eyes and same direct tone. She held her hand out for the ticket and when he handed it to her, she shoved it into the handbag.

"I'll be going soon enough, young man, don't you worry."

"It isn't of concern to me, but it is to someone I care about. You need to meet her."

Martha disagreed. If Dorothy wanted her to know about children and grandchildren, Dorothy would have told her.

"Christie only found out you existed a few weeks ago," The man spoke as if he could read Martha's thoughts. "She's been doing everything in her power to find you and put together the pieces of a rather big puzzle your sister left behind."

"Well, why are you here instead of her?"

"Oh, I'll let them explain when they get here."

"Them?"

The horn of a car tooted from the carpark. Elizabeth appeared a moment later near the steps, waving.

"My ride," Martha announced. She began to stand, realising with some irritation she was going to struggle. Already on his feet, the man extended his hand. She ignored it.

"What is it about you Ryan women?"

Martha glared at him and Martin almost laughed, the fire in her eyes was so like Christie's. She reluctantly allowed him to support her, muttering "Thanks" under her breath. He gave her the handbag and held his arm out, which she pretended not to see.

The growl of the Lotus drew near and stopped. Martha glanced up at Martin. "That's her?"

"That's Christie."

Martha stopped, troubled. "She came to Palmerston."

"I told you, she was searching for you."

"Elizabeth lied to me."

"I'm afraid a lot of people have been lying to you. Will you wait here a moment? I'll be back." Without waiting for an answer, he sprinted to the steps, meeting Christie as she reached the bottom.

"Where is he?" Martin's heart sank at the distress in Christie's eyes.

"Stubborn old man! He wouldn't come with me. How is she?"

"Stubborn old lady." Martin squeezed her hand. "She's leaving in a minute."

"I'd better say hi."

Christie turned to wave to Martha, who was shuffling through the sand toward her.

Martha waved back. Emotion overwhelmed Christie, a bursting of happiness that she had found her great-aunt. It was only when her vision got blurry she realised she was crying. Again.

She raced across the distance and threw her arms around Martha. For a long moment, they hugged, strangers from different generations, brought together by blood, secrets and determination.

"Hello, Auntie."

Martha released her and they gazed at each other, faces alight with joy.

"I believe you've been searching for me?" Martha said. "I fear my friend may have lied to you to protect me."

"So many people have lied, and I'm so sorry to tell you Gran was one of the worst."

The horn of Elizabeth's car tooted again.

"Stay. Please stay a while?" Christie held Martha's hand.

"I can't, dear. My plane won't wait, but I want you to visit me. Come to Ireland."

Martha started walking again, gripping Christie's hand.

Do I tell you?

Christie's mind worked overtime.

Will it hurt you too much?

With sudden clarity, Christie knew. The truth had been withheld for long enough.

She stopped. "Auntie? Please, just for a moment, listen."

Martha stopped and turned to face her. "I'm listening."

"That night...the night you fell in the ocean and left Thomas?"

Martha glanced behind Christie at the jetty. "How do you know about that?"

"Gran was here on the beach. She and Frannie planned everything, and when you were thinking of coming home, Frannie lied about Thomas marrying her."

Martha shook her head. "He married her."

"Well, yes. But she'd told him you'd married a boy from school."

"She did what?"

"There's so much more you need to know. I have to tell you about Thomas."

"No. No, I have to leave now. Besides, it all stopped mattering the day he died."

Over Martha's shoulder, a movement caught Christie's eye at the top of the cliff.

"Martha!" Thomas' voice boomed across the beach.

Martha's eyes widened as she stared at Christie's face.

"That's what I was trying to tell you." Christie took Martha's arm and gently turned her around. "He's alive!"

~

Thomas almost fell down the last few steps, so intent was he on reaching the beach, but Martin grabbed his arm and steadied him.

As if he was a young man again, Thomas flew across the sand.

On Martha's face, there was no smile, no welcome. Just utter shock. She swayed as if on the verge of collapsing, but Christie put an arm around her. "It's real. He's real."

Thomas slid to a stop, gasping for air, as if unable to believe his own eyes. Martha was right there in front of him.

A step at a time, Thomas and Martha closed the distance through a stillness encircling them. As though not even one day had passed.

"I waited for you." There was a question in Thomas' words.

"I found out today."

Thomas dropped to his knees before Martha. "Forgive me."

"Oh, Thomas, it's me who needs forgiveness. But I never stopped loving you."

She reached out her hands and so tenderly, Thomas took them in his and kissed one, then the other. He kept her left hand in his and rummaged around in a pocket. There it was. As brilliant and beautiful as the day it was made, her engagement ring.

Martha gasped.

"If this goes on your hand, it stays there. Understood?"

"Yes, Thomas. Oh, yes!"

Thomas slipped the ring on Martha's finger and clambered to his feet with the strength of a man reborn. His eyes were alive with love as he pulled Martha into his arms. After a lifetime apart, their lips touched and finally, they were together again.

Christie had retreated to the steps, where Martin waited. She joined him, unable to meet his eyes in fear of what she might see. What if he never forgave her for reading those letters?

"Give it time, Christie," he said as if reading her mind. She nodded.

When Thomas put the engagement ring on Martha's finger, Christie burst into tears.

"I've never met a woman who cries so much." Martin gave her a handkerchief.

"I don't think I ever cried before I met you."

A few moments later, Martha and Thomas wandered across the sand, hand in hand. They stopped at the bottom of the steps.

"Does this mean you might stay a bit longer?" Christie teased Martha.

"Oh, my flight. I'd better ask Elizabeth to cancel it for now."

"What do you mean, for now?" Thomas growled.

"I have a house in Ireland to sell, dear, unless I leave it to someone? Maybe you, Christie?"

"I'm a bit over inheritances, Auntie. Although I've always wanted to visit Ireland and I don't have anything stopping me from travelling." Christie said it to get a response from Martin.

As though he had not heard her, he offered Martha his arm and headed back up the steps. All the joy of the moment disappeared, and Christie realised she wanted Martin in her life every bit as much as Thomas and Martha wanted each other in theirs.

They were together. The terrible secrets belonged in the past, and finally, almost everything was right again.

A PROMISE KEPT

*O*n the first Saturday in January, on the jetty, Thomas married Martha. Against the backdrop of the Great Southern Ocean, they exchanged the vows written almost fifty years ago. Promises both decided still applied to their love and future marriage.

Thomas had insisted the wedding start in the early evening to avoid high tide. He had no intention, he told Martha, of fishing her out of the sea again.

The ceremony was short and simple. They exchanged loving words, promises, and rings, followed by a kiss so tender even Martin had to blink a little more than usual.

With Christie as bridesmaid and Martin as best man, Martha and Thomas posed for a photographer patiently, but their eyes rarely left each other. Since reuniting, they had not spent a day apart, as if afraid this was a dream from which they would waken.

Back on the beach, Elizabeth threw her arms around Martha, while George, grinning broadly, slapped Thomas on the back. Daphne kept dabbing her eyes and John was exactly the same as he had been at the funeral, except with a smile. Belinda—who had done Jess and Sylvia's makeup under Christie's guidance—fussed around checking everyone was at their best for the ongoing photographs. Even Randall wore a doggie bow tie.

Watching them all so happy, so united, mixed feelings surged through Christie. Such joy for Martha and Thomas. Almost unbearable sadness for their lost years. Residual anger at Gran, more so than Frannie. Frannie, after all, loved Thomas and could not see past her own needs. Gran should have known better. Underneath all of that was an emptiness. As though Christie had lost something important.

"This must belong to you." Martin was beside Christie, and she started. He raised an eyebrow and held up a strand of jasmine.

"Oh, that's from Martha's bouquet."

"No. I'm sure it belongs here." Martin touched Christie's hair, braided colourfully to one side with flowers. Weaving the jasmine around the braid, his hand brushed Christie's skin, shooting tiny sparks of electricity through her. "There, that's better. Jasmine sea."

Wide-eyed, Christie gazed at him.

You remember!

The scent from the jasmine mingled with the sea air, as it had the evening she'd joked about becoming a candle maker.

Martin wandered back to the group as though nothing happened.

Randall trotted to Christie, and she knelt on the sand to cuddle him. He licked her face, making her giggle, but inside, butterflies played havoc with her stomach.

Since that day on the beach when Martha and Thomas reunited, Martin had been polite, but distant. They spent plenty of time together, helping plan the wedding and even sharing Christmas at Palmerston House, but it was always with company and Martin showed no interest in seeking Christie out alone.

This was the first time they touched in ages, and it took all of one light brush of his fingers to crash back through the barriers she had rebuilt. Her hand strayed to her hair.

Stop wishing.

∾

Guests waited in the near-darkness of dusk on the wide, timber verandah of Palmerston House, as a horse and open carriage turned into the driveway.

Martha gasped in delight at the fountain, which lit from within, flowed with tumbling streams of ever-changing coloured water. Trees around the homestead twinkled with fairy lights, and as the carriage drew near, each guest held up a lantern.

She grabbed Thomas' hand. "This is for us!"

There was wonder in her voice, and Thomas did not trust himself to speak. All he could do was gaze at his bride. Martha was his wife. She was real.

As the carriage stopped, the verandah erupted with clapping. Thomas climbed out and offered his hand to Martha. Christie rushed to help with the dress and Martin joined them for another round of photographs.

The foyer was large enough for the reception and a small dance floor. When the formalities and meals were finished, the lights dimmed, and Thomas escorted Martha to the centre of the room.

Christie watched them from the top of the steps, her phone at the ready to video this poignant event. Martin wandered up the staircase, stopping when he was at her eye level. He held out a crisp, white handkerchief.

"What's this for?"

"You'll need it."

"Why?"

"Always a question." he sighed. "Just take it."

Christie accepted the handkerchief and slipped it into her bag. The music began, and she turned her attention to the dance floor.

After the bridal waltz, Martin stood on the edge of the dance floor, hand extended to Christie. As the music began, Martin took Christie into his arms. Aware of the eyes on them, she kept herself from melting into him the way her body ached to. When he tried to draw her closer, Christie stiffened, and he gave her a puzzled glance.

"Smile," he suggested. "I'm not going to bite."

I can think of worse things.

Christie forced a smile and let her body relax. Martin slid his hand a little lower and tightened his embrace. The strength of his arms and oh-so-masculine scent played havoc with whatever remained of Christie's barriers, and she gave up. She loved Martin, and for once, she would believe he loved her in return.

Too soon, the dance ended as if to remind Christie not to dream. The music changed tempo, and other guests joined Martha and Thomas, who continued to waltz regardless of the world around them. Martin led Christie off the dance floor by a hand and held it to keep her attention as he leaned down to speak over the music.

"We need to talk."

"We are talking."

"Don't be difficult, Christie," Martin spoke in the mild tone that usually meant something else. "Tomorrow. Come to the house, there's something I need you to see."

Heart racing, Christie tried to read his expression. Why had he insisted she take a handkerchief from him, warning her she would need it? Had he worked out how she felt and did not reciprocate?

"Can you tell me now?"

"I can't show you something here that is at my house." For a moment, it seemed as though those shutters would come down again and he would change his mind.

"I'll be there." Christie agreed. "I love what you gave them as a present." She needed to normalise things again. Martin squeezed her hand before releasing it.

"All I did was restore it. Thomas is responsible for creating it."

"You undersell yourself." Christie flashed a smile at Martin. "Coming?"

Before he could answer, she crossed the dance floor, laughed at something Belinda said and slipped through the partly open door leading to the front living room.

Inside it was a little quieter, and she paused, eyes closed, to gather herself. Whatever happened tomorrow, she still had this beautiful evening to spend with Thomas and Martha. And Martin.

"What are we doing in here?" Martin spoke from right behind Christie. She opened her eyes, heart speeding up at his voice. As always.

"How can you say all you did was restore it? Thomas told me there was a hole right through it!"

On an easel in the middle of the room was Thomas' painting of Martha in the meadow in springtime, flowers in her hair and love in her eyes. It was framed and could have been painted a week ago, so fresh and vibrant the colours.

"Slight exaggeration, but it was damaged. Like the seascape, somebody mistreated the canvas, and it was pure luck I found it in time."

Martin took a step or two around Christie to touch the frame and tilted his head at her. "Do you see the love in this painting? How could Martha have thought for one second Thomas was anything other than deeply, desperately in love with her?"

Why are you telling me this?

Christie was too afraid to ask. "And I knew. From his letters."

"You shouldn't have read them."

Christie lifted her chin. "I am sorry it upsets you." she kept her eyes on his, refusing to back down. "I am not sorry I read them, given the result."

Martin reached out and brushed a stray hair from Christie's eyes. "Good for you," he said. He dropped his hand again as the music changed to a faster beat. "Tonight belongs to Thomas and Martha. Let's celebrate with them."

"Of course." Christie murmured. "I'll be right there."

She wanted another moment with the painting and when Martin left, took a deep breath to clear her head. If only he felt the way about her Thomas did about Martha. But true love just comes once in a lifetime, and this painting might represent the only time she would see it in hers.

A WORK OF LOVE

*M*id-morning and it was already warm. Wearing a sarong and sandals, hair loose in soft waves, Christie carried the seascape across the meadow to Martin's house.

Randall came hurtling around the corner, yipping in delight. His bow tie was gone, and he smelt doggie and wagged his tail like crazy.

Martin was not at the house. Randall by-passed it, running instead to the studio. Christie followed, curious about Martin's creative space, but worried about intruding.

The studio door was wide open.

"Hello?" Christie called.

"Come in."

Christie stepped inside the door, staring in wonder at the incredible artwork in the room. Stunning pieces radiated colour and magical concepts. In the centre of the room was a sheet-covered easel.

"Don't tell me it needs repairing again." Martin got up from the sofa near the window.

"Huh? Oh, this? No, of course not. It's for Thomas. Please make him keep it this time."

Martin laughed shortly as if to say good luck with that, but he wandered across to take the painting. Their fingers touched, and fire shot through Christie. Eyes on the seascape, she said the first thing that came into her mind. "I never understood why Thomas sent this painting to Martha. It was a reminder of how bad things were. Why not send her the portrait?"

"There was a reason behind it, but that's one to discuss with him."

Martin settled the painting on an empty easel and turned to gaze at Christie. She played with her hair, unsure of herself as she viewed one painting after another.

"Christie? Look at me."

Christie feared this was the moment. He was about to break her heart, and she was too afraid to do as he asked.

"Will I need that handkerchief?" she asked with a short laugh.

"Look at me, please."

When she did, there was something unexpected in his eyes.

Uncertainty.

"I want to show you a painting I did."

"A painting?"

"If it sends you away, I'll live with that, but what I learned recently is there should be no secrets."

"What do you mean?" Christie's voice was almost inaudible.

Her hand in his, Martin led Christie to the covered easel in the centre of the studio. Positioning her in front of it, he slipped the cover off. She gasped.

Martin had taken his sketch of Christie on the stone steps and turned it into a stunning oil painting. Randall was at her feet; she gazed out over the ocean and wore Martin's T-shirt and the pendant from the jewellery store.

This was a work of love. Every stroke of the brush revealed a powerful emotion. Desire. Admiration. Respect. Trust. Love.

"This is me?"

Martin said nothing.

"You see me this way?"

"I was wrong about you, Christie. I made unfair judgements, and I'm sorry."

Christie thought she misheard him. "Did you just apologise?"

"Don't get used to it."

"This painting…why?"

"Thomas shows love through his art and apparently, so do I."

Still, she was too afraid to believe what she thought he meant.

"Christie, last night after you told me you weren't sorry for reading those letters, I wanted to pull you into my arms and kiss you. Standing up for what you believe in yet still having the grace and empathy to acknowledge the effect it had on me."

He took both of Christie's hands in his. "You have courage."

"I do?"

"And spirit, a warm heart and kindness. And a sense of right. Well, most of the time." Martin chuckled. "Randall loves you. So, there it is." He pulled Christie against him, releasing her hands to slide his arms around her waist.

"I don't know what to say." Her voice was little more than a whisper.

Martin responded by capturing her lips. With a tiny sigh, Christie surrendered, her arms winding around his neck, her hands through his hair. He kissed her until she was breathless and lightheaded, and powerless to resist. Then, he released her mouth, kissing the tip of her nose.

"Say you'll lock doors when you're told to."

He kissed her forehead.

"And eat properly."

He kissed her neck where it met her shoulder.

"And you love me too." He threw that in casually, loosening his arms enough to gaze at her.

"Okay." Her eyes sparkled with love.

"Okay?" Martin squeezed her in mock warning.

The heat and scent from his body radiated through her, over-loading her senses until all she could do was whisper, "I love you too."

Instead of kissing her again, Martin lifted her into his arms and carried her to the sofa. Sitting with her nestled in his arms, he brushed his lips against her forehead. "I love you, Christabel Ryan."

Eyes closed, she snuggled into his embrace, listening to his heartbeat. Randall padded over and climbed up beside them, dropping his head onto Christie's lap.

"You asked me once why I was still in Rivers End." Christie's fingers stroked Randall's ears.

"And?"

"I needed to find my home."

"You found it."

Yes. I did. Here, with this man and his dog, she was home.

ABOUT THE AUTHOR

Phillipa lives just outside a beautiful town in country Victoria, Australia. She also lives in the many worlds of her imagination and stockpiles stories beside her laptop.

Apart from her family, Phillipa's great loves include the ocean, music, reading, the garden, and animals of all kinds.

www.phillipaclark.com

ACKNOWLEDGMENTS

To Nas Dean, my deepest thanks for always driving me to do my best, and being a wonderful teacher and friend. As editor of this edition, you've taken *Cottage* to a new level.

My love and thanks to my fabulous family and friends, Helen Sibbritt (cheerleader extraordinaire), the amazing authors I count as lifelong friends, and the readers who make every moment worth while.

Thank you to my husband and sons, who fuel my dreams.

RECOMMENDED READING ORDER

The Rivers End series includes four main books (The Stationmaster's Cottage, Jasmine Sea, The Secrets of Palmerston House, The Christmas Key), plus three short books.

Taming the Wind can be read anytime. Before or after the others will still make sense.

Martha is best read after Cottage and some readers enjoyed it more after reading The Christmas Key.

～

There are also two spin-off series to enjoy.

The Charlotte Dean Mysteries begin shortly after The Secrets of Palmerston House. They are best read in their series order.

The Daphne Jones Mysteries are set after The Christmas Key. These also are best read in series order.

∽

Last Known Contact is a stand alone crime suspense, unrelated to the other series.

Simple Words for Troubled Times is a non-fiction short book to offer comfort and happiness.

∽

Future books include a fantasy trilogy, a new crime suspense, and more in the various series.

Thank you for reading one of my stories - I am so thrilled you took a chance on me and hope you enjoyed your time in my world.

CPSIA information can be obtained
at www.ICGtesting.com
Printed in the USA
LVHW040433120122
708315LV00005B/127